SANDY TOES

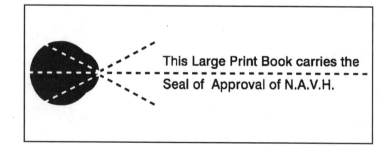

This Large Print Book carries the
Seal of Approval of N.A.V.H.

CHRISTY & TODD, THE BABY YEARS,
BOOK 1

SANDY TOES

ROBIN JONES GUNN

THORNDIKE PRESS
A part of Gale, Cengage Learning

Farmington Hills, Mich • San Francisco • New York • Waterville, Maine
Meriden, Conn • Mason, Ohio • Chicago

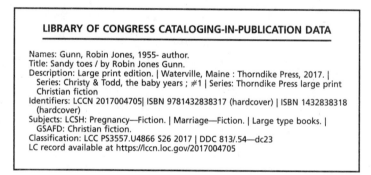

LIBRARY OF CONGRESS CATALOGING-IN-PUBLICATION DATA

Names: Gunn, Robin Jones, 1955- author.
Title: Sandy toes / by Robin Jones Gunn.
Description: Large print edition. | Waterville, Maine : Thorndike Press, 2017. | Series: Christy & Todd, the baby years ; #1 | Series: Thorndike Press large print Christian fiction
Identifiers: LCCN 2017004705| ISBN 9781432838317 (hardcover) | ISBN 1432838318 (hardcover)
Subjects: LCSH: Pregnancy—Fiction. | Marriage—Fiction. | Large type books. | GSAFD: Christian fiction.
Classification: LCC PS3557.U4866 S26 2017 | DDC 813/.54—dc23
LC record available at https://lccn.loc.gov/2017004705

Published in 2017 by arrangement with Robin's Nest Production, Inc.

Printed in the United States of America
1 2 3 4 5 6 7 21 20 19 18 17

For Stacey with hope and much love.

"How precious are your thoughts about me, O God. They cannot be numbered! I can't even count them; they outnumber the grains of sand."

— Psalm 139:18

ONE

Christy sat alone in the doctor's office and flipped through the pages of a home-decorating magazine. Her gaze kept darting toward the door, waiting for it to open and for Todd to enter.

He said he would be here. Where is he?

Drawing in a deep breath, Christy pulled her long, nutmeg-brown hair back into a twist and secured it with a clip. Perspiration swerved down her neck. She wished she had a mint to calm her stomach.

The woman across from her in the waiting room rested her hands on top of her large, rounded midriff while the man next to her focused on his phone. She caught Christy's eye, and they exchanged tentative half smiles.

This first visit to the OBGYN wasn't going the way Christy had imagined it would. She thought she and Todd would be seated side by side, holding hands, whispering to each other, and sharing the sacredness of this moment.

More than a month ago, when the home pregnancy test was positive, Todd's response was everything Christy had hoped it would be. He had stared at the wand, stared at Christy, and then burst into loud, manly sobs. He scooped her up and hugged her so close she could barely breathe. Then he kissed her, and she kissed him back, and they both laughed. No words were exchanged between them in their upstairs bathroom on that landmark morning. They didn't need to speak. Their kisses contained every nuance of their unspoken messages.

In the hours that followed that life-altering home test, Christy and Todd decided not to tell anyone until they had seen the doctor and the results were confirmed. It had taken weeks to get this appointment, and the waiting had been agony for Christy. Waiting now for Todd to show up was even worse.

Christy was about to check her phone again when the door to the examination rooms opened and the medical assistant stepped out. "Christy Spencer?"

Christy followed her down the hall to a scale where she was weighed and then ushered into a small, highly air-conditioned room. In the center was an examination table with metal stirrups attached to the end. Christy hadn't thought about how thorough this exam might be. She suddenly felt clammy, and a familiar wave of nausea followed.

The nurse left, and Christy changed into the paper-thin examination gown. She positioned herself on the edge of the examination table, crossed her bare feet, and rubbed them together to warm them. Her nervousness about the exam overpowered her frustration with Todd for not being there.

A tap sounded on the door. Christy looked up hopefully. It was the nurse again.

"I'm afraid I have bad news for you, Christy. Dr. Avery had to go to the hospital for an emergency with one of her patients."

"Oh." Christy hoped her startled expression hadn't given away the rush of fear she felt when she heard "bad news."

"I apologize for the inconvenience, but we'll need to reschedule your appointment. I'll go ahead and take your vitals. We can at least put all your starting numbers in your file." The nurse slid the blood pressure cuff over Christy's bare arm, and she felt it tighten.

"Did you get the lab work back?" Christy asked. "Are you able to at least tell me if I am pregnant? I mean, definitely pregnant?"

The nurse removed her stethoscope and checked Christy's file. She looked up and offered a professional smile. "Yes. Your results are positive. From the information you gave us, it looks like you're about six weeks along."

Christy nodded. "That was my estimate, too. Are you able to tell me anything else?"

"You'll have an exam at your next appointment, and you should be able to hear the heartbeat then. Be sure to start on a prenatal multivitamin, if you haven't already. Let us know if you have any questions or concerns. We'll see you soon." The nurse exited quickly, closing the door behind her.

For a moment Christy didn't move.

I'm really pregnant.

The rushed appointment had not made the grand confirmation feel as grand as she had expected it to be. Her phone chimed, and she quickly reached for it to read the text from Todd.

JUST GOT HERE.

Christy texted back. I'M DONE. DON'T COME IN. I'LL MEET YOU IN THE PARKING LOT.

She slipped her clothes back on and stopped at the front desk to reschedule her appointment. Todd was waiting for her at the entrance of the large medical building.

"Hey." He wrapped his arms around her and pulled her close. "Sorry, Christy. There was an accident on the 405. It was all backed up. What'd the doctor say?"

"I didn't get to see her. She had to go to the hospital so I rescheduled."

Todd's silver-blue eyes narrowed. "So, we still don't know for sure?"

Christy grinned slowly. "No, the nurse confirmed it. We're definitely going to have a baby."

"We are? Really?"

Christy nodded.

Todd encircled her with his muscular arms once again and pulled her close, pressing a steady string of kisses against the side of her head. Christy drew back and offered him her lips. Todd kissed her tenderly.

"We're having a baby," she whispered.

"Are we going to start telling people now?" Todd asked.

"Yes. Who should we tell first?"

"Everybody!" Todd tried to catch the attention of an older woman as she was entering the medical building. "Hey, we're having a baby!"

The woman smiled politely and kept walking.

"Todd!" Christy playfully gave him a fwap on the chest. "Our parents should be the first ones we tell, don't you think?"

"Too late. I already told that lady."

"Be serious. Come on, don't you think we should call my mom right now?"

"If you want to. Sure."

"My dad won't be home but . . ." Christy reached for her phone and then paused. "Maybe we should wait and do a fun announcement at the end of the month at Uncle Bob and Aunt Marti's when my parents come up."

"Okay."

"But you probably want to tell your dad and Carolyn before then, right?"

"We can tell your parents first."

Christy bit her lower lip. "I told Katie she'd be the first to know, so maybe . . ."

"You know what?" Todd put his arm around her and started walking toward the parking lot. "I'll leave all that up to you. Just tell me when you want me to get on the phone. Are you hungry? We have time to get something to eat, don't we?"

Christy stopped walking and looked up at her husband's boyish expression. How could his thoughts turn to food so quickly while she was still enraptured with the happy confirmation and eager to finally tell people?

Todd's sandy-blond hair had grown long over the past few months, giving him the look of a sailor who had been out to sea a little too long. He had been working extra hours at the warehouse where he shaped old surfboards into park benches. Christy knew he was trying his best to keep up with everything, but she really wanted him to stay in the moment a little longer. This was a big deal.

"What?" Todd asked. "What's wrong?"

Christy noticed that his eyes were puffy and his left eye was bloodshot. If she had learned anything over the past few years of their marriage, it was that timing was everything with her husband. If he was hungry, the best course of action was to hold off on discussing any important topics.

"Nothing," Christy said. "I love you."

"I love you, too." He gave her a quick kiss and kept walking. "What about fish tacos?"

Christy felt her stomach do a long, rolling flip. "No thank you."

"You sure?"

"Yes, very sure. I need to get back to work. I'll stop to pick up a smoothie on the way. See you at home tonight."

"Oh, hey, did I tell you that Trevor and

Brennan are coming over around seven to work on music for the Friday Night Gathering?"

Christy tilted her head and gave him a teasing look. "No, I don't believe you mentioned that."

"You don't mind, do you?"

"No. Of course I don't mind. I just like a little warning ahead of time so I can make sure I have enough food for you guys."

"We don't eat that much, do we?"

Christy stopped beside her car and gave her teasing husband a look that said, "Do you really want me to answer that?" She pressed the unlock button on her key chain and kissed Todd. "I'll see you later."

Todd patted her flat belly tenderly as if he were saying good-bye to their new little miracle. "Yeah," he said with a grin. "Later."

Christy sat in the warm car for a moment with her phone in her hand. She thought about texting her best friend, Katie, and setting up a video call, but it was the middle of the night in Kenya where Katie and her husband, Eli, lived. Plus, something in her said she should tell her mom first, before anyone else. Even Katie. However, if Christy told her mom now and her mom told her dad, which of course, she should, then would her dad leak it to Christy's aunt and uncle? If he did, that would ruin any surprise announcement Christy might want to make later.

Leaning her head against the headrest, Christy realized she had another slight complication. Her manager, Eva, was friends with Aunt Marti. If Christy went back to the White Orchid Spa now and gave any hint of her news, Eva would surely tell Aunt Marti, and Marti would waste no time in telling Christy's mom. The last thing Christy wanted was for her aunt to find out and tell her mom before Christy had a chance to tell either of them.

Pushing a button on her phone, she did something she had rarely done before. She called in to work and said she needed the rest of the day off.

"Is everything okay?" Eva asked.

"Yes. I'll be at work in the morning. I just need to take a half day of personal time."

"Oh, okay. No problem. We'll see you in the morning, Christy."

Feeling like a free bird, Christy started the ignition. For a moment, she considered trying to catch up with Todd at his favorite fish taco hangout. Then a better idea came to her.

She drove the short distance to their home in Newport Beach and changed out of her work clothes into shorts and a cotton top and tied her Rancho Corona University hoodie around her waist. Christy tossed a few snacks and a bottle of ginger ale into her tote bag and grabbed a beach chair from the garage. She felt as if she was having her own personal ditch day as she took her time walking the few short blocks to the beach.

Just last week she bemoaned that she and Todd lived so close to the sand and surf, and yet they rarely took the time to walk on the beach. This afternoon was perfect for taking a front-row seat to the most gorgeous view in the world and doing some important thinking.

The early spring weather was breezy, but the sun had baked the sand to a golden warmth. Christy felt happy the minute her bare feet stepped onto the long stretch of toasty beach. To the left was a familiar lifeguard station, and in the far distance she saw the pier. Her aunt and uncle's beach-front house was about a fourth of a mile to the right along the walkway.

Drawn like a magnet toward the water, Christy traipsed past her two favorite palm trees and settled in the sand with a perfect view of the vast ocean. She snuggled her bare feet into the comforting sand and popped open the bottle of ginger ale.

The colors fed her soul. She loved the ombre effect of the caramel sand as it met the blue Pacific and stretched out effortlessly before melding with the pale blue of the cloud-streaked sky.

Pressing her hand on her stomach, Christy smiled. *Thank You. Thank You so much.*

Her small prayer was simple and heartfelt. She felt deeply grateful, and yet, if she was honest with herself, she would admit that she was also nervous. Ever since she took the home pregnancy test, she had kept her emotions and her conclusions on the lowest level possible. She had given no hints to anyone because she didn't want to build up too many hopes and then be heartbroken if she wasn't pregnant. Plus, one of the massage therapists at work had recently had a miscarriage, and Christy knew that was always a possibility.

She looked down and wiggled her feet, watching the way the sand clung to her toes.

What is that verse about the "grains of sand"? Something about how God thinks about us more times a day than all the grains of sand? Something like that. Where is that verse?

She looked at her feet again and tried to count the tiny grains of sand on just her big toe. She couldn't. There were too many, and the grains were all smushed together. Christy lifted her sunglasses and stared at all the sand around her feet. Then her gaze expanded to the sand around her, stretching as far as she could see in both directions.

Her heart felt overwhelmed. The precious reality settled on her.

I'm pregnant. Todd and I are going to have a baby.

Christy knew then that she couldn't wait another minute. She fumbled with her tote bag and pulled out her phone. She tapped on one of the buttons and waited. Her call was answered on the second ring.

"Hi, Mom," Christy said in a timid voice. "Do you have a minute? I have something to tell you."

Two

"Sorry, Christy, but this isn't a good time."

"Oh, okay."

"Your father just came home from work and told me some unsettling news. I need to call you back."

"That's fine. Is everything okay, Mom?"

"I . . . I'm not sure. I'll let you know."

The call ended abruptly, and Christy's phone went silent. She gazed out at the ocean and thought about how her mother was usually such a calm, matter-of-fact sort of person. Her answer of, "I'm not sure" was unsettling. Christy whispered another prayer. This one was for her parents.

Reclining her beach chair, Christy treated herself to what felt like the ultimate luxury of taking an afternoon nap on the beach while being lulled by the soothing sound of the waves. She slept deeply for only about twenty minutes, but that was exactly what she needed.

The rest of Christy's afternoon felt equally decadent as she strolled back to the house around four o'clock and treated herself to a long bath. She took her time putting together some food for the guys. Todd came dashing in the door just five minutes before Brennan and Trevor showed up with their guitars.

Christy had put out a large platter of loaded nachos and freshly made guacamole for Todd and the guys. They inhaled it before shuffling into the living room and tuning their guitars. Christy loaded the dishwasher and was humming along on the first song when her mom called back.

"Hang on, Mom," she said. "Let me go upstairs so I can hear you."

"Is this a bad time?"

"No, this is a great time. It's just that the music is live at our house tonight so I can't turn it down, if you know what I mean."

"It sounds nice."

"I know. I love this song. These guys are getting better all the time." Christy took the last stair and slid into the master bedroom. She closed the door and settled in her snuggle chair by the window. "There. I can hear you better now. What's happening with Dad? Is he okay?"

"There have been some changes for him

at work. He'll need to make a decision soon about whether he'll take an early retirement."

"Retirement? Dad's not old enough to retire, is he?"

"Well, according to some people he is."

Christy guessed that the "some people" were the decision makers at the small dairy where her father had worked ever since they had moved from Wisconsin to Southern California almost twelve years ago. She remembered hearing her parents talk about how extraordinary it had been for him to find work in his area of experience and how Uncle Bob had helped make it happen.

"When does Dad have to decide?"

"Soon. In fact, he's pretty much already decided that he needs to take the offer."

"What will you do?"

There was a pause on the other end of the phone. Christy was pretty sure her parents didn't have a lot of savings. They had rented the same small house in Escondido for the last decade, and even though Uncle Bob was a successful Realtor, he hadn't managed to convince them to buy a house. Christy had a feeling it was because Uncle Bob would have wanted to help out financially and Christy's dad was proud enough to want to provide for his family in his own way, even if it meant living by humble means.

"We have some options," Christy's mom said. "Your dad could find another job. We could move into an apartment, now that your brother is out on his own. Or we could move back to Wisconsin."

"Wisconsin?"

"It's an option." Christy's mom cleared her throat. Christy knew that meant she was trying to remain steady and not show her emotions.

"Wow, Mom, this is a lot for you and Dad to have to figure out."

"Yes, well, we need to sleep on it. But let's not talk about all that now. You were starting to say that you had something to tell me when you called earlier."

Christy hesitated. She wasn't sure if this was the right time to share her good news with her mom. Would it affect her parents' decision about what to do next? One thing was certain in her mind: They couldn't move to Wisconsin. She wanted them to be close by. Their home in Escondido was an hour-and-a-half drive from where Christy and Todd lived in Newport Beach. That was already too far away for them to be actively involved as grandparents. She couldn't bear the thought of their being thousands of miles away right before her first child was born.

But for some reason she couldn't bring herself to come right out and say, "We're having a baby." Instead, Christy said, "Um, I . . . well, I wanted to talk about when you guys come up to Bob and Marti's in a few weeks."

"Yes?"

"Well, I thought maybe we could do something together, just you and me."

"That would be nice."

"Maybe you and Dad can stay here overnight." Christy made a pitch for their downstairs guest room. "I finally put up new window shades after the old ones were broken when Doug and Tracy were living here. I think I told you how much Daniel loved to pull on the strings."

"I'll talk to your father and see what he wants to do. We don't have any responsibilities at church on that Sunday the way we usually do. It would nice to stay over and enjoy the time with all of you."

"We'd like that, too, Mom. The weather has been nice. We could ride bikes on the beach pathway or go over to Balboa Island. Todd would love it if we'd make s'mores out on our deck. He could play some of his new songs for you."

Christy's mom chuckled. "You don't have to plan activities for us. I think your father would be content to take a nap on your couch and just be with you. It's been a while since we've gone up there."

"I know. I don't think you've been here since Thanksgiving, and that was kind of a circus because we had so many people here."

"Do you have lots of guests coming in the next few weeks?" her mom asked.

"No. We don't have anyone coming until the last weekend of July. Shawna is going to come stay with us."

"I don't think I know Shawna. Is she a friend from college?"

"No, Shawna is Alissa's daughter. Do you remember Alissa, the girl I met on the beach the summer I first came here to stay with Bob and Marti?"

"I'm not sure."

Christy realized that during her teen years she kept a lot of things to herself and rarely told her mother anything that she thought might upset her or cause her to restrict Christy's involvement with the teens she had met at the beach. Alissa getting pregnant at sixteen was the sort of detail she didn't share with her mom.

Aunt Marti, on the other hand, knew most

of the specifics of Christy's comings and goings and her friendships. So did Uncle Bob. They didn't know everything, but they knew enough to be informed.

Christy explained that Shawna was going to stay with them while her parents were at a convention in Anaheim. "We did a video call with her parents last week and made all the arrangements. Shawna came on for part of the call. She seems pretty shy. We'll meet her face-to-face for the first time, though, when she comes in July."

"Will you get to spend much time with Alissa and her husband after the convention?"

"No. See, Alissa is Shawna's birth mom. But Shawna was adopted when she was a baby. Her parents are Andrew and Jacqueline, and they're staying at a hotel in Anaheim for the weekend. Just Shawna will be staying here with us."

"Oh, I see." Christy's mom paused. "How old is Shawna?"

"She'll be twelve in a few weeks."

"Twelve."

Christy guessed that her mom was doing the math. The gaps in her mother's understanding of the whole story made Christy want to sit down and tell her mom everything. Maybe when her parents came to stay with them she could share more details about Alissa and Shawna and why Todd decided before Shawna was even born that he wanted to stay involved in her life. It didn't feel quite right to start that conversation now on the phone. Christy went a different route and told her mom that Todd had a soft spot for kids like Shawna who were an only child, the way he had been.

"Todd always appreciated the people who spent time with him when he was growing up since his mom was gone and his dad was working all the time. He wants to do that for other kids. Especially Shawna."

"You and Todd are both very giving." Her mom seemed content not to go into all the details. That was a quality Christy had always appreciated about her mom. She allowed Christy the time and space to share what she wanted to share, when she wanted to share it. "I'm sure Shawna will enjoy staying with you very much."

"Well, I hope you and Dad will also enjoy staying with us very much," Christy said. "Try to talk him into it, okay?"

"I will. I should get going. We'll see you in a few weeks."

"Love you, Mom."

Christy knew her mother wasn't accustomed to saying, "I love you" so she didn't wait for the echo at the end of the call. She did feel loved, though. She also felt a little desperate at the thought of her parents moving. She wanted to share so many things with her mom now, starting with telling her that she was going to be a grandma.

I wonder if I should have told her. Why did I hold back?

Curled up in her cozy chair by the window, Christy lingered upstairs while the music floated up to her and brought back a flood of fond memories of their close friends Tracy and Doug who had lived with them last year. Doug and Todd often played guitars together and filled the house with praise music.

Christy thought about how rich and yet how difficult that season had been for all of them. The upheaval started when Tracy's parents left Newport Beach and moved to Oregon. Their move eventually prompted Doug and Tracy and their three little ones to move to Oregon after the twins were born. Christy couldn't imagine following her parents if they moved back to Wisconsin. She also couldn't imagine having a baby without her mom being close enough to be involved in an ongoing way.

There is no way my parents can move to Wisconsin. They have to stay nearby.

The music had stopped so Christy headed back downstairs to see if the guys were leaving. There was so much she wanted to talk with Todd about.

"Were we too loud?" Brennan asked.

"No, it sounded great. I had to take that call from my mom."

"How's she doing?" Todd asked.

Christy made a grimace.

"Is everything okay?"

Without thinking, she asked, "How would you feel about my parents moving in here?"

Todd looked surprised. "Before or after the baby comes?"

Christy froze.

"Baby?" one of the guys repeated.

Christy and Todd locked eyes. She held him with a tight stare. It was evident that he realized what he had just leaked out.

"Are you guys having a baby?" Trevor asked.

"Hopefully," Todd said calmly, plucking a few strings. "Someday."

Christy glanced at the high school guys. The topic of babies carried no further curiosity for them. Trevor strummed his guitar, picking up a chord based on the notes Todd had just played. His long, straight blond hair fell over his eyes as he looked down.

Christy switched the topic and asked the guys how their summer jobs were working out. They answered in short sentences, and Todd got up and went to the refrigerator. He pressed his cup against the dispenser to get some crushed ice. The clanging ended the awkward conversation, and Christy slipped away to pull a load of towels out of the washer and put them in the dryer.

Later that night when Christy and Todd were in bed, Christy reached over and gave Todd a playful pinch.

"Hey, what's that for?"

"That was for your loose lips! You almost blew it tonight. I don't want a couple of grommets to be the first ones we share our big announcement with."

"They're not grommets."

"Well, they're not our closest family and friends."

"They're my friends. I thought you liked them."

"I do. But . . ." Christy paused. "You're trying to change the subject, aren't you?"

Todd's dimple showed as he repressed a grin. "Maybe."

"Well, I'm not handing you a get-out-of-jail-free card quite yet, Mr. Loose Lips."

"I smoothed it over, didn't I?"

"Yes, but we still have to watch what we

say. I almost told my mom on the phone tonight."

"Why didn't you?"

"Because I think we should wait until the dinner at Bob and Marti's."

"So, that the plan then?"

"Yes. We've waited this long. We can wait a few more weeks and tell everyone at the same time."

"You're sure, then."

Christy hesitated. "Don't you think that's the best way to make the announcement? And after we tell them we can call your dad and Carolyn?"

"We could call my dad right now."

"Now?" Christy felt like her emotions had turned into a flurry of bouncing Ping-Pong balls. "But, Todd, I really think I should tell my mom first."

"Okay." Todd propped himself up on his elbow and, reaching over Christy, he unplugged her phone from the charger. "Let's call her now."

"No, we can't call my parents now. They'll be asleep already." She grabbed her phone from him.

"Then we'll call my dad." Todd reached for his phone.

"No, wait. I think we should wait."

Too late. Todd had already placed the call.

He put the phone to his ear. Christy's phone suddenly chimed. She looked at the screen and saw that Todd was calling her. Going along with the joke, Christy answered, "Hello?"

"Hey, it's your husband. You're making me crazy with this announcement thing. I'm calling to ask you if you'll call your mom tomorrow and get it over with."

"Okay." Christy hung up and borrowed the playful answer he had given her earlier by adding, "Maybe."

Todd returned his phone to the nightstand and acted like he was going to go to sleep. Instead he reached over and tickled Christy under the covers, causing her to curl up and giggle. Todd leaned over and started kissing her neck, which tickled even more from the scruff on his unshaved face. She broke into a loud belly laugh. Todd took advantage of her vulnerability and tried to plant a kiss on the lips while still tickling her.

Christy wiggled and turned her head from side to side, delighting in her husband's spirited antics. He caught her midway between her flips and gave her a big smack of a kiss on the lips. Christy lifted her head and kissed him back in a way that she knew Todd would recognize as an invitation.

Todd pulled away, his expression turning

serious. "What about the baby?" he said in a whisper. "Is it . . . ?"

Christy nodded and offered him a comforting grin. "Yes, it's fine."

He placed his rough hand on her flat stomach. "Are you sure?"

"Yes. I checked in one of the books Tracy left here when they moved. Books about pregnancy."

"We should get some more books."

"Okay."

"We need to read everything we can. And we need to always go to the appointments at the doctor's together, in the same car, so that what happened today can't happen again." Todd smoothed back her long hair that had swept across her forehead when she was writhing with laughter.

"I'm sorry I wasn't there for you, Kilikina."

"It's okay." Christy's heart always melted a little when Todd called her by her Hawaiian name.

"I want to be there for you. I want to do whatever I can for you. I want to be a better husband."

"Todd." Christy felt tears coming to her eyes. She smoothed her palm around the curve of his handsome face. "You are a wonderful husband. You are! And you are going to be a wonderful dad."

Her whispered words of deepest affection seemed to go through him like the best kind of shiver. A shiver of happiness and anticipation.

They held each other's gaze for a peaceful moment before Christy stretched her arm over her husband's side and turned off the lamp on the end table. She kissed him on the earlobe and on the cheek before extending her invitation to him once again with a definitive kiss on the lips.

This time Todd didn't hesitate before responding with the kind of RSVP that could only be expressed at the soul-deep level by a husband to his wife.

THREE

The next morning when Christy went downstairs, ready for work, she found Todd foraging through the cupboard.

"I thought you were going to make some oatmeal for us."

"I was. I am. The water's hot. I just can't find the packets."

"What packets?"

"You know, the kind you can tear open and there's oatmeal inside."

Christy remembered that Todd had spent most of his life eating only instant food or something that came in a box that could be microwaved for three minutes on high.

"We don't have any instant oatmeal." Christy opened the pantry cupboard and took out a large canister filled with oatmeal.

"What's that?"

"Oatmeal." She pulled out a saucepan and poured the recently boiled water from the electric kettle into the pan.

Todd looked closely at the large flakes in the canister. "Is this like oatmeal in the raw or something?"

"Yes." Christy grinned. "Something like that."

"It looks different than the kind in the packets. Are we going organic now?"

"I don't know if this is organic. It's what we have." Christy sprinkled a bit of salt into the water and went to the pantry for cinnamon and raisins. It still amazed her sometimes how clueless her husband could be about the most basic things. She had a feeling they were in for a world of adjustments when their baby came.

Todd opened the dishwasher and unloaded dishes while Christy stirred the boiling oatmeal. He pulled out two bowls and placed them on the island counter so Christy could scoop the oatmeal into them. He reached for the aqua bowl that had a row of white dots around the rim on the inside and a pink peony artfully curved around the outside.

Just as quickly he pulled his hand back and grinned. "I forgot. This is your favorite bowl."

"You can use it."

"Nah. It's all yours. I'll settle for this manlier green bowl with the white rose on it instead of the pink rose."

"This is a pink peony. And that's not a rose; it's a gardenia."

Todd looked at his bowl more closely. "How can you tell?" He opened the cupboard and looked at their other three bowls. "We need to get some bowls that have surfboards on them. Or maybe cartoon characters."

"Cartoon characters?"

"Yeah, our son isn't going to want to eat cereal out of a bowl with a flower on it."

Christy gave Todd an exaggerated "oh brother" sort of look. She knew he was teasing. But not completely.

Todd chose a new topic before Christy had a chance to say something about the bowls or about the way Todd was referring to their unborn child as their "son."

"So, what's going on with your parents? Last night you asked if they could move in with us. Why would they want to do that?"

Christy gave Todd the update on her dad's work situation while Todd scarfed down the hot cereal.

"They can't move back to Wisconsin." He put his emptied green gardenia bowl in the sink and rinsed it out. "We need them around here. Especially because my dad and Carolyn live on the other side of the world.

Our son needs grandparents nearby."

"I know. That's why I held back from telling my mom about the baby. I wasn't sure it was fair to influence them when they have such a big decision to make."

Todd gave her a funny look. "That's even more reason to tell them. Go ahead. Our son should influence their decision to stay here."

Christy couldn't let the "son" reference slip past her again. She put her hand on her hip and gave Todd her best playful look. "You keep saying, 'our son.'"

Todd poured a glass of milk and downed it in one long slosh. Without looking at Christy, he made an "mm-hmm" sound of affirmation.

"You're convinced that we're having a boy."

He wiped his mouth with the back of his hand. His clear-blue eyes gave her a "yes."

"What if we have a girl?"

Todd shrugged slightly.

Christy wasn't exactly sure what that meant. "You'll be happy if it's a girl, won't you?"

"Of course." Todd's even-keeled expression broke into a hint of how much he was enjoying getting a reaction out of Christy with his comments. "But he's going to be a boy."

Christy shook her head and took another bite of her oatmeal. Her gaze stayed fixed on Todd. He folded his arms and gazed back at her with a look of seasoned affection that had grown only stronger between them over the years. Both of them shot each other silent grins. Todd took a few steps closer to Christy.

Taking hold of her by cupping his large hands around both her elbows, Todd leaned in until they were forehead to forehead, nose to nose. Christy's bowl of oatmeal was still in her hands and was now wedged between them.

"Cole Bryan Spencer," Todd whispered with conviction. "You'll see."

Cole Bryan was the name the two of them had come up with in an unexpected and humorous way last summer while they were on a camping trip after the wedding of their friends Sierra and Jordan.

"Yes, well, you're right about one part of that declaration," she murmured back.

"What's that?" Todd pulled back and looked her in the eyes.

"The part about 'we'll see.' " She scooped another spoonful of oatmeal into her mouth.

"I guess we will." Todd kissed her on the

forehead, and when he pulled back he had a serious look on his face. "When do we find out? Did one of Tracy's books say when we'll find out if it's a boy or a girl?"

"They probably do, but I haven't read that far yet."

He reached for his phone on the counter. "I bet we can look it up. How far along are you? Six weeks?"

"Yes. I think it has to be at least five months before they can tell. Maybe it's more than that. I honestly don't know."

"It says on this app that you can find out the sex of your baby between sixteen and twenty weeks." Todd looked up, appearing quite pleased with his speedy answer.

"You have an app? A baby app?"

"Yeah. You need to get it on your phone. Bones told me about it."

Christy put her bowl on the counter with a defining thud. "Bones? The old surfer guy, Bones? You told him we were having a baby?"

"No, I didn't tell him. He was at work yesterday afternoon and was talking about how his daughter is having a baby, and she was telling him stuff every week like, 'It's as big as a pear,' or 'This week the lungs are being formed.' He put the app on his phone and was showing it to me. I thought it was

41

pretty cool."

"If somebody sees that app on your phone, they're going to figure out that we're expecting."

"Nobody is going to see it on my phone. And so what if they do? You're going to tell your parents today, right?"

Christy glanced at the clock on the microwave and avoided giving him a final answer. "I have to get going."

"Me, too. I'm going to be late tonight. We're behind on a big order, and I need to stay at the shop until we get the last bench finished." He gave Christy a brush of a kiss and exited through the door that led to the garage. Over his shoulder he called out, "Call your mother!"

Christy grinned and ran water into her bowl and the empty saucepan. She noticed that Todd hadn't finished emptying the dishwasher. He had pulled out the two bowls and then got sidetracked. She didn't have time to do anything now except make sure the house was locked up before she set off to work.

That evening Christy had plenty of time to do the dishes and the laundry and clean the kitchen floor. She put her favorite music on and cheerfully tidied up the living room. She hadn't called her mom yet, but she had thought a lot about it during the day. She still felt unsettled about telling anyone.

Is it because I'm afraid I might have a miscarriage?

Christy knew she shouldn't be afraid, but all she could think about was how deeply the loss had affected the massage therapist at work. She had told everyone and was talking about her pregnancy all the time. Then the baby was gone. It was terrible, and Christy didn't want to think about how she would cope if she lost this baby.

Denial seemed to be her closest friend right now.

Todd texted Christy twice that evening, letting her know they were still hard at work at the shop. Around nine thirty she texted him and said she was going to bed and hoped the project would wrap up soon.

The bench-making business had remained brisk ever since Todd went into partnership last fall with an older guy named Zane. The two of them worked well together, and Todd had brought on some of the guys he surfed with. Zane's wife did all the bookkeeping and was the one who had arranged for them to move into a better warehouse and workshop space as soon as the orders started rolling in.

The setup was good and so was the work

environment, but Christy knew that making benches out of surfboards wasn't what Todd wanted to do for the rest of his life. They were both thankful that it was bringing in so much money for them right now because they were better off financially than they had been their whole married life.

Christy went to bed alone that night. She smoothed her hand over her belly and decided it was time for her to be brave.

"Hello, little one," she spoke softly in the darkness. "How are you doing in there? I love you. Your daddy loves you. We can't wait to meet you."

She reached for her phone on the end table and clicked open the app Todd had told her about. She had downloaded it during her lunch break and spent ten minutes checking the images and information on what was happening inside her at the six-week stage. Her baby was the size of a pea. Its heart was the size of a grain of sand and already was working, pumping blood.

"That's amazing," she whispered. "You are so tiny. So, so tiny."

Christy put her phone back on the night-stand and stared at the ceiling. It was perhaps the first time she had thought about the wonder of what was being created inside her. Up until now it had seemed as if she had viewed her pregnancy as having a "condition." Something was happening to her body, and she felt the effects of the change with nausea, emotional swings, and weariness.

But that afternoon, when she looked at the images of a baby at six weeks, Christy connected with the reality that she was hosting a tiny life inside her. A real person was developing in her. A human with a heart the size of a grain of sand.

Christy reached for her Bible in the nightstand's drawer. She flipped through the Psalms on the hunt for the verse she had thought of at the beach about God's thoughts toward us being like a grain of sand.

She found it in Psalm 139. Christy got comfortable and decided to read the whole chapter aloud, as if she were reading her baby its first bedtime story. She loved this chapter and smiled when she reached the verses she already had underlined.

" 'You made all the delicate, inner parts of my body and knit me together in my mother's womb. Thank you for making me so wonderfully complex! Your workmanship is marvelous — how well I know it. You watched me as I was being formed in utter seclusion, as I was woven together in the dark of the womb. You saw me before I was born. Every day of my life was recorded in your book.' "

A few verses later she found the part about the grains of sand.

" 'How precious are your thoughts about me, O God. They cannot be numbered! I can't even count them; they outnumber the grains of sand!' "

The upstairs bedroom window was open a few inches. Christy listened for the sound of the waves and remembered how she felt yesterday afternoon when she sat on the beach and tried to count the sand on her toes and then looked around, taking in the immensity of how many grains of sand surrounded her.

You think about us that much, God? I can't even fathom it. More than all the grains of sand. And You've already started thinking about this little baby with that same endless compassion. Please protect this tiny life. Please, Father.

Christy lay quietly for many minutes. Her emotions had been all over the place the past few days. At the moment she felt settled. Safe. Secure. At peace.

She found her thoughts sifting through memories of Alissa and tried to imagine what it must have been like when she found out she was pregnant with Shawna. Christy's heart softened toward Alissa more than it ever had before. At the time she felt sorry for Alissa because her dad had passed away and her mom was in rehab for substance abuse. But when Alissa went to Boston to live with her grandmother, Christy didn't think about her much.

How difficult it must have been for Alissa to go to a doctor's appointment like the one Christy went to, alone, and find out that the results were positive. Christy couldn't imagine going through the pregnancy alone and then giving her daughter up for adoption.

I wish I could see Alissa now and sit down and have a long conversation with her.

The two of them had connected via phone and e-mail a few months earlier, but Christy wished they could be together and talk face-to-face. Her conversations with Alissa now would be much different than the sparse ones they had had over the years. It made Christy appreciate Todd even more because, from the beginning, he had reached out and been there for Alissa.

Maybe Todd and I should go to Oregon this summer. We could see Alissa and Brad as well as Doug and Tracy since they all live in Glenbrooke. I wonder how much time Todd will be able to take off from work. Maybe we could go in July. I won't be too jumbo by then, will I? We could stop in Santa Barbara and see Sierra and Jordan. It could be our last big camping adventure before the baby comes.

Christy fell asleep with happy memories floating around her from the camping trip she and Todd had taken last year in their renovated VW Bus, affectionately named "Gussie." She could see Todd's happy expression in her dreams as she pictured him strapping his surfboard to Gussie's roof and they took their time driving up the California coast, stopping whenever the waves kicked up. California dreamin' at its best.

Sometime in the middle of the night, Christy awoke feeling thirsty and unsettled. She turned over and saw that Todd's side of the bed hadn't been ruffled. She squinted as she checked her phone. 3:52 a.m.

"Todd?" Christy called out. She cleared her dry throat and called out again.

No response.

Taking her phone with her, Christy shuffled her way downstairs. The light in the downstairs bathroom was on and the door was open halfway. Christy had left it that way when she went to bed. She thought it would provide enough of a nightlight so

48

when Todd entered through the garage, he wouldn't step into a dark kitchen.

"Todd?"

Again, no reply. Christy dialed his cell and waited for him to answer.

"Hey, what are you doing up?" Todd asked.

"Are you okay?"

"Yeah. We're almost done here. Another couple of hours, and we'll be finished."

Christy frowned. "I didn't realize you would be there all night."

"We had some problems with the resin finish on some of the boards. We figured it out, though. It's just taking longer than we thought. Are you okay? What are you doing up?"

"I was thirsty. And I wanted to make sure you're okay."

"I'm good. Get some sleep, okay?"

"Okay. I love you."

"Love you, too."

Instead of going back upstairs, Christy made a cup of herbal tea and curled up on the couch. She pulled out a bag of granola and munched on it in the silence. It felt strange for everything to be so quiet in this space that was usually brimming with some sort of comings and goings.

She turned on the TV and found an old

movie just starting. Pulling a throw blanket over her feet, Christy settled in and watched the plucky heroine deliver her lines. Her words were quite different than the way people talked now. Christy wondered if the life that was being portrayed in the movie was really the way life was back when the film was made. Or was it all exaggerated? Did people really gather around a table for dinner every night and pass around bowls heaped with potatoes that had been mashed by hand and platters of crispy chicken fried in a cast-iron skillet?

I remember eating dinner with our family when I was growing up on the farm. Todd and I hardly ever sit at the table when we eat now. What will our lives be like when we become a family of three?

That was Christy's last hazy thought before she fell asleep on the couch and slept deeply until the light of the new day flooded the living room.

She squinted and looked around. "Todd?"

Christy got up and trotted into the kitchen. The light was still on in the down-stairs bathroom, and the door was still ajar. It was after eight o'clock already, and she knew she would be hard-pressed to get to work on time. She hurried upstairs and phoned Todd as she started the water in the shower. He answered just before the call would have gone to voice mail.

"Hi. How's it going?" she asked.

"Slow. We hit another wall. Are you on your way to work?"

"No, I'm running late." Christy felt a wave of nausea rolling over her. She leaned against the bathroom counter and closed her eyes. "I just wanted to make sure you're all right."

"I'm good. I'll let you go so you won't be late. I'll text you later."

"Okay." Christy barely got the word out and the call cancelled before the remains of her midnight granola party took over the moment.

She knew this was going to be a rough day.

FOUR

Over the next week Christy tried to push through the returning waves of morning sickness without drawing attention at work. Thankfully, she always felt better by around ten o'clock or at least by eleven. She found that if she ate a few plain crackers on her way to work, they helped to calm her stomach. Drinking sips of ice-cold water throughout the worst of it also helped.

Fortunately, Eva spent most of her time in the back office and wasn't at the front desk during the flashes when Christy felt about to be overcome by queasiness and the beads of perspiration swerved down the sides of her face.

Todd's workload hadn't let up. A second rush order had come in on the heels of the last big order. He was usually out the door by six in the morning, and many nights he wasn't home until after she had gone to bed. They had barely seen each other for the past five days. Almost all their communication had been through their phones. He seemed to have forgotten about Christy's indecision about when to tell their family and friends about the baby, and she was grateful for the chance to let it rest as she worked to release her fears about having a miscarriage.

As she and Todd drove to the doctor's office together, he looked more exhausted than she had ever seen him. His eyes were bloodshot and his skin pale since he hadn't been outside for so long.

They entered the doctor's office hand in hand. Christy was given a specimen cup and directed to the bathroom. When she returned to the waiting room, Todd was sound asleep in the chair. His chin rested on his chest.

Part of her felt embarrassed. Another part of her felt terrible for him. She wished they could both go home and sleep for two days straight.

She took the chair next to Todd and flipped through the pages of a magazine. It didn't matter what the other five people in the waiting room might think of her or of Todd right then. This was what their life looked like. She might as well own it.

"Christy Spencer?" The efficient medical assistant stood by the opened door with a fixed smile on her face.

Christy nudged Todd. He didn't stir.

She knew that he could awaken like a wild man if he was jolted out of a deep sleep so she tried a technique that had worked once at home. She rested her hand on his arm and softly said, "Todd, we're at the doctor's office. We can go in now."

He opened one eye and then the other. A dollop of drool had formed at the side of his mouth. He sat up straight, blinked, and wiped his lips. "Now? Where?"

"This way." Christy slipped her hand in his and led him through to where the assistant was waiting for Christy to get on the scale.

"You're down two pounds. Have you had a lot of morning sickness?"

Christy immediately felt concerned. She explained her symptoms and asked if it was normal to lose weight instead of gain during the first trimester.

"It varies. We'll keep an eye on it," the nurse said. "Try to eat a little something every few hours. Small meals work best. Mild foods, even protein drinks, are good for you at this stage." She led them into the examination room and gave Todd a small smile.

Christy introduced Todd as her husband,

and they exchanged hellos while the nurse wrapped the cuff around Christy's arm. She recorded Christy's vitals, instructed her to put on the paper gown, and assured her that Dr. Avery would be right with her.

When the door closed Todd said, "I didn't know I'd be coming in here with you." He looked away awkwardly and seemed to be studying the blood pressure chart on the wall.

Christy felt nervous. She handed him her stack of clothes and suggested that he sit on the chair and hold them for her. She positioned herself on the edge of the examination table. The paper covering crumpled as she adjusted herself.

Todd sat down with a plop. He appeared slightly relieved to have a job to do and rested his arms on Christy's folded clothes as if he were protecting them.

"This is creepy," Todd said.

"Creepy?"

Todd gave a nod to the sterile-looking surroundings and the movable tray in the corner that held some stainless-steel instruments all lined up. "They're not going to use any of those, are they?"

"I don't know." Christy felt aggravated, but she noticed again how exhausted Todd looked. He had told her on the way over that he wasn't going to go back to work that night. The other guys had ordered him to go home and go to bed. They assured him they could finish up without him.

"This is all new and frightening for me, too." The edge of frustration and fear was evident in her lowered voice. "I keep having these terrible thoughts about having a miscarriage. What if the doctor tries to find the heartbeat today, but it's not there?"

Todd reached for her hand. "We can't live in fear, Kilikina. We just can't. We have to take this a step at a time. If there's no heartbeat, no life, then all we can do is trust God for what's next, just like we trusted Him to get us to this point."

Christy blinked quickly so her tears wouldn't be evident if the doctor walked in right then. She knew Todd was right. She also knew she should have said something to Todd sooner instead of carrying the fear around inside for so long.

Todd let go of her hand and leaned back in the chair. "Just trust. Don't be afraid."

A tap sounded on the door. A middle-aged woman with short, bleached-white hair entered wearing an equally bleached-white doctor's jacket. She had a row of silver-stud earrings along the rim of her earlobe and a colorful protective cover on the electronic tablet she held in her hand. She looked up over the top ridge of her lime-green reading glasses. "Hello, Christy. I'm Dr. Avery. I understand we had to reschedule your first appointment. I apologize for that."

The doctor glanced over her shoulder as if intending to politely acknowledge the guest seated in the chair. She stopped and stared at Todd.

"Linda?" Todd suddenly looked more awake than he had been in two weeks. "Hey."

Dr. Avery looked at the chart again. "Spencer. Christy Spencer. I didn't make the connection." She turned to Todd and smiled warmly. "Todd, how are you? How's your dad?"

"He's doing great. He got married. He's living in the Canary Islands now."

"Really." She looked stunned.

Christy couldn't tell if the surprise was because Todd's dad was married or that he had moved so far away. She wondered if Dr. Avery had gone out with Todd's dad at some point and that's why Todd treated her with such familiarity.

Dr. Avery returned to her professional mode and focused on Christy as she went through a list of questions. The unexpected connection between the doctor and Todd felt awkward to Christy, but both of them seemed comfortable with the familiarity, whatever it was.

The nurse wheeled in a cart with a monitor and keyboard for Dr. Avery. All Christy had to do was lie back and follow the doctor's instructions. Todd stood by her head and took her hand in his.

A blip appeared on the screen. A light blinked. Then they heard it — a fluttery whooshing sound.

Dr. Avery smiled at Todd first and then at Christy. "That's your baby's heartbeat."

For one eternally-sacred-the-world-just-stood-still moment, Christy squeezed Todd's hand, and both of them seemed to be holding their breath in perfect union as they listened to the sound whoosh in and whoosh out with steady determination.

"He's alive," Todd whispered.

"Nice and strong," Dr. Avery said with medical efficiency. "That's always a good sign this early on. Do you know your due date yet?"

Christy couldn't speak. She felt as if she were spinning — as if she had fallen off the planet and was tumbling though the galaxy. Her baby. Their baby. The child growing inside of her was alive. Its tiny heart, the size of a grain of sand, was already beating.

A brand-new, eternal soul was being formed in the cavern of her body.

Christy wanted everything to stop so she could sit in the immense gravity of this holy moment. Her thoughts kept orbiting her heart like the moon, and her tears fell like shooting stars. Everything was in motion. Life was happening.

Todd's choked laughter pulled her back to earth and anchored her once again. He was crying unashamedly but was laughing at the same time. "Wow," Todd said. "Wow!"

It was all he could say, over and over, even after the monitor was turned off, and the sweet sound of their baby's heartbeat had returned to the cosmos. "Wow."

Dr. Avery gave them a moment to bask in the wonder while she checked Christy's chart. Lifting her chin, she delivered the important data to them with unemotional ease.

"It looks like your due date will be around November 20. I'd like to see you every month between now and then, unless you have any difficulties. If you do, call our advice nurse. She'll be able to answer a lot of your questions, and she can set up additional appointments, if she feels you should come in between your monthly visits." Dr. Avery smiled at them warmly.

"Congratulations. I'm very happy for you."

"Thanks, Aunt Linda." Todd initiated an awkward side hug with her.

"Say hi to your dad for me." Dr. Avery left and closed the door behind her.

"She's your aunt?" Christy didn't know Todd had any aunts living in the area.

"She's my mom's sister."

Christy let the information sink in. "I didn't know your mom had a sister."

"She has two. I haven't seen Aunt Linda in a long time. I didn't know she lived here. The last I heard, neither of them had any contact with my mom. Not since she moved to Florida."

The event of hearing their child's heartbeat was nearly eclipsed by this stunning news of Todd having two aunts, one of them a doctor who was going to deliver their baby.

"My mom ripped them off," Todd said in a matter-of-fact tone. "When I was about six, my mom convinced their dad to change his will. He died when I was nine and left everything to my mom. My dad said it was a significant amount. I don't know how much, but she took it all and moved to Florida."

"Wow." Now Christy was the one who was stunned. She knew that Todd's mom had left his dad when Todd was very young. She had remarried, and when Todd was a teen, he had lived off and on with her new family in Tallahassee. He had never told Christy much about that experience, only that it had gone poorly and was a bad idea. As far as Christy knew, Todd's mother hadn't made any significant efforts to be in his life. She didn't come to his graduation from high school or college. She told him she was going to come for their wedding, but she didn't.

Todd looked at Christy. Remnants of his earlier tears of happiness still glistened in his eyes. He leaned in and gave her a tender kiss. His heart seemed to be fixed on the promise of their future that they had just heard in the baby's heartbeat. If he harbored any resentment toward his mother and their broken relationship, he showed no evidence of the hurt. All that mattered in his world was right here in front of him, and his expression made it clear that he was filled with hope. No fear. Just hope.

Over the next few days Christy thought many times about the extraordinary visit to the doctor's office. Sometimes she pondered the marvel of hearing their child's heartbeat and how the doctor had said it was strong and steady and that was good.

Other times she thought about what her

husband's childhood must have been like without a mom. He seemed to have moved past a lot of the destruction and pain that must have been caused by his mother's choices. Christy didn't want to try to make him talk about any of it or relive any of the losses. But now that they would soon become parents, she wanted to make sure she and Todd had a mutual understanding of how they would parent their baby.

Thoughts of Todd's fractured childhood made Christy appreciate her own parents even more. It also made her eager to tell her mom about the baby. She wanted the announcement to be a special connecting time between the two of them. This was important. Her mother deserved more than to be part of a group announcement.

When Christy returned to the house from work three days after their doctor's appointment, she found that Todd was already home, which was unusual. He was stretched out on the couch, half asleep and half watching a movie with a noisy car chase.

Christy waited until the commercial and then positioned herself across from Todd in one of the living room chairs. "I want to tell my mom now."

"Okay."

"I'm ready. I want her to know now before

we tell everyone else."

"Good choice." Todd turned the volume to mute and gave Christy his attention. "That's how it should be between a mom and her daughter."

"Todd?" Christy tried to form her question carefully. "Do you ever regret that you didn't get to have a relationship with your mother?"

"Of course. I've thought about it a lot after seeing Aunt Linda." Todd pulled himself up to a seated position. His expression was serious. "My dad did a good job raising me. I realize that now. He had all his own stuff he was working through, but I never felt like he didn't have time for me or that he didn't want me around. We were more like brothers than father and son. The closest thing I had to a mom was Leilani."

Christy had heard bits and pieces about Leilani. For a short season, when Todd was in third grade, he and his dad moved to Maui. His dad's girlfriend, Leilani, had been an important woman in Todd's life.

"Leilani treated me like a son. It was awful when she died. I was too young to know how hard that loss was on my dad. I'm just glad he found Carolyn and that they have a good life together now."

"Even if their life is on the other side of

the world," Christy added.

Todd looked at his rough hands and rubbed them together. "Yeah, even if it is on the other side of the world. I'm happy for him."

Christy heard a rare sort of sadness in his voice. "Why don't we call your dad and Carolyn right now and tell them?"

Todd looked up. His eyes were puffy and red. "You call your mom first. Then we'll call them."

Christy went into the kitchen to retrieve her phone from her purse. She noticed a check sitting on the counter and was surprised at the amount.

"This isn't your paycheck, is it?" she called out to Todd.

"No, it's my percentage."

Christy picked up the check and carried it back to the living room. "Percentage for what?"

"Zane set it up when we first started making the benches that I would receive a percentage after we hit a certain mark in sales. I think he called it a designer commission. Something like that. I get a residual on each bench we make."

"Is this a one-time check?"

"No, I'll get a commission every quarter based on how many benches they sell."

"Todd, this is wonderful!"

His demeanor was still nonchalant. He never had been very motivated over money, whether it was the lack of it or the blessing of a bonus like this. For Christy, this kind of passive income was a huge blessing. She hadn't yet let her worry-woman thoughts turn to what they would do about their financial situation once the baby came. That was a conversation for another time.

Todd pointed at the check. "We can use some of it to buy a crib. I want to go shopping with you to pick it out."

Christy gave Todd a playful look of surprise. "Wait. Did my husband just say he wanted to go shopping with me?"

Todd reached for her hand and pulled her down next to him on the couch. He circled her with his arms and kissed her. Pulling back, he smoothed his hand down Christy's long hair and looked at her sincerely as he said, "I want to do this together. All of it. I don't know anything about babies or what we need. All I know is that this is our child, and we're going to raise him together from the start."

Christy's lips formed a grateful smile. She took note that Todd was still calling their baby a "him," but she decided this wasn't the time to point that out again.

"Call your mom." Todd stood up. "I have to go."

Christy reached for his hand. "You're not going back to work, are you?"

"No, I need to run to the grocery store. I'll be right back. Do you need anything?"

Christy smiled. "Just you."

Todd leaned over and kissed her again. "How about if I pick up a pizza for dinner?"

"That would be great. No onions or bell peppers, though."

"Got it." Todd strode to the kitchen and scooped up his keys off the counter.

Christy watched his cute backside as he exited through the door into the garage and thought, *I am married to the most wonderful man in the world.*

FIVE

Christy listened to the familiar chug-chug sound of Gussie's engine as Todd backed out of the garage and drove off to the nearby grocery store. She sat in silence for a few moments before dialing her parents' phone number. Her mother answered, and Christy drew in a deep breath.

"Mom? Todd and I have some very big news, and I wanted to tell you first."

"Oh?"

"Mom, we're going to have a baby."

"You are? Oh, Christy, that's wonderful! Norman, come here. Christy, say it again. I have you on speaker now."

"Hi, Dad." Christy's eyes had glazed over with tears. "Todd and I wanted to let you guys know that we're having a baby."

A pause followed on the other end of the phone. Christy blinked and wished that she had driven down to her parents' home and delivered this news face-to-face. Or at least convinced her parents to do a video call with her. She wanted to see their faces right now.

Her father's choked voice came over the phone. "We couldn't be happier for you. When is it coming?"

"November. The end of November. We just heard the heartbeat at the doctor's this week, and it's strong and steady." Christy grinned broadly as her tears fell. "You're going to be grandparents!"

She heard her parents laugh the best kind of shared joyous laughter.

"That's wonderful news, Christy," her mother said. "Your father and I needed some good news right now."

"You guys can't move to Wisconsin," Christy blurted out. "We need you here."

Another pause followed. Christy's reminder of the ominous decision looming over her parents seemed to have stifled all the gladness of the moment. She quickly tried to pull back what she had said.

"I just meant that, well, Todd and I hope, that . . ."

"Does your aunt know?" Christy's dad's voice sounded back to normal. Firm and a little gruff.

"No, I was going to wait until you come up this next weekend so I could make an announcement to everyone at dinner. But Todd and I talked about it, and we wanted to tell you before then. I wanted you to be the first to know, Mom."

"Thank you, honey. I appreciate that. We're so happy for you and Todd. This is wonderful news. Is Todd there?"

"No, he ran to the grocery store." Christy wished she had asked him to wait so he could have been in on the call with her.

"Your mother's right, Christina. It was considerate of you to tell us first." An ease had returned to her father's voice. "Tell Todd we're happy for you both."

"I will."

"Your mother said you had asked earlier if we could stay over with you next Saturday night."

"Yes. We'd love to have you stay with us for as long as you want."

"Okay, we'll stay with you Saturday night. You can put me to work painting the nursery or putting together the crib or whatever you need."

Christy grinned. "We're not quite at that stage yet, but thanks, Dad. Oh, and if you guys don't mind, could you not say anything yet to anyone? We're going to call Bryan and Carolyn in a little bit and tell them. But, if you could wait until after we make an announcement next Saturday, that would be great."

Christy's mom assured her they would both keep their lips sealed and joyously offered another round of congratulations before the call ended. Christy kept smiling as she headed upstairs to change out of the black top and pants she had to wear as a uniform for work. She was very glad she had told her parents. The only problem now was that she wanted to tell everyone else. She remembered how Todd wanted to tell everyone after her first appointment confirmed that she was pregnant.

Katie is going to freak out. I've avoided setting up a video call with her for more than two weeks. She's probably figured out that something is up. Tracy is going to be so happy for us. I wonder what Aunt Marti will say? She'll probably immediately buy designer baby outfits. Uncle Bob will cry. I know he will.

Christy washed her face, folded her hair into a side braid that hung over her shoulder, and smoothed her favorite coconut-and-mango-scented lotion over her arms. The best part about working at a spa was that she received a discount on expensive, scrumptious body care products. She also had learned to treat herself to small kindnesses that made her feel relaxed and lovely and very much at home on evenings such as this. The long, flowing beach dress she changed into made her feel even more relaxed.

The sound of the automatic garage door opening beneath their bedroom meant that Gussie was returning to her shelter. Christy smiled at her contented reflection in the bathroom mirror and then headed down to the kitchen. She felt as if she were floating down the stairs.

Christy stopped on the second to the last stair. Todd was standing in the middle of the kitchen with a big bouquet of white carnations, fresh from the grocery store with the clear cellophane still wrapped around them.

He held them out to Christy and grinned. She went to her adorable man, took the bouquet, and pressed a warm kiss on his lips. The spicy, sweet fragrance wafted to her nose and connected her heart to every memory she had of falling in love with Todd.

"Thank you," Todd said as he pulled back.

She lifted her eyes. "Are you thanking me for being pregnant? Because you had something to do with that, too, you know. Should I get a thank-you present for you, too?"

"Naw." Todd grinned. "I saw the flowers at the store, and I just wanted to say thank you for being my wife." He sniffed the air. "Smells good in here."

All Christy could smell were the fresh carnations. Her heart was filled to overflowing.

Todd suggested that they eat their pizza outside on the deck. The evening was beautiful and mild. They settled into the low beach chairs side-by-side at the fire pit and sipped from bottles of a select variety of cream soda Todd had discovered a few months ago. The drink was a little sweet for Christy's liking, but it was Todd's current favorite so she gladly clicked the neck of her bottle with his and smiled again at their small celebration of life, love, and all that was to come.

Todd had texted his dad earlier about a good time to set up the video call. The reply came back that it would work for them the next day. With the time difference, that meant Christy and Todd would be getting up earlier than usual to place the call, but neither of them minded.

They set the alarm that night and got up early enough so Christy had time to wash her face and brush her hair. She pulled on her old Rancho Corona hoodie over her pj's and positioned herself next to Todd at the kitchen counter with her arm around his shoulder. She could see in the smaller upper box that Todd was grinning as broadly as she was.

The call went through on the first try, and Todd's dad, Bryan, and his wife, Carolyn, appeared on the screen. They were in their beautifully renovated home in the Canary Islands. The buttery glow from the lamps in the living room made it clear that nighttime was upon them, and their contented expressions reflected that all was well in their corner of this golden world.

Carolyn greeted them with an eager grin and immediately said, "We are so happy for you!"

Christy looked at Todd. "Did you tell them already?"

"No, I didn't tell them. We're telling them now. Go ahead."

Christy looked into the camera and delivered what felt like an afterthought. "We're having a baby."

Bryan and Carolyn beamed and said all the right words of congratulations.

Christy looked at Todd and then looked back at her in-laws. She didn't feel like she could be mad at him for enthusiastically giving away their big news. She just wanted to know what he had said and why he hadn't waited.

Turning back to the screen, Christy asked, "What did he tell you?"

"It was all the emojis in his text that gave it away," Carolyn said. "I loved the one with the crawling baby and the long line of baby bottles."

Christy looked at Todd. "You used emojis in a text? That's how you told your parents?"

"I was waiting for the pizza," he said.

Christy laughed and shook her head. She was too happy to give him a hard time.

"Tell us all the details," Carolyn said. "When are you due?"

Christy shared about the due date, how it felt when they heard the heartbeat, and how the only people they'd told so far, besides them, were Christy's parents. She asked if they could keep it quiet until she and Todd had a chance to tell Aunt Marti and Uncle Bob and then make an official announcement online. Carolyn's daughter was married to one of Christy's childhood friends from Wisconsin. If Tikki found out and told other people, Christy was afraid the news would circle back to Marti before they had a chance to make an announcement Saturday.

"We'll wait until you give us the all-clear signal." With a laugh Carolyn added, "You can send us a text with more emojis, Todd.

I'm sure you can find some we've never seen before."

He glanced at Christy and gave her a chin-up sort of nod. "I have a few hidden talents you don't know about."

"I guess you do."

Over the next few days Christy had to use considerable effort to restrain herself from setting up a video call with Katie or sending a text to Tracy. She knew it was important to tell her aunt and uncle first, but the stress of delaying the news was wearing on her. Most of the stress seemed to be based in her inability to think of a clever way to make the announcement. She watched video clips of other couples' baby announcements and checked social-media boards for fun ideas. The possibilities were overwhelming, and so were the elaborate ways many people made their announcements.

The posts of how couples did grand reveals of their babies' genders were even more overwhelming.

"When did our culture get so crazy?" Christy asked Todd Friday night. They were on their way back from the usual Friday Night Gathering that was held in the large, empty garage at Trevor's house.

The worship time had been especially meaningful that night because of the new songs the guys had been working on. One of the girls read a poem she had written, and one of the younger guys bravely asked the whole group to pray for him because his parents were getting a divorce. Christy loved seeing the group of more than fifty teens rally around the guy and show him so much support.

Todd talked to the group about friendship that night. He talked about how friends were such an important part of their formation and that's why they should choose their friends wisely. Christy had heard him talk about that topic to groups several times over the years, but she always appreciated hearing it because Todd and her other Forever Friends were such a significant part of the formation of her life and values when she was a teen.

As Todd drove them home that night, he said, "It's harder now to find a good friend than it was a decade ago when we used to hang out with Doug and Tracy and the rest of the God Lovers. Trevor told me that two of the guys who used to surf with us have dropped out. They've gotten in with a rough crowd. That really bothers me."

"I'm sorry to hear that," Christy said. "Hopefully they'll reconnect with your guys."

"That's what I'm praying," Todd said.

Christy circled back to the thought that had prompted her original comment. "I haven't figured out how to make the announcement special tomorrow when we have brunch at Bob and Marti's."

"It's the miracle of new life, Christy. Isn't that special enough?"

"I wanted to do something fun. Something clever, like you did with the emojis for your dad."

"That wasn't planned."

"I know, but it was memorable." She told Todd about the many ideas she had seen online of how couples shared their baby news. She told him it was too late for them to print T-shirts or order mugs made for Bob and Marti. "And besides, that's not their style. I want it to be distinct. I want to do this right."

"You know what I think?" Todd parked Gussie in the garage and turned off the engine. He adjusted his posture and looked at Christy in the passenger's seat. "I think you're worried about hurting your aunt or making her nervous because she and Bob lost their baby daughter all those years ago."

Christy let the thought settle on her. It was true. She was nervous about telling her aunt and uncle their good news. She hadn't felt nervous about telling her parents. She hadn't felt flustered when they told her in-laws, and she couldn't wait to tell Katie and Tracy. But Todd was right.

"It's because you love them," Todd said. "But here's the thing. Losing their baby was their experience, not ours. They have dealt with it over the years in their own ways. It's not something we can change or make easier for them. You and I need to fully live out our lives. This is our baby. Our future."

Christy nodded. She agreed. Their experience should not be compared to her aunt and uncle's.

"You have a tender heart, Kilikina. I know you want to be sensitive to their feelings, but you and I are full of hope. That's what we feel. I think that's what they'll feel for us."

"You're right." Christy leaned her head back and stared out the windshield at the stack of boxes and assorted clutter that had accumulated in their garage. Even though Todd's statements should have settled the topic, her hormones seemed to be feeding her brain a flurry of unprocessed ideas.

"Although, maybe I could buy a little pair of baby shoes and put them on the table at brunch. Or better yet, a pair of baby flip-flops. Don't you think that would be cute?

And simple?"

"Sure."

Christy felt a crazy-strong urge to purge all the baby announcement thoughts that had been crammed inside her for weeks. She talked fast and used her hands in an animated way as if she were tagging all the ideas as they flew out of her mouth.

"So, what do you think?" Christy glanced over at Todd. His eyes were closed and his head was leaning against the window. "Are you asleep?"

"Almost." He opened both eyes and tried to focus on her.

"You're fried, aren't you? Let's go in." She realized she had overanalyzed this topic with her exhausted husband. Her brain wanted to keep going, and she had enough energy to talk about it for another hour. But her patient husband had reached his limit.

Todd opened the car door and came around to Christy's side. He opened her door and offered her a hand out. It was his new thing. He told her it made him feel like he was doing his small part in helping with baby care.

"Let's just tell them, Christy. We don't have to make T-shirts or release a bunch of balloons. We can start a whole new trend and just say, 'Hey, we're having a baby. Be happy for us.' We'll post that online and get a million likes."

"Yeah, a million likes from a million guys who wish their wives wouldn't try to be so creative," Christy said.

"Hey, I like your creativity."

"I know. But you're right," Christy said as they entered the kitchen and turned on the light. "It's best to keep things simple. We should just tell them."

"What time are we going over there tomorrow?"

"Ten. Are you going surfing tomorrow morning?"

"No. I told the guys I couldn't make it. I have to get some sleep." He kissed Christy on the forehead and made his way upstairs with slow footsteps.

Pouring herself a glass of water, Christy leaned against the kitchen counter. She pulled her phone from her purse and saw that she had missed a text from Katie.

ELI AND I HAVE BIG NEWS! VERY BIG NEWS! WHEN CAN WE SKYPE?

Christy's heart took off flying. She was certain this could only mean one thing. A little dream she and Katie had shared for years was about to come true. They were both pregnant at the same time!

"Todd," Christy called out. "Don't go to

bed yet. We have to call Katie and Eli!"

She hurried upstairs to their bedroom and found her husband stretched out on his stomach on his side of the bed, still in his clothes, sound asleep. Christy smiled to herself and went back downstairs. She set up her laptop in the living room and clicked the familiar buttons that would connect her with her best friend.

The call went through, and Katie's freckled face appeared, filling the entire screen.

"Christy, you're not going to believe this! Guess what?"

"You're having a baby!"

Katie looked stunned.

Christy couldn't hold in her announcement another second. "Me, too, Katie! When are you due?"

An odd expression had come over Katie's face. She pulled back from the screen, and her facial features seemed to be caving in as her smile diminished. Eli appeared in view. He gave Christy a slight wave.

"Christy, I'm not pregnant," Katie said.

Six

Christy collected her thoughts and reran in her mind what had just happened. How did she arrive at what seemed such an obvious conclusion and yet have it all wrong?

"You're not pregnant?" Christy asked. "I thought when I saw your text that . . ."

"Wait." Katie's red hair swished as she glanced over her shoulder at Eli and then fixed her view back on the screen. "Did you just say you're pregnant?"

Christy nodded.

"You're pregnant!? Really? Honest?"

Christy nodded again. Her smiled returned and so did Katie's.

"Christy, I can't believe it! You're going to have a baby! Are you sure?"

"Yes, very sure. We're due in November."

"Wow, Christy!" Katie's expressions made it clear that the news was finally sinking in.

"Congratulations," Eli said.

"I would have called you sooner, Katie. I

almost did right after we found out. But Todd and I thought we should tell our parents first. We told them the other day, and now we're going to tell Bob and Marti in the morning. When I saw your text, I thought your good news was the same as our good news."

"No." Katie looked at Eli over her shoulder. "No babies for us. Not yet."

"So, what's going on? What's your big news?"

Katie leaned in closer to the camera. "We're coming back to California in the fall!"

"You are? For how long?"

"At least six months. Maybe a year. We're going to work on recruiting service teams at different universities and set up a more organized system for fund-raising with a base in the States. The best part is that we can do this from anywhere so of course we want to live near you guys."

"Katie, I can't believe this! I'm so excited!"

"I know." Katie's green eyes filled with tears. "Can you believe this? Of course you can believe this. This is a God-thing of cosmic proportions. You said you were due in November? That means we'll be there when your baby is born. This is what you and I have both wanted since we were roomies at Rancho."

"I know." Christy felt the tears welling in her eyes. "When will you get here?"

"We hope to come in August."

Eli leaned in and placed his hand on Katie's shoulder as if trying to calm her exuberance. "It's not finalized yet. We should probably make that clear. We're waiting for the budget to be approved. But the initial proposal was accepted at the board meeting today."

"It'll happen." Katie looked undaunted. "It has to all work out. It just has to."

Christy tried to read Eli's hesitant expression. He always had been the more cautious one. Christy decided to side with Katie's effusive optimism on this one. She hoped with all her heart that Katie would be in California by August or at least by November. It would be so great if Katie and Eli could move into their guest room. Christy started thinking through the possibilities but then knew she needed to talk with Todd about everything.

"Let us know as soon as the budget is approved and when you're ready to make your plans," Christy said. "I'll tell Todd your good news in the morning. I tried to wake him up so he could be on this call, but he's been working way too many hours, and he's dead asleep."

"Tell him hi for us. And don't worry. We'll keep you updated on all the details and let you know the minute we book our flights," Katie said. "I'm so excited for you guys and the baby. I can't wait to get there. This is going to be amazing, Christy. I still can't believe you're pregnant!"

"It took me a while to believe it, too," Christy said.

"Do you hope it's a boy or a girl?" Katie asked.

"Either."

"Or both? Like Doug and Tracy had with their twins?"

The possibility of twins had flitted through Christy's thoughts before, but it sounded so daunting when Katie said it aloud. "I don't think we'll have twins."

Katie took on a mischievous look. "We never know what surprises God might have waiting for us just around the corner."

Eli said something about how they would all have to wait and see what happened. Katie blew her a kiss, and Christy went to bed smiling over the possibilities ahead.

She woke two hours later to go to the bathroom and realized her dreams had been of the sort she and Katie had fabricated during their high school and college years whenever they made wishes together. They wanted to both marry around the same time, which they had. They wanted to live near each other and raise their children together and always share the happy and sad moments of their lives together. They had done that in bits and pieces while Katie finished college, but everything changed when she moved to Africa. Now their lives would soon be back in sync in an everyday rhythm.

Christy couldn't be happier.

She told Todd the good news as soon as he woke up, which was after nine o'clock. He immediately agreed that Eli and Katie should come live with them and wanted to call them and make sure they knew they had a place to stay.

Christy knew how long a call like that could last. "We probably should wait and call them later because we need to get to Bob and Marti's in half an hour. I'm almost ready to go."

While Todd showered, Christy finished dabbing on some mascara and then went downstairs to tidy up the guest room. She wanted to make sure the bathroom had plenty of clean towels and a new bar of soap in the shower for her parents.

It struck Christy that her life had unfolded in many of the ways she always had hoped it would. She liked to be hospitable, and Todd loved to teach and lead teens. When they first talked about getting married, when they were still in college, Christy pictured them doing some sort of ministry together as a couple, the way Katie and Eli were doing with digging wells in Africa to provide clean water. Christy saw herself hosting, cleaning, and cooking to facilitate some sort of group of young people that Todd would oversee as a youth pastor or ministry leader.

Everything they both wanted to do was happening, but none of it was happening the way they thought it would.

On their short drive over to Bob and Marti's beachfront home, Christy asked Todd, "Are you happy with what you're doing now?"

He shot her a surprised look. "It's okay. I'm grateful for the steady income."

"I know, but making benches is not what you really want to do with your life, is it?"

Todd paused before saying, "Friday night is my favorite part of the week. The Gathering is what I like doing most."

Christy reached over and gave his arm a squeeze. "Thank you for being willing to do work you don't really love. I appreciate that you're always thinking of us and how to bring in the income we need."

A slight smile hung on the edge of his lips and seemed to halt what he was about to say next. Todd hadn't always felt the weight of doing his part to provide for them. A few years ago they had gone through a horrible stretch during which Todd struggled with his identity after stepping away from a difficult situation in a church where he had served as the youth pastor. He loved his role there, and in many ways it seemed to define who he was.

When that anchor was pulled up, he drifted on the sea of possibilities for a long time. Christy believed with all her heart that it had been God's provision and His answer to a lot of prayers that had opened up the job for Todd to make surfboard benches with Zane.

Something inside Christy nudged her to pray for Todd. She felt she should pray that he would be able to move into a job that would make him feel fulfilled. She guessed that would be some sort of position where he would teach teenagers and be involved in their lives in a significant way.

"It's been a while since you've checked on any openings for youth pastor positions in this area." The words were out of Christy's mouth before she had thought through how they might sound to Todd. The nudge in her spirit had been for her to pray, not for her to come up with logical solutions to what she saw as a problem for her husband.

"Yeah. I haven't been on the hunt for a job like that." Todd's expression and his response appeared calm. But Christy felt an undercurrent of tension that had been there between them in the past when they had talked about this topic. "Let me get your door," he said.

Christy pressed her lips together.

Pray. Just pray. That's all you have to do.

Christy linked her arm in Todd's as they walked up to Bob and Marti's house. She leaned close and was grateful for their shared expressions of solidarity and alliance because as soon as they entered Bob and Marti's spacious home, she felt a kind of tension in the air. Her aunt, a determined woman who was much more forceful than her petite frame indicated, was in one of her hyper modes.

Marti greeted them at the door wearing a flowing, sheer poncho over a low-cut, sleeveless top and pair of designer jeans. She looked as if she were about to play the role of a butterfly in an interpretative dance performance.

"It's so lovely that everyone could be here today." Marti kissed Christy on the cheek and then showed the same gesture of culture and glib hospitality to Todd. "Come in, come in. Don't worry at all about being late. Everyone is on the patio. Bob is starting us off with sparkling beverages. Join us."

Christy turned to Todd and whispered, "Are we late?"

He shrugged.

Marti flitted ahead of them toward the patio at the back of the house that faced the wide beach and the ocean. Christy and Todd exchanged humored glances. It seemed as if Marti was hosting one of her special fund-raising events and not simply serving brunch to her four closest relatives.

Christy's mom and her dad got up from the table when they saw Christy coming their way. Her mom was grinning broadly and seemed eager to place her hands on Christy's stomach, which she did in a subdued way.

Christy's dad kissed her on the side of her head and gave Todd a brief side hug, which was unusual for him.

Christy's uncle was his usual warm self. He gave Christy a hug and a kiss on the cheek and then slapped Todd on the back with a friendly thwap as the two of them hugged, surfer-guy style.

"My! Aren't we all happy to see each other today?" Marti exclaimed. "It's been far too long, hasn't it? Please sit down. The food is on the table. Let's not wait another moment."

The group complied, and Bob asked if they would all hold hands around the table so he could offer a prayer of thanks.

The words, "In Jesus' name, amen," were barely out of his mouth before Marti lifted her knife and gently tapped the side of her fluted glass, as if she needed to do so to get everyone's attention.

"I'm so glad it worked out for us to all be here today because Robert and I have something we've been eager to tell you."

Christy and Todd exchanged poker-face glances.

What is going on? I thought we were going to be the ones with the big news. And what about my dad's news about being forced into early retirement? Do Bob and Marti know about that already?

"We bought a new house!" Marti looked at each guest around her table as if in search of shock or praise or some sort of effusive response.

"Tell them the details," Bob said. "There's

a lot more to it."

"As you all know, we sold our two condos on Maui earlier this year. We decided to use the profit to invest in a home in this area that needed renovations. We'll have the renovations done and then sell the house at a grand profit." Marti looked at everyone again as if she had been the first person to ever come up with this idea.

"The house we found is on Balboa Peninsula," Bob said. "It's only a few miles from here, and it's in bad shape. We put an all-cash offer in and it's looking like we'll get it."

"I was going to tell them that part," Marti said, taking the reins again. "It's newer than this house and much larger. I'm working on the decorating selections, and as I said, our plan was to simply make improvements and sell it."

Marti glanced at Uncle Bob. "However, just last night we decided that since we like the way the renovation plans are shaping up, we think we'll move into it and rent this one."

Christy's thoughts immediately ran to her parents as well as Eli and Katie's upcoming need for housing. How wonderful it would be to have either one of them only a few blocks away. She wondered if her aunt and uncle would be able and willing to set the rent at an affordable rate.

"Well?" Marti was still waiting for a response. "What does everyone think? It's the biggest news we've had in a long time. We're moving into a new house in a few months."

Each of them offered their congratulations. Christy bobbed her head in agreement to the words of praise the others were offering. She wondered how she and Todd could slip in their big news about the baby. It made her wish that they had done some sort of gift like a mug, so she would at least have a box to place in front of her aunt when it made sense to change the subject.

Marti held fast to the subject of the new house during their entire meal. She described the floor plan, the current style of kitchen appliances, the square footage, the way they were going to create a new master suite upstairs, and then she started in on her color palette and the virtues of her choice of Italian marble countertops in the kitchen and bathrooms. She talked about the renovations as if this were her life's work.

In a way, maybe it had been her life's work. Marti had renovated their current home a half-dozen times. Maybe more.

At last Christy chimed in. "It sounds

exciting, Aunt Marti. It's a lot of work, but I'm sure the end results are going to be gorgeous."

Then, because she had been trying to think of a simple way to slide in their big announcement, Christy added, "Do you think the new house might be finished by, say, around November 20?"

Marti clasped her hands together. "Yes, good thinking, Christy. Thanksgiving will be at our new home this year. Is it on November 20 this year?"

"No." Christy felt like she was dropping the first clue. "Thanksgiving is on November 24 this year."

"That would be nice," Bob said with a nod of satisfaction. "I think it's possible to have the work done by then. The dining room has a great view. I like the idea of all seven of us gathering around the table and giving thanks. Wouldn't that be great, Marti?"

Before Marti could answer, Christy jumped on her uncle's comment with a more obvious clue. "Actually, this Thanksgiving there will be eight of us around the table."

"Eight?" Marti looked intrigued. "Are you saying that David has a girlfriend?" She looked at Christy's parents, who were both trying to conceal their smiles. "No one told me David has a girlfriend. When did this happen?"

"David doesn't have a girlfriend," Todd answered before Christy could. "David won't be the one bringing a guest to the dining room table this year for Thanksgiving."

Marti looked befuddled.

Christy reached across the table with both hands and took Bob and Marti's hands in hers. "Todd and I will be bringing a new family member to Thanksgiving this year. Lord willing, we'll be bringing our baby."

Marti's mouth slowly opened, but no words came out.

Bob gave Christy the same grin he had bestowed on her for years as a silent way of telling her how proud he was of her. She knew the secret message in his look because the corners of his eyes always crinkled in an upward pattern, as if his smile were rising on his expression like the sun. And yes, he cried, just as she knew he would.

Todd put his arm around Christy's shoulders and gave her a squeeze.

Todd was right. This was perfect. Simple. To the point. All we needed to do was tell them we're having a baby.

Christy let the reality sink in one more time.

We're having a baby.

If felt so good to no longer keep the news to themselves. Christy caught her mother's gaze and felt instantly warmed by her proud and nurturing smile. Christy was so glad she had told her mom about the baby first.

Now they could tell the rest of the world.

SEVEN

The first Tuesday in June proved to be an important day for Todd and Christy. It was the day they would be able to find out if they were having a boy or a girl. The problem was that they hadn't come to a mutual decision on whether they wanted to know the sex of their baby.

Ever since the brunch at Bob and Marti's a month and a half earlier, the entire family had been engaged in a lively discussion as to whether they should find out ahead of time or go the old-fashioned, simple route and find out when the baby arrived.

Marti, of course, was adamant about knowing right away so she could shop for clothes and nursery décor. Her plans to renovate the new house were in full swing, and at one point she told Christy it would be too stressful for her to not know the gender until November.

Marti's reaction to Christy and Todd's

baby news hadn't surprised Christy. She had hoped Marti would be more excited and congratulatory, but instead the new house and not the new baby occupied Marti's mind.

Christy's mom, on the other hand, was enthusiastic and supportive in every way. Christy's dad had been given an extension until the end of the summer to make his work decision. On August 31 his forced retirement would go into effect. The extension seemed to give Christy's mom and dad the time they needed to think through the options without panic.

The reprieve also gave Christy's mom an eagerness to check in every few days with a call or text to see how Christy was feeling. She had confided in Christy about how the decision-making process was going and the possibilities they were considering about where to live. This new level of friendship with her mom prompted Christy to tell her they weren't sure about finding out the sex of their baby.

Her mom said she hadn't found out what she was having when she was pregnant. She liked not knowing until Christy and David were born because it allowed her the chance to form her opinions of them on first sight, not several months ahead of time.

Christy had told Eva at work and was surprised at how supportive Eva was about the baby and the possibility that Todd and Christy might not find out the baby's sex until the moment of birth. She gave Christy a gift bag filled with all Christy's favorite lotions and candles from the spa gift shop and told her to start nurturing the baby now with "tranquil moments" and "peaceful meditations."

As Christy told her coworkers and other friends she kept up with online, all of them had asked if she was hoping for a boy or a girl. Her answer was the same as it had been for Katie and Eli. "Either."

Todd kept saying it didn't matter to him if they found out now because he knew it was a boy.

When they had told Doug and Tracy, Tracy gave her prediction that it would be a girl. Doug laughed. "Or you could get one of each the way we did."

"Katie said the same thing," Christy told him. "I'm sure we're having only one baby. We only heard one heartbeat."

Doug still teased her, saying the second one might be hiding in there.

When Christy and Todd rode together to the doctor's appointment on that first Tuesday in June, they still hadn't decided whether to have Dr. Avery reveal the gender to them.

"The way I see it," Todd said, "you're the one who needs to make the call on this, Christy. I don't need to know."

"Aunt Marti wants to know."

"Of course she does. This is our decision, not hers."

"I know." Christy thought a moment and added, "Your dad also said he would like to know."

"That's true."

"But I agree with you. It's our baby. We should decide."

Todd glanced over at Christy. "Don't overthink it. If you need to know, then say so."

"I don't need to know." The answer tumbled out of Christy's mouth. As soon as she said the words, she felt settled on the subject. "I really don't."

"Then that's our final choice." Todd pulled into a parking spot and turned off the engine. "Let me get your door."

Christy was becoming used to Todd opening the door for her, even though she still felt he didn't need to. She waited until it opened and then slipped her hand into his when he offered to help her out.

"Final decision, right?" he asked as they

walked into the doctor's office.

"Yes, final decision."

As she went through the pre-exam routine and changed into the examination gown, Christy reminded herself of all the times she had been glad that she had trusted her instincts or followed in the direction she felt God's Spirit was subtly leading her.

This time it was an especially good thing that she and Todd had arrived at their conclusion ahead of time. Dr. Avery entered the exam room with a smile and seemed warmer and friendlier that she had been at previous appointments. She seemed excited and vested in the results.

"Big day!" she said. "Are you ready to find out if it's a boy or girl?"

"Actually," Christy gave a final glance at Todd, "we'd like to wait and be surprised."

Dr. Avery was the one who seemed surprised. "Okay, that's not a problem. Not many mothers wait anymore. Is there a reason you've come to that decision?"

Christy looked at Todd, hoping he would say something. He returned her gaze.

When she didn't reply, Todd answered firmly and confidently for both of them. "It's what we decided."

"All that matters to me," Dr. Avery said, "is that we use the technology we have available to assure that your child is as safe and healthy as can be."

"Agreed," Todd said.

She smoothed the slippery gel over Christy's stomach and turned on the machine. With the probe in her hand and her eye on the screen, Dr. Avery rolled the device across Christy's skin in smooth lines.

Christy was partially reclined on the examination table. When she looked down at her stomach she noticed that she definitely had the beginnings of a baby bump. Whenever she stood in front of a mirror, smoothed down her top, and took in her side view, she could tell her middle was getting thick. In this position, she noticed that her skin was taut across the lower part of her midriff. It wasn't the same sort of pooch she would get if she ate too many tortilla chips and the salt made her bloat. Her body was changing.

The sound that had begun to be an anticipated comfort to her at every visit pulsated through the speaker and filled the small room. The steady, fluid sounding *whoosh, whoosh, whoosh* made her want to cry.

From the size of a grain of sand to a growing, beating heart. So amazing.

Glancing at the monitor, Christy could make out the rounded shape of their baby's head amongst the shadowy lines. Todd placed his hand on her shoulder and gave her a squeeze. The image on the screen beside them resembled the pictures they had studied in their shared research of their baby's development.

By their estimates, Christy was seventeen weeks along. Their baby was about five inches long and the size of a pear. She knew those facts based on the pictures on the app, in the books, and from the video clips she had watched online. Those details were astounding in general. When she connected the information to the image of their own child, who was growing inside her, Christy's spirit became very still.

"Look at his little arm," Todd whispered. "That is his arm, right?"

"Mmm-hmm." Dr. Avery kept her attention fixed on the monitor. Her view changed directions as she expertly moved the device across Christy like an Olympic skater gliding across the ice.

"Everything looks perfect." Dr. Avery gave Christy and Todd another warm smile.

"You know, don't you?" Todd asked. "You could tell."

"I thought you didn't want to know."

"We don't. But you know, don't you?"

"I have a pretty good guess. I'll form a

more educated opinion after your next visit." Dr. Avery tapped some information into the tablet in her hand. Without looking up, she said, "It's none of my business, Todd, but on a personal note, what have you two decided about your mother?"

"What about my mother?"

"Are you going to tell her about the baby?"

Christy tried to read the answer in Todd's expression. It seemed to her that he hadn't even considered it. "I don't know," he said flatly. "Maybe after the baby is born. We could send an announcement or something."

Dr. Avery switched her attention from Todd back to Christy. "I shouldn't have asked such a question. That's personal. I'm here to serve you as a professional. I apologize."

"No need to apologize," Todd said. "You can be as professional as you want as our doctor, but you'll still always be my aunt. We're blood relatives. That's not going to change."

"That's true."

"The way I see it, Aunt Linda, God connected us, and I want to stay connected." Todd's voice picked up steam. "We're family. You can ask me anything you want. You can also be as involved or uninvolved in our lives as you want. Christy and I want our relationship with you to continue after the baby is born. We hope you want to stay in our lives, too."

"I'd like that." The expression on Dr. Avery's face carried a hint of pain. Christy thought it had to be the shared pain she and Todd felt over the loss of their relationship with Todd's mom.

Once they were back in Gussie and Todd was driving Christy to work, she noticed that his expression had clouded over, and his jaw appeared set in a forward position. It was the first hint that he was angry about something.

"Are you okay?" Christy knew that Todd's usual way of processing things was inward. He would become quiet and think for a long time, wrestling with the issue, before coming to a conclusion.

"How can a mother go through everything you're going through and be so connected to her baby and then walk away?" His voice was a low, gravelly murmur. "I just don't get it."

She cautiously asked, "Is it hard for you to see your aunt each month at our visits?"

"Seeing her keeps bringing up the past." His jaw flinched. "I don't know if Linda feels the same way since she got burned, too, but I've felt more anger toward my mother in the last few months than I have in years. It's something I have to work on."

Christy saw the continued symptoms of Todd's aching heart spill over again a few days later on Saturday morning. Todd had gone to work early so Christy had agreed to shop with some of the teen girls from the Friday Night Gathering. She returned home around noon and found Todd on the couch watching a TV news channel. Christy pulled out a box of baby announcements and eagerly showed them to Todd.

"Aren't these cute? I love this little giraffe. I was thinking it would be fun to decorate the nursery with a baby giraffe theme. That works for either a boy or a girl."

Todd glanced at the box of announcements. "Do you think only one box will be enough?"

"Yes, I think so. Most of our family and friends will know all the details as soon as the baby is born so I don't need to mail out announcements to them. I thought we could send these to some of my relatives in Wisconsin and to other people we don't keep in close contact with like Rick and Nicole and . . ." Christy cautiously added, "your mom."

As soon as she suggested they send one to

his mother, Todd sat up and pointed the remote at the screen with a straight arm, as if it were a bow and he was trying to shoot an arrow at an enemy. He looked at Christy with bloodshot eyes and ignored her comment about his mom. "I'm going surfing."

Todd hadn't surfed for weeks. Christy was glad he was going. He did his best thinking and processing while bobbing on the salty water, waiting for the next wave.

Todd grabbed his navy-blue hoodie from where it was wadded up on the kitchen counter. "I'm going to San Clemente."

Christy was surprised he wasn't going to the beach just a few blocks out their front door. It would take him close to an hour to drive down the coast to San Clemente at this time of day. Maybe he wanted the time alone on the drive as much as he wanted to get out in the ocean.

"Call me when you're on your way back home," Christy called out.

Todd strode back to the counter and picked up his cell phone that he had left there recharging. "I will. I love you." It sounded more like a low growl than words of endearment.

"I love you, too." The door to the garage closed with a loud thud. Christy wasn't sure if Todd had heard her.

I know he wants to work through all these feelings about his mom by himself, but it kills me to see him like this. Plus, he's so dead tired after all the long hours at work. I hope he's going to be okay.

Christy lowered herself into the comfy chair next to the couch and prayed for her hurting husband. As she silently prayed, she ran her fingers across the dusty top of the end table and sighed. The last thing she felt like doing was cleaning. Christy kept praying for Todd, for his mother, for their baby. She didn't see any possibility of restoration of their mother-son relationship so she prayed for resolution for Todd.

The peace that rested on her after she prayed prompted her to stretch out on the couch and take a nap. The throw pillow was still warm from where Todd had been resting. The fabric carried his scent. Christy smiled, feeling close to her husband even though he was driving farther away from her down the freeway as she was falling asleep.

When Christy awoke, the afternoon sun was coming in through the sliding glass doors that led out to the deck. She sat up and rested her chin on her arm that stretched across the back of the sofa. The surroundings were so quiet. Swirling dust particles did a lazy dance in the shaft of light that spilled out on the floor like golden vapor.

For a long moment Christy let the hazy serenity cover her like a shawl. Over the past few years, this living room had been the scene of what seemed like a steady stream of noise and activity. The walls had been christened with much laughter, music, and most importantly, eternal conversations. The floors had been blessed with Scriptures written on the cement before the new carpet had been installed. Tracy and Doug's toddler, Daniel, had knocked over lamps and left marks and dents in the furniture. The air had often been filled with the lingering fragrance of baby wipes and dirty diapers after Doug and Tracy's twins spent the first few months of their lives in this space.

Now all was calm. All was bright and cheery and ready for the sounds and smells of a new baby. Their new baby.

Christy stretched and checked her phone. No texts from Todd. She prayed for him one more time and tried not to worry about him. She had a feeling he was heading for Trestles, a surf spot south of San Clemente that was notorious for bigger waves than any other location in the area. Even if he was surfing with a lot on his mind, Todd was a true waterman. He took precautions. He was wise. He wouldn't take any risks. Especially not now that he was soon to be a father.

Christy's phone vibrated in her hand. The incoming call was from Aunt Marti.

"Are you home?" Marti's voice came through the speaker at a high pitch.

"I'm here," Christy said. "Todd is surfing."

"Would you be willing to entertain a guest for a short visit?"

Christy took her aunt's words to mean that she was looking for a guest room for someone to stay in. "We have someone coming at the end of July. I told you about Shawna, didn't I? She's staying with us for that weekend."

"Yes, yes, you told me all about Alissa's daughter coming. I'm not asking about your bed-and-breakfast calendar. I'm asking if I might come in. I'm parked in front of your house."

"Oh! Yes, of course." Christy sprang into action. She scooped up the shopping bag with the birth announcements and cleared an empty paper plate and glass from the coffee table. "You're always welcome, Aunt Marti. Any time."

"I wasn't sure you were home."

"I'm home. I'm here." Christy stubbed her toe on a kitchen stool as she tried to move the bowls left over from breakfast into the sink. "But I appreciate your calling."

"I'm walking up to the door now."

"Okay, I'm hanging up now."

"I'm on your doorstep."

Christy pressed the end button with her thumb and placed her phone on the counter. She instinctively wiped the crumbs off the counter into her hand and dumped them into the sink before hurrying to open the door. What unnerved her about her aunt's visit was that Marti owned this house. She'd bought it from Todd's dad after he had helped renovate it. Even though she was, for the most part, an unobtrusive landlord and hadn't raised the rent on them, she still always looked around with a critical eye whenever she came in.

Christy had a feeling her aunt's visit today would be no different.

EIGHT

"Hi. Come in!" Christy offered an unbalanced sort of hug as Marti released a kiss into the air somewhere in the vicinity of Christy's right earlobe. "What are you up to this afternoon?"

"Plans and more plans. I'm up to my chin in tile samples." Marti's dark gaze was darting around the open space. "I thought I'd be past all these decisions by now, but there are so many details when you're renovating a house as large as this one. The bathrooms have been the worst. I have to make all the choices for all four of the bathrooms, Christy. Four!"

"That's a lot of bathrooms."

Marti ushered herself over to the comfy chair next to the couch. She sat down and placed a large binder on the coffee table. Flipping to a specific, marked section, she said, "I need your opinion. I've looked at the sink options too many times. I can't decide which one would work best for the downstairs entry bathroom."

"Would you like something to drink?" Christy offered before taking a seat on the couch. "Water? Juice? I think we have some lemonade in the freezer. I could make that for us if that sounds good."

With a wave of her hand, Marti dismissed the options. "Hot tea will be fine. Earl Grey. No honey, but lemon, please."

Christy didn't remember offering hot tea as an option. No matter. She knew she didn't have Earl Grey tea. She checked the cupboard and saw that she had mint, English Breakfast, chamomile, and a special herbal blend she had bought at the health food store. It had soothed her nausea more than once during her first trimester, but she hadn't had any in a while since the upset stomach symptoms had passed. The only touch of morning sickness that remained was when she awoke every morning. She had to sit on the edge of the bed for a few moments because she felt as if she were driving down a curvy mountain road at an unsafe speed.

"I don't have Earl Grey," she called out. "How about some English Breakfast?"

Marti looked up. "No Earl Grey? None?"

"No."

"Never mind, then. I don't need a drink."
Marti focused on the binder and muttered,
"Actually, maybe that's exactly what I
need." She looked up again. "You don't
happen to have a nice chardonnay, do you?
Chilled?"

Christy laughed. She couldn't help it.

Marti seemed to know the answer to her
question and waved her hand again as if
dismissing the entire topic of beverages.
"Come look at these sinks, will you? I didn't
stop in for refreshment. I need your opinion.
What do you think of this one?"

Christy obliged. She took her place on the
couch with the heavy binder balanced on
her knees while she spent the next hour
looking at pictures of sinks. She never realized so many sink styles existed in the
world.

Only after they had discussed every option and Marti had narrowed it down to
two free-standing pedestal styles did the
subject change. Marti marked the pages,
closed the binder, sat back, and with a
continued woman-on-a-mission tone she
asked, "Have you changed your mind yet?"

"About what?"

"About the baby. About knowing the
gender ahead of time."

"No, we're going to wait until he or she is

born. We'll find out then and not before. That's our final decision, and our doctor is honoring it." Christy tried to sound authoritative, but she knew she could never pull off the same "don't cross me" tone that her aunt had perfected.

"Well, then, I have a solution."

"We don't need a solution because there's not a problem." Christy still attempted to sound forceful, but the tone didn't sound natural to her voice.

"If you and Todd do not want to know the sex of your child, that's your choice."

"Yes, it is," Christy interjected quickly, as if trying to retain the hill where she had planted her flag.

"I honor your choice, Christina." Marti's voice turned melodic. "And I trust you and Todd will honor mine."

Christy waited for the punch line.

"I'd like you to give me the name of your doctor so I can contact him and be informed ahead of time whether it's a girl or a boy." Marti quickly put up a hand as if to stop Christy's protests. "You don't have to know. I certainly won't tell you. But I need to know so I can make the proper arrangements."

Christy had heard some stunning pieces of logic roll out of her aunt's mouth before, but this one topped them all. "What arrangements are you talking about?"

"For the nursery. For the layette. Am I shopping for blue or pink? If you want to know my opinion, I believe you and Todd are selfish to withhold this information from those who are closest to you and are contributing to your child's future."

Christy couldn't believe what she was hearing. She had no response. It felt as if she were tumbling headlong down the hill she thought she had taken a few moments ago.

"Don't you see, Christina?" Marti's voice turned soft again. "This is something I'm doing for your child. I need to know if it's a boy or a girl so I can do my part. I need to have everything in readiness for the baby at the new house, and you are making it impossible for me to move forward."

The gravity of Marti's words settled on Christy as Marti went on to explain how she planned to turn one of the many rooms at the new house into a nursery, and she wanted to settle on a decorating theme that matched the rest of the house.

"I wasn't going to tell you, but you might as well know." Marti looked quite pleased with herself. "I've narrowed it down to a sailor theme with navy-blue and white if it's a boy and apricot and cream if it's a girl. The theme would be a tea party for the girl. I've already found the sweetest little china tea set that's child size and has pink peonies at the bottom of each teacup and on the teapot. It really is the most adorable thing you've ever seen."

Christy was feeling the same nauseous sensation she'd felt early in her pregnancy. Moistening her lips before she spoke, Christy tried to find her firmness and courage once again. "Todd and I have an agreement in our marriage that whenever it comes to important decisions like this, we always talk with each other first and make sure we are on the same page."

A scowl creased Marti's flawless skin.

"Let me talk with Todd about this tonight. We'll give you an answer tomorrow. I promise."

Marti left that afternoon appearing pacified but certainly not satisfied. She insisted that Todd and Christy come for dinner soon so Uncle Bob could be part of the discussion. Christy wondered if her uncle had any idea that Marti was designing a nursery in the new house.

She did something she didn't remember ever doing before in a situation like this. She called her mom and told her about the conversation she had had with Marti and how it felt imbalanced to her.

"Do you think Aunt Marti is going through something in all this that is related to the baby girl she lost?" Christy asked.

"I don't think so. If she is, you certainly can't try to process her feelings for her."

"I know. And it probably sounds crazy, but doesn't it seem over the top to you? Who would plan a whole room around a theme just because her niece is having a baby?"

"You've always been more than just a niece to her, Christy, you know that."

"Yes, I know."

"It may seem extravagant, but I think this has almost always been my sister's way of showing her love and support. It means a lot to her that she can be involved in your life."

"I know. But it still feels a little weird."

"Think of it as her way of being a sort of grandmother to your child."

"But, Mom, you're the grandmother."

"I know."

Christy took a long sip of ice water and walked outside to the deck. "Does it ever bother you the way Marti sort of invents her own place of importance in our family?"

Christy could hear her mother chuckling softly. "It bothers your father very much. It always has. It doesn't bother me anymore because I think my sister needs this. She needs us. We're her family. Not just extended family. We are her family."

Christy lowered herself into one of the beach chairs by the built-in fire pit and remembered what Todd had said to his Aunt Linda about being family. What her mom was saying made sense.

"Let me ask you a question, Mom. If you lived near me, and you had money, and if you had a house with a spare room, would you turn it into a nursery for your grandchild?"

"If all those things were true, especially about having the house and the money, then yes. I'm sure I'd turn a spare room into a nursery of sorts. I don't have your aunt's knack or desire to decorate so I wouldn't need to know if you were having a boy or a girl. But I'd probably put up a crib, buy some toys, and eventually buy a high chair. I'd want to make my house a special place so our grandchild would want to come and visit."

The way her mom was spilling out so many details about what she would do if she had a house made Christy realize how

119

painful this topic must be for her. She and Christy's dad didn't know where they would be living by the end of the year when the baby came. They didn't have the freedom to even dream about a spare room or a place to set up a high chair.

"Mom, are you okay talking about this?"

"Yes, of course. I appreciate your calling. It's good to be able to share these things with each other, isn't it?"

"Yes. It means a lot to me, too, Mom." Christy regretted once again that she hadn't been closer to her mom during her teen and college years. She was grateful for the way the baby and this new season for both of them was providing the chance to talk more. The late-afternoon sun was fading, and it felt chilly on the shaded deck. Christy went back inside as she and her mom chatted a few more minutes before Christy felt as if she had climbed back up her small hill of determination and was planting her flag once again.

"I appreciate all that Aunt Marti does, but I don't think she needs to know if it's a boy or a girl. She can wait until after the baby is born and decorate then. It might even take some pressure off her if she doesn't have to rush into creating a nursery for her new house, don't you think?"

"I think you'll find out when you and Todd have dinner with them."

Christy felt energetic after her call with her mom. She tidied up the house, pulled a chicken out of the freezer, and started an easy Crock-Pot meal for dinner. She folded the towels that had been in the dryer for several days and put a load of laundry in the washing machine.

Since she was still feeling motivated, she cleaned both bathrooms, vacuumed the downstairs, and cleaned out the refrigerator after discovering a fuzzy cucumber in the vegetable bin. Todd came in just as she was putting away her assortment of all-natural cleaning products under the kitchen sink.

"How was surfing?"

"Didn't go." Todd opened the refrigerator and appeared to be on the hunt for something to drink. "Looks nice in here."

"I went through a cleaning frenzy while you were gone. Aunt Marti came by. She invited us to go to their place for dinner tomorrow night."

"Okay."

"I also had a long talk with my mom." Christy sidled up to him and gave him a kiss on the cheek. "Did you go to work?"

"No." Todd reached for the rest of the orange juice and drank it from the bottle.

Christy leaned against the counter, waiting for him to say more.

"I stopped by Brennan's to see if he wanted to go with me." Todd took another long swig of the high-pulp orange juice. "He wasn't there, but I had a long talk with his dad, Mike. It was significant."

Christy raised her eyebrows, waiting for him to explain what he meant.

"Mike suggested that I apply for a job that will open up in the fall at South Coast Believers Academy."

"A job? Doing what?"

"Teaching Old Testament for both junior high and high school."

Christy felt a sudden tingling sensation at the back of her throat. It was as if a flock of questions were all fluttering about at once. How much did the position pay? Was it full-time? Would Todd's BA be enough, or would he have to go back to school for more education before he would qualify?

She swallowed and said, "What did he have to say?"

"Mike is the principal at South Coast. He said he's heard Brennan tell him stuff I've talked about at the Gathering on Friday nights, and he thought the job might be a good fit for me. He's an alumnus of Rancho Corona, so that was a good connection."

"What do you think?"

Todd tossed the emptied orange juice bottle into the recycle bin next to the trash. "You know how we've been praying for a while about my going back into full-time ministry?"

Christy nodded.

"I thought I'd end up on staff at a church again. I never thought about teaching at a large, private Christian school. It makes sense, though. I would have a chance to do a lot of the things I love to do."

"And you would have time off in the summer," Christy added. "And at Christmas."

"Or I could teach summer school, if we needed the money. The main thing is that we would have health benefits after the baby comes, and hopefully you wouldn't have to work. At least you wouldn't have to work full-time."

All the possibilities spun through Christy's thoughts. Todd would have regular hours as a teacher. They wouldn't be in a bind after losing her health-insurance benefits at the spa. He could teach God's Word to teens every day. The position seemed too good to be true.

"I told Mike that you and I would talk about it, pray about it, and get back to him on Monday. I need to put together a résumé, and I need to enroll for some online classes right away to get the credits I need for a teaching credential."

Christy realized that the whole time Todd had been relaying this unexpected and exciting news, his facial expression had remained the same. He looked steady. A bit hesitant. He didn't seem to feel excited about the opportunity the way she was.

Taking four steps over to where Todd was standing with his hands in the pockets of his Rancho Corona hoodie, Christy looped her arm through his and pulled him close. "What do you think?"

He looked down at her, his expression still solemn. "It's a lot, you know?" Todd drew in a deep breath.

Christy tried to figure out what he meant by "a lot." Was it the additional classes needed that were overwhelming him? The expense of the online schooling? Or was it the extraordinary blessing of a steady job opportunity in his area of interest?

"Growing up is shocking," Todd said.

Christy tried not to laugh.

"I mean, being responsible and figuring out how to provide for our family — it's heavy stuff. Mike laid it all out in front of me." Todd pulled back and looked at Christy with an even more tense expression. "We need to get life insurance. And we need to have a will. I mean, Christy, I never even thought about this stuff before. What if both of us were hit by a bus? Who would we want to raise our son?"

The tone of Todd's voice ruffled a few panic feathers inside of Christy. Her thoughts grew serious. "We can work on that," she said. "We'll make a list and go through everything we need to do."

Todd leaned over and kissed Christy with fierceness. It felt to her as if he thought he was going to lose her, and he had to make every moment count.

She looked up into the cloudy silver-blue eyes of her favorite surfer boy. The carefree, summer-fun, playful boyfriend part of her husband was being eclipsed by a responsible, fully grown, serious husband and father who had just been called into action.

Something changed in their lives during that conversation. Christy could feel it. They had left the season of being slightly naïve newlyweds and stepped together into the world of being adults with responsibilities outside their fairly easy lives as a couple. If they were going to be prepared for what was just around the corner for them, the future required a little less dreaming and a lot more doing.

Christy realized that her dream of driving Gussie up the coast to Oregon that summer would be impossible now. Thoughts of lots of sunset walks on the beach with Todd and coming home to make s'mores on their patio evaporated.

Christy felt a strong urge to slip away from their reality-infused conversation and go upstairs. She wanted to flop on the bed and mourn the loss of the first season of their marriage that was now changing into a season of even more work and scheduling and responsibilities.

Such actions, however, were a luxury given to fifteen-year-olds. That season of her life had long passed. She needed to finish making dinner.

After all, she was eating for two.

NINE

Dinner at Bob and Marti's house on Sunday night didn't go the way Christy thought it would. Instead of eating outside on the beautiful patio that faced the ocean and always offered gorgeous sunset views, the four of them gathered at the small table in the kitchen. Their meal wasn't the usual gourmet efforts of Uncle Bob at work on the grill, and the food didn't include any new special seasoning that Marti had hunted down in one of her favorite shops on Balboa Island.

They had an extra-large, double-everything Sicilian-style pizza and root beer that came in a large plastic bottle. Most surprising was that they ate off paper plates. Christy couldn't remember ever eating off paper plates at her aunt and uncle's home.

Everything felt scattered. Especially Aunt Marti. She waved off Bob's offer for a slice of pizza, saying she would eat something later. Her glass wasn't filled with root beer, and her focus wasn't on the meal.

"We spent the morning testing paint samples on the walls of the new house," Marti said. "Then we had to dash home to change before going off to a birthday party this afternoon for one of your uncle's real estate associates. They have a lovely home in Laguna Beach. We barely made it back here before you arrived."

"We could have rescheduled for another night, Aunt Marti," Christy said.

Marti gave Christy a nervous shake of her head. "Not when we're on such a tight schedule. We need to stay on track. Otherwise the time will get away from us."

Turning to Todd, Marti said, "I've narrowed the design down to nautical for a boy and a tea party for a girl. I don't know if Christy told you that yet."

"She told me you want to contact my aunt."

Marti scowled. First at Todd and then at Christy. "What aunt? I don't want to talk to your aunt. I don't even know your aunt."

"Dr. Avery is my aunt. She's my mother's sister."

"Oh. Oh my." Aunt Marti looked as if she had been thrown off track.

"Todd hasn't seen her in decades," Christy

said. "My insurance company assigned me to her as a preferred provider in our area. She's really great."

"How about that," Bob said.

"I think it's pretty cool," Todd said. "She's fine with our choice not to be told if we're having a boy or a girl."

Marti's thoughts seemed to be spinning as she looked at Todd and then back at Christy. "This is perfect! If your aunt knows, Todd, then certainly there's no harm in Christy's aunt knowing." Marti looked pleased with her conclusion.

"We didn't tell my aunt," Todd said. "The only reason she knows is because she was doing her job."

"I would like to be able to do my job as an aunt as well!"

"Marti, we're not going to find out. *You're* not going to find out." Todd's voice and expression were firm. "Everyone except our OBGYN will be surprised the day our baby comes into the world. That's it."

Marti's voice elevated to a high pitch, as she listed all the things she had done for Christy and Todd over the years. She wanted them to understand why they owed her this one small favor and how unreasonable they were to withhold it from her.

Christy felt sick to her stomach, but Todd

kept eating and went for a second slice of pizza. When Marti finished, Todd said, "We appreciate all the ways you've been generous to us over the years."

"Then I don't understand why you wouldn't return the kindness and do this one thing for me so I can do something for you and have the nursery ready ahead of time. The two of you are being selfish."

"Aunt Marti, we're not trying to be selfish. We're . . ." Christy wanted to say more, but she wasn't sure which direction to go.

Todd leaned closer to her and took the lead. "I'm sorry you see things that way. That's not the way we see it. We're not going to change our decision." Todd's jaw was set, and his tone was firm.

Christy glanced at Uncle Bob. His face was getting red. A tightness pulled at the edge of his mouth. "It's their choice, Martha. Leave it alone."

"Fine." Marti got up and went to the cupboard from which she took one of her latest weight-loss meal bars. Christy had seen her aunt and uncle work out their differences of opinion before and knew this was usually the point in the conflict when Marti would retreat upstairs to her room.

This time Marti returned to the table, and it was Christy who felt the need to retreat.

Her stomach definitely felt unsettled. She pushed her chair back and said she needed to be excused.

"Are you okay?" Todd reached for her hand and gave it a squeeze.

"I think I just need to stretch out for a few minutes. My stomach isn't very happy."

"We should have picked up something less spicy," Bob said.

"Would you like a protein bar?" Marti asked.

"No, I'll be okay. Thanks." Finding solace in the quiet living room, Christy lay on the sofa and rested her hands on her midriff. She felt the urge to protect her baby. The taste of bell peppers lingered in the back of her mouth, and concluded that what she thought were sun-dried tomatoes on the pizza had actually been red bell peppers. That would explain the intensity of her nausea. This wasn't the first time in her pregnancy that bell peppers had not been friendly to her.

Smoothing her palm over her small baby bump, Christy hoped the tense conversation and her uncle's firm words, along with Todd's stand, had settled the matter once and for all. She didn't want to spend the rest of her pregnancy feeling pressured by her aunt to reveal the gender.

"Christy, darling."

Christy looked up and saw her aunt coming toward her with a contrite expression. "My apologies. The men seem to think that I've upset you and the baby."

Christy blinked but didn't respond right away. She could only remember a few times when her aunt had apologized to her.

"Actually, I think it's the bell peppers on the pizza. They don't want to stay down."

Marti stood over Christy, examining her expression. "You're deflecting, you know. The issue is not the pizza."

Christy drew in a slow, deep breath through her nostrils. She didn't mean to, but she started crying. Her hormones were playing with her as if they had been let loose in an inflatable bounce house.

Marti settled herself calmly in one of the armless chairs facing the couch. She looked concerned. For a moment neither of them spoke as Christy reined in her tears.

Marti squared her shoulders. "Your uncle is right. It's your baby, and it's your choice. That's the end of it. Please tell me you accept my apology."

Christy offered her aunt a calm nod and let the corners of her closed lips turn up into an agreeable expression. What she really wanted to do was open her mouth and let out a huge belch. It wasn't the first time she had felt that sensation during her pregnancy. She did her best to keep her lips sealed while her stomach rumbled.

Marti seemed to take Christy's silent nod as her acceptance of the truce. She ruffled her backside into the chair like a roosting hen and offered Christy a transformed expression. Marti lowered her voice and asked, "What do you make of this Linda?"

It took Christy a moment to catch her aunt's meaning. When she did, she closed her eyes and drew in another long breath. She had no interest in discussing Todd's aunt at this moment. Especially when another wave of nausea was coming over her.

"I'm sorry but my stomach is . . ." Christy murmured. "I need to use the restroom." She hurried to the downstairs powder room. The strong floral fragrance from an air freshener overpowered the small space. Christy held her breath and exited the bathroom. She went directly into the kitchen and placed her hand on Todd's shoulder. "I'm not feeling well. I need to go home."

Todd got up immediately. "You okay?"

"I feel nauseous, that's all." Christy gave Uncle Bob a weak smile. "Sorry."

"No need to apologize." Bob was on his

feet and following Christy and Todd to the front door. "Let us know if you need anything."

Christy nodded and took Todd's arm, letting him lead her to the car.

They had driven only a block before Christy commanded, "Pull over!"

Todd had taken a short cut down a narrow one-way street and there was nowhere to pull over. He stopped the car in the middle of the alley. Christy opened the door and leaned her head out. She was certain that she was about to lose her half a slice of vegetarian pizza and the root beer.

She didn't. Fortunately she was able to swallow enough times to convince her body to wait until she reached home before the inevitable, unpleasant moment overtook her.

Todd pulled into the garage. Christy opened her own door quickly, and it happened. She didn't even make it inside to the bathroom.

Christy felt Todd's arm around her. She leaned on him for support and tried not to look at the puddle she had left on the garage floor. "I'm sorry. I'll clean it up. I just need a minute."

"I've got it. Don't worry. Come on," Todd said gently. "Hold on to me. Let's get you inside."

Todd headed for the downstairs bathroom, but Christy told him she wanted to go to the couch. "I'm fine now. Really. I'm sure it was just the bell peppers."

"I'll get you some ice water."

Christy stretched out on the couch. She sipped the water and tried not to feel embarrassed that her husband was in the garage cleaning up after her.

I guess this is real life. Real married life. I know he's going to tell me I don't have to keep apologizing and telling everyone I'm sorry. And he's right. I can't help it though.

Christy took another drink and thought about the times she had seen Todd clean up after a few gruesome moments at youth events over the years. She was grateful stuff like that didn't gross him out too much. When the baby came, she knew she could count on him to help with diapers and other messes.

"Feeling better?" Todd asked after he had come back inside and was washing his hands at the kitchen sink.

"Much better. Thank you for cleaning up."

"You want some toast or crackers or anything?"

"Toast sounds really good. And do you mind making some tea? You'll find tea bags in a blue canister that has bird on it."

"This one?"

"Yes. Thanks, Todd." Christy watched her husband adeptly make his way around the kitchen. Her heart warmed with a growing sense of appreciation for this man who she had loved for almost half her life already.

The tea helped. The dry toast helped. Christy soon felt much better.

Todd had made himself a bowl of popcorn. He sat down, but instead of turning on the TV he asked, "Do you mind if we talk about a few things?"

"No, I don't mind."

"You know that list we made of all the things that need to happen if I get hired at South Coast Believers Academy?"

Christy nodded.

"I looked into the class I need to take online, and I have to start tomorrow to complete it in time."

"Are you feeling pretty certain then about taking the position?" Christy asked.

"They have to offer it to me first." He had a shy look. "All I can do is apply along with whoever else is applying and see what happens. But if they do hire me, I'd have to take this class for the teaching credential."

"It sounds like you should take the class then."

"It means I'd have even less free time in

the evenings this summer, if I keep up the same hours at the warehouse with Zane. You and I would see each other even less than we have been."

Those weren't encouraging words. But Christy knew that if that was what Todd needed to do so they would eventually have more time together after the baby came, now was the time to put in the hard work. She shared those thoughts with Todd and reminded him that they had prayed together about the opportunity many times. Even though it was a surprise, it had God's fingerprints all over it.

Todd reached over and gave her arm a squeeze. "You're a gift to me. Do you know that? I always feel like you support whatever I do."

"Well, almost always." Christy gave him a grin. "It helps when you're making a little money at whatever you do. That's when I'm the most supportive."

"There have been a few times when I wasn't doing my part. I'm sorry that I put you through that. I don't want you to feel insecure."

"You know what was good about those rough times? The uncertainties about the future made me trust God. I mean, trust Him even more than I felt like I could trust you at the time, if that makes sense."

Todd moved closer to Christy on the sofa. He stretched his arm around her shoulders, drawing her close. "I get what you're saying about how you need to trust God more than you trust me. I think that's a good, foundational piece for any marriage between two believers."

Christy snuggled up to Todd as he wove his fingers into her hair cascading over her shoulders.

"I want to be reliable and trustworthy," he said. "But I'm sure I'm going to mess up a lot.

"I will, too."

"We have a lot to figure out as parents." Todd smoothed her hair and twisted a long strand around his finger.

"I know," Christy agreed. "We need to make so many small decisions now because they could have long-term repercussions."

"Right," Todd said. "For instance, how do you feel about organized sports? At what age do we put our son on a soccer team or Little League team?"

Christy chuckled. The topics she had in mind were along the lines of newborn decisions. She listed a few of them for Todd. Sleep training? Diapers: cloth or disposable? Pacifier or no? What if she had difficulty nursing? Should she buy a pump now?

For the next few hours, they talked and cuddled and talked some more. Christy could not remember having this long of a serious conversation with Todd nor could she remember the last time they had spent the evening in shared communion. Usually the TV was on or one of them was wiped out and ready for bed, or lately Todd was working at the shop and not even home until after Christy had gone to bed.

They talked about all kinds of possibilities of what they needed to buy or do before the baby arrived. They talked about the new songs Todd was writing and Christy's thoughts on improving their diet in the months ahead. They talked about their future and their past and the sweetness of the present.

It was one of the most romantic, heart-filling evenings Christy ever remembered having with Todd. She was glad they had left Bob and Marti's early. She was also glad they had held their ground on not revealing their baby's gender. It made it feel as if she and Todd were more of a team than ever before.

That night, as Christy fell asleep in Todd's embrace, she thought, *If I weren't already in love with this man, I think I would have fallen in love with him tonight. I can't imagine loving Todd more than I do at this moment.*

TEN

One of the biggest changes Christy implemented after the unsettling pizza night at Bob and Marti's was to adjust what she ate. She looked up which foods were least likely to cause indigestion during pregnancy. Each website and blog she visited for tips on a healthy diet for pregnant moms led her to another source and then another until she had more information than she could process.

Her new eating plan wasn't too complicated. She would go for organic foods whenever possible, focus on vegetables and fruits, choose whole grains, avoid shellfish, anything extra spicy, and no processed meats. She would buy items that had the least amount of preservatives, salt, and refined sugar.

Christy was a few weeks into her new eating plan when Marti called to ask if she could meet Christy during her lunch break.

Marti suggested they go to one of her favorite restaurants in Corona del Mar. Christy asked if they could meet at a casual place called Ollie's instead. The eatery was within walking distance of the spa, and Christy liked their fresh-to-table salads. She also had a few favorites in their large selection of smoothies made from local fruit.

When Christy arrived at Ollie's, Marti was staring up at the menu in the cafeteria-style salad line. "What did you possibly find on this menu that was to your liking, Christina?"

"I come here often. Everything I've had has been really good." Christy offered an apologetic look at the young man behind the counter who was waiting for them to order. "I'll have the sweetheart smoothie."

Marti frowned. "You do realize you're ordering a smoothie that has beets in it."

"It also has blueberries and orange juice. It's very good."

Marti blinked and turned to the server behind the counter. "I've tried to get her to eat this way her entire life. You must have some secret ingredient you add to your smoothies. Would you mind telling me what it is? She would never agree to drink anything remotely like the items on your menu when she was a teenager."

Christy wished they had gone to Marti's restaurant choice in Corona del Mar so they could have slid into the dark leather booth and had a more secluded conversation. Marti continued her comments yet the people in line behind them clearly weren't interested in Christy's preference for waffles over protein drinks or the quality of Marti's professional-style blender.

"Would you like to order something?" the server asked impatiently.

Marti brusquely ordered a cup of tomato bisque soup and a bottle of water. Christy added a specialty salad called the "808" to her order but asked them to hold the feta. By the time they sat down, they only had twenty minutes to eat before Christy had to be back at work.

Marti leaned across the small table. "I want you know, just to ease your mind, that I've ordered everything we need for both the nautical theme and the tea party theme. It's all on hold until the baby comes. I can cancel whatever we don't need."

"Aunt Marti . . ." Christy realized that she may have walked into a trap by agreeing to meet her aunt for lunch. This wasn't what she wanted to talk about. Her mind raced to come up with a topic that would serve as a good detour.

Marti flicked her fingers as if shooing away whatever Christy was about to say. "Your uncle made me promise I wouldn't focus our conversations today on the nursery, and I'm not. Not at all. That's why I'm putting your mind at rest on the matter so we can go on and talk about something else."

"Okay, good. What should we talk about?"

Marti picked up her soup spoon and held it as if it were a paintbrush and she were trying to decide which part of the conversation canvas she wished to paint next. "You know, I was thinking on the way over here, you and I have come a long way, haven't we, Christy darling?"

Christy nodded. Her mouth was too full to reply.

Marti lowered her spoon into her soup bowl and stirred slowly. "When I think of all we've experienced together, particularly the summer you came to live with us, I have to admit I feel a sense of pride in the way you've turned out."

She looked at Christy with a soft smile. "You're very much your own woman now. As a matter of fact, the more I've thought about it, the more pleased I am that you have found a way to make such an important decision about your baby and stand firm on your opinion. Decision making wasn't always your strength."

Marti paused. "That is, as long as keeping the sex of your child is your decision and not Todd's."

"Yes, it's our decision, Aunt Marti. Our mutual decision. And didn't you just say we should talk about something else?"

Marti glanced to the side but seemed unable to come up with a new topic.

"Let's talk about the rest of your new house," Christy suggested. "How is the kitchen coming along?"

"If you don't mind, I'd prefer we didn't talk about the house."

"Okay." Christy took a long sip of her smoothie. "I talked to my mom a couple of days ago. Have you talked to her lately?"

"Yes, as a matter of fact, we spoke this morning."

"I'm sure she told you then that my dad's last day at work is going to be the end of August. I've been praying for them. I'm sure it has to be really difficult."

"Your uncle offered your father a job."

"He did? When?"

"This morning."

"Doing what?" Christy thought her aunt sounded surprisingly disinterested in this bit of important news.

"Robert needs a reliable cleaning service that will take care of the new commercial property he acquired. You know how strong and capable your father is. Robert thought it would be a reasonable first step, and soon Norman could move up to become the supervisor of grounds maintenance of a larger complex."

"Uncle Bob offered my dad a job as a janitor?" Christy could only imagine how humbling that must have been for her father.

"That's not exactly the job title. But it doesn't matter. Your father wouldn't even consider it. He said he didn't want to jeopardize the family relationships." Marti shook her head. "If you ask me, your father is jeopardizing the relationships by turning down the chance to take the position. At least they could have moved here to Newport Beach and been near you and the baby."

Christy swallowed and felt disappointed that she was hearing all this from her aunt and not from her mother.

Marti shrugged. "We told them they could rent our house as soon as we move into the new one. We assured them that we would keep the rent affordable, the way we have for you and Todd. But your father wouldn't even consider it."

A swirl of emotions rolled over Christy. On one hand, Bob and Marti's solution was ideal. Christy's parents would have a beautiful place to live, they would be nearby, and her dad would have a job. If she had been asked to come up with a happy solution, this would have been it.

On the other hand, Christy knew that her dad would feel obligated to Bob and Marti under such conditions and that would take all the joy out of him. He took pride in caring for his family with his own two hands and making ends meet on his meager salary. It would kill him to be under Bob and Marti's roof, paying them rent and cleaning his brother-in-law's office buildings.

Christy sighed. She didn't mean to, but the weary sadness over what already felt like a stalemate between her family members took all the energy out of her.

Marti looked offended by Christy's sigh. "You can't possibly think that we didn't try our best to convince them to move into our house for your sake. We were as generous as we could be."

"I'm sure you were."

"Perhaps you can talk some sense into them. I'm about to give up on trying to do anything nice for anyone anymore." Marti leaned back and put up both her hands for emphasis. "All we want to do is help. No one in the family seems to realize that."

"I know." Christy slid her phone out of the side pocket of her purse and tried to inconspicuously check the time.

"Do you have to leave now?"

"Yes. I have to get back to work."

"That was certainly a short lunch break."

"I know. It always goes quickly. Maybe we can get together this weekend." Christy stood up and folded the lid on the box that held the remainder of her salad so she could take it with her.

Marti pushed her chair back and looped her designer-label purse over her arm. "I have to be going as well. Call me about this weekend. And try to convince your father to reconsider, will you? Why can't he see that this would be the best for all of us?"

For the rest of the afternoon Christy thought about Marti's conclusion that it would be "the best for all of us." She wasn't sure that was true. It seemed as if it would be best for her and Todd. But would it be best for her mom and dad? What did her dad want to do? Had anyone asked him? Was he still thinking of returning to Wisconsin? And if he did, shouldn't his wishes be considered?

Christy called her mom as soon as she left from work. She was sitting in her hot car in the employee parking lot and had rolled down all the windows. No one answered so she left a message and asked if they wanted to come up and stay for the weekend.

Christy knew she should have run that idea past Todd first. But he was working as much as ever and spending all his spare time studying for his online class. He still hadn't heard back from the school if they even wanted to interview him for the teaching position. He knew he might be taking the class for no immediate good reason, but he was determined to finish it.

Christy had used the alone time to work on some sewing projects and to sleep a lot. To her it seemed like a good idea to have her parents come for a visit. That is, until she started driving home and remembered that Shawna was coming to stay with them the weekend after that. Maybe it would be too much to have company two weekends in a row.

Before she had time to convince herself that she had made a mistake in inviting her parents to come, Christy's phone rang. She had just pulled into the parking lot of one of her favorite health food stores. Or as Todd called it, the "Crunchy Market" due to the amount of granola she brought home out of the scoop-it-yourself bins.

She quickly parked and picked up the call right before it went to voice mail. "Hi, Mom. How are you and Dad doing?"

"We're fine. How are you?"

"Good. I had lunch with Marti today, and she told me about the job offer Uncle Bob gave Dad. I wanted to hear how you and Dad felt about it. Is there any way you would consider moving up to this area? Because I think you can guess that, for me, it would be a dream come true."

Christy's mom paused before answering. "It makes me happy to hear that, Christy."

"Well, it's true. Of course. I'd love it if we could live closer, especially after the baby comes."

"Did Marti ask you to try to convince your dad to reconsider the job offer?"

"No. Well, actually, I think she did make a comment along those lines. I'm not saying Dad should work for Uncle Bob or that you guys should rent their house. All I'm saying is that I wish we could live closer. That's all."

"We'd like to be closer to you, too. We've talked about it a lot. Bob's offer, though, was too binding for your dad. He doesn't do well when he feels that he's in someone's debt, and that's how the arrangement would have been."

"I understand. Believe me."

"I know you do."

Christy wasn't willing to leave it at that. "There has to be some way to get around the high rent and low job possibilities in this area. We need to get creative."

"Well, actually, I —"

"Because, Mom, you know there's no reason you and Dad couldn't live in our guest room for a while. At least until you figure out what you want to do permanently. I mean, if it turns out that you need a place temporarily, you should stay with us. I mentioned it to Todd several weeks ago, and he didn't have any objections."

"We appreciate that, but what I was going to say is that I did come up with a new possibility for us this afternoon."

"You did? What is it?"

"I need to run it past your dad before I say anything. But it's an interesting option."

Christy wanted her mom to tell her the details, but she knew that if her mom said she was going to wait, then she wouldn't budge. It was a quality Christy admired in her. Christy saw how her mother had always done a good job of honoring her husband by going over everything with him first and including him on all important decisions.

Christy wanted to develop more of that trait in her marriage because she knew how much easier things went when she didn't leap ahead on decisions but rather waited and talked through the details with Todd. Which reminded her of her impulsive invitation for the weekend.

"Mom, about you and Dad coming this weekend . . ."

"We won't be able to come, honey."

"Good." Christy caught herself. "I mean, okay. Whatever works best for you and Dad."

Her mom laughed. Christy liked it when her mom laughed. It made it feel like they were conversing in their "friend" mode when her mom responded with laughter to something Christy had said.

"Honesty is the best policy, Christy. Have you over-scheduled yourself for this weekend?"

Christy explained about Shawna coming the following weekend and Todd spending all his free time studying. "I should have talked to Todd about it before saying anything. You're really good at waiting until you discuss things with Dad. I'm working on it, but I'm not there yet."

"I think you do a very good job of honoring your husband, Christy."

"Well, I learned it from the best, Mom."

Christy's mom deflected the compliment, as she usually did. "The following weekend is a possibility, if that works for you and Todd. Your brother wanted to get away from camp and said he hopes to have next Saturday off. If it works out all the way around, we could meet up at your place for the day. Or you and Todd could come down, and we could all gather here in Escondido."

Christy leaned back in the driver's seat and unfastened her seat belt. "I'll talk to Todd about it. That's the weekend Shawna is coming to stay with us so it would be better to meet at our house rather than yours, if that's okay."

"That's right. You just said that's the weekend Shawna will be there. We don't want to overload you."

"It wouldn't overload us. Not if you just came for the day. I think it would be fun. I'll ask Todd to see what he thinks."

An hour and a half later Christy ran the plan past Todd as he was chomping into a veggie burger. "They would only come for the day. What do you think?"

Todd nodded, took another bite, but didn't say anything. Christy wasn't sure if he was agreeing to the weekend plans or approving the new brand of veggie burgers she had brought home. This brand was plumper than the last ones they had tried. Todd had said he didn't mind the taste, but there wasn't enough "meat" to the patty. This time she added lots of lettuce, tomato, onion, and pickles, and he clearly was enjoying it.

"So, what do you think? About my parents coming, I mean."

Todd swallowed, still bobbing his head. "It's fine with me, but I think it might be more than you're imagining right now."

"What do you mean? More work to get the house together and the food made for everyone?"

"All of it."

"I don't think it will be too much. I like doing all that."

"I know. And you do a great job. That's why people love coming to visit. I'm just saying that we don't know if Shawna is going to need a lot of attention and supervision." Todd took another big bite.

"Supervision?" Christy laughed. "She seems like the most timid, well-mannered twelve-year-old on the planet. Every video call we've had with her and her parents she has been so reserved. I can't picture her needing supervision to make sure she doesn't sneak out in the middle of the night."

Todd gave her a side glance and a shrug. "I guess we'll soon find out."

ELEVEN

By the time the last weekend in July arrived, Christy's pantry and refrigerator looked like they belonged to a certified vegan. She set up a video call with Katie to show her how impressive her pantry looked.

"I'm trying to figure out how to give you a hard time about this," Katie said once the quick tour concluded.

"Why would you give me a hard time? I hoped you would be impressed."

"Payback, that's all. Have you forgotten how many times you rolled your eyes at me when I went through my vegan phase in high school? Don't you remember awkward encounters at the Organic Tomato?"

"Oh, yes. The Organic Tomato. You know, I did forget about that. What's funny is that I seem to have no problem remembering the chocolate bar fund-raiser for the ski trip and how one of us bought more candy than she sold."

"Hey! Those were good chocolate bars. You have to admit, they were worth the big bucks they cost."

"No they weren't! I thought they were terrible. I never understood how you could keep eating them." Christy gave a little shiver at the memory of the entire ski trip. That was a time in her life she didn't want to hone in on.

Returning to the topic of cooking, Christy told Katie she was enjoying coming home and trying new recipes and food combinations with ingredients such as quinoa and brussels sprouts. She even had tried some no-bake cookies made from peanut butter, oatmeal, and maple syrup when the guys came over to play guitars. "They devoured them and never asked what was in them."

"You're a star mama," Katie said. "Does this mean you're going to grow yams and pumpkins in your backyard and puree them into baby food a year from now?"

"I thought you weren't going to give me a hard time."

"I never promised that. Besides, we grow pumpkins here, and if I had a kid, I would make baby food."

Christy pulled out a kitchen stool and sat down. "So, tell me how the plans are coming along for your trip here."

Katie shook her head. "I don't know. They're making a lot of changes in leadership, and one of the decision makers at the top now thinks we shouldn't be gone for a long time because there's so much to do here."

"Are you saying you might not come at all?"

"No, we're coming. It just won't be in August like we had hoped."

"Do you think you'll be here by November?"

"Yes, we have to be there by November. I told Eli if there was ever a nonnegotiable in my life, it's this. I will be there for you, Christy. I promise. You can count on me. This is deal-breaker stuff."

Christy felt uneasy about Katie's choice of words after their conversation ended and thought about what Katie meant. What kind of "deal breaker" was she talking about? Had Katie placed the trip to California above her position with the clean-water ministry? Was being with Christy somehow more important now than being with Eli?

She decided that after Shawna's weekend stay, Christy would call Katie again and ask what she meant.

With Christy's renaissance in her kitchen, the only person she worried about feeding was Shawna. She guessed Shawna might be a picky eater and not crazy about the selection to be found in the refrigerator.

"If she doesn't like your rabbit food," Todd had said, "I don't have a problem doing pizza and drive-through the whole time she's here."

Christy mentally prepared herself to dine on drive-through burgers and fish tacos all weekend if need be. That didn't bother her. What did bother her was that both her parents and her brother had decided not to come on Saturday to spend the day with them. That meant that if Christy ran out of ideas on how to entertain Shawna, she would be on her own, without backup from her family.

She left work early Friday and stopped at her favorite farmer's market so she could stock up on fresh vegetables and fruits. She decided to take a chance with the veggie burgers Todd had liked and do a simple barbecue Saturday night with baked potato chips instead of potato salad and lots of bowls of grapes, watermelon, and cherries. She knew Todd would eat plenty of carrot sticks, celery, and zucchini if she put out a bowl of ranch dressing for dipping.

Christy carried in the groceries and called out to Todd. He didn't answer, but she could hear the shower running and didn't bother to go upstairs to let him know she was home. Instead, she went to work in the kitchen and had barely put most of the groceries away when a knock sounded on the front door.

Christy left the bunches of carrots and celery in the kitchen sink with the fresh green carrot tops sticking up like an organic hedge along the kitchen counter. Quickly wiping her wet hands on the vintage apron she had put on over her black work clothes, she opened the front door with a big smile.

"Hi! Welcome. Come in. Please."

Shawna's adoptive parents, Andrew and Jacqueline Lane, were both tall and slim. They had a quiet demeanor about them, and ever since their first video call, Christy had thought of them as affluent professionals. Her view was confirmed by the way they responded sedately to Christy's casual, beachy welcome.

Shawna hung back, her dark eyes quietly taking in everything. Her blonde hair was the same shade as Alissa's but instead of long and flowing over her shoulders the way it had on their last video call, her hair was now short and pulled back into a stubby ponytail.

For a moment, Christy couldn't speak.

She stared at Shawna without blinking. Shawna's real-life appearance was more to take in than Christy thought it would be. She wore no makeup, had not yet shaped or plucked her thick, distinctive eyebrows, but she was a natural beauty already. Seeing her in person startled Christy. There was no mistaking that she was Alissa's daughter.

"Would you like us to leave our shoes here at the door?" Jacqueline asked, looking at the haphazard collection of beach flip-flops next to the welcome mat.

"No. No, that's fine. You're welcome to leave your shoes on."

Both Jacqueline and Andrew looked at Christy's feet and saw that she was barefoot. They chose to effortlessly slip off their shoes and gave Shawna a nod. She followed their lead and left her canvas slip-ons at the front door before she stepped inside and silently took in everything as if she had to memorize the details for a test.

"I made fresh lemonade with blackberries and wild honey. Would you like some?" Christy started for the kitchen, hoping they would follow her. She always felt more at ease entertaining people if she had offered them something to eat or drink. That way all of them had something to do with their hands and something to do with their

161

mouths if they didn't know what to say.

The Lane family stood on the border between the living room and the kitchen. She took off her apron and hung it on the hook on the side of the refrigerator. Then she motioned toward the glass pitcher of lemonade and the beverage glasses she had set out on the counter, indicating that they should come help themselves. Christy wanted her visitors to be at ease, but she wasn't sure how to make that happen.

Todd came down the stairs just then, his bare feet thumping loudly. As soon as he came into view, Christy's jaw dropped. Todd had cut his hair. Short. Really short. As in, buzzed-off short. Christy had never seen his hair like that before. For a moment she wasn't sure she was looking at her husband.

"You're here," Todd said warmly. "Good to see you."

Their expressions warmed when they saw Todd, and their postures relaxed as he gave big bear hugs to each of them the way Doug used to always give bear hugs and make Christy and her friends feel relaxed and welcomed.

He looked over at Christy, who stood behind the kitchen counter with her hand on the pitcher of lemonade. "How about something to drink?" Todd asked. "Do you guys like lemonade?"

Christy poured a glass and set it on the counter. Now that Todd had put everyone at ease, her meager offering of organic homemade lemonade didn't seem like enough refreshment. She pulled from the refrigerator a large sheet of brownies she had made from a mix that morning for the snacks at the Friday Night Gathering. After cutting small squares, she placed them on one of her fancier serving plates.

"Please, help yourself," Christy said.

Shawna looked at the brownies and with a serious expression she asked Christy, "Are these made with fair-trade chocolate?"

"Fair-trade chocolate? Ah, I don't know. I made them from a mix." Christy had never been asked a question like that, even by the pickiest teens at the Gathering. "The lemonade is organic, though. So are the blackberries, and I used local honey."

"I'll try some of the lemonade, then, thank you."

Christy poured a glass for Shawna. She tasted it, declared it "delicious," and then Andrew and Jacqueline both said they would like to try some. None of them took a brownie. Todd, however, took two and suggested they go sit in the living room.

Once they were clustered around the coffee table, the conversation picked up. Andrew talked about the surgeon's conference he was attending in Anaheim, and Jacqueline shared about how much she was enjoying the summer break before returning to her position as a university professor in Seattle.

Shawna sat quietly with impressive posture. She was wearing a summer dress with a full skirt that fanned out. Around her neck hung a dainty flower charm accented by some small, colorful glass beads strung on a long chain. She reminded Christy of a ballerina the way her legs were turned to the side and crossed at the ankles and the polite way she was holding her glass.

Shawna's demeanor reflected her refined upbringing, and her answers to all of Todd's questions sounded more mature than would be expected of a twelve-year-old. However, the flitting look in her eyes and the curious way the corners of her mouth turned up hinted at a more youthful personality hiding inside.

Christy decided in that moment that she wanted to make room in her heart and in her life for Shawna. Whatever it took, Christy wanted Shawna to know that she was already loved for who she was, and she would always be wanted and welcomed into

Todd and Christy's lives.

Their visit lasted less than an hour. Andrew thanked Todd and Christy for their hospitality and assured them that Shawna had been looking forward to this weekend.

"We're the ones who have been looking forward to it." Christy smiled and hoped Shawna could hear the warmth in her words. "We want you to feel at home here in every way. Would you like me to show you the guest room where you'll be staying? It's all ready for you."

"Yes, thank you."

"I'll go out to the car for your luggage," Andrew said.

Without a change of expression Shawna stood and followed Christy into the downstairs guest room adjacent to the kitchen. Jacqueline followed. Christy noticed that Shawna smiled for the first time when she entered the guest room and spotted the vase of gerbera daisies on the nightstand. The flowers' bright colors matched the teen-style throw pillows Christy had made earlier that week and arranged on the bed. One of the pillows had an S on it in bright pink, and the pillow was positioned at the very center of the others.

"The S is for Shawna, of course," Christy said. Then feeling self-conscious again, she pointed out the downstairs bathroom. "Our room is upstairs. I can show you that now, if you would like."

Shawna nodded so Christy took Jacqueline and Shawna on a grand tour of the upstairs. She opened the door to the small room across the hall from their bedroom as if she felt responsible to offer Jacqueline full disclosure of the environment her daughter would be staying in. "This is my messy craft and sewing room right now, but we'll turn it into a nursery."

"You're going to have a baby?" Shawna's eyes grew wide. "I didn't know that."

"Yes. In late November. Can you tell?" Christy smoothed her black work tunic over her middle and stood to the side. "I'm just beginning to show."

"I love babies." Shawna's smile had grown wider.

"I do, too," Christy said.

"Are you going to work on the nursery while I'm here? I could help you if you would like."

"Well, I'm not sure exactly what we'll be doing this weekend. We thought you might like to hang out at the beach or maybe ride bikes or go shopping on Balboa Island."

"If that's what you and Todd were planning to do, then that's fine with me."

"We can decide later." Christy closed the door to the spare room and led the way back downstairs. "What do you like to do, Shawna?"

"I like to read."

Christy smiled. "Your mom liked to read a lot, too, when she was a teen."

As soon as the words were out of her mouth, she felt a rush of panic. Christy's first thought had been of summer days on the beach with Alissa who always had a paperback romance novel she was reading.

In the fastest recovery she had ever made of a bumbled statement, Christy glanced at Jacqueline as the three of them reached the bottom of the stairs. "I, of course, assumed you were an avid reader when you were younger, since you're a professor."

If Jacqueline was offended by Christy's comment, she didn't indicate it. Her expression actually softened as she looked at Christy. "I was an avid reader. But I thought you were referring to Shawna's birth mother. Was Alissa an avid reader, as well?"

"Yes. Yes, she was." Christy's face felt warm. The three of them stood in a small circle, each catching the gaze of the other.

Jacqueline placed her hand on Shawna's shoulder in a tender, motherly way. "I hope you have a chance to learn all kinds of interesting details about your birth parents this weekend. I'm sure Todd and Christy will be able to tell you lots of things your father and I don't know."

Christy knew that Andrew and Jacqueline had made it a point to be open about Shawna's adoption. They had spoken freely on early video calls. But the comment surprised her. It comforted her to see the way that Jacqueline was both a polished professional and a caring mother. Christy was glad she had a glimpse of that side of Jacqueline.

Shawna didn't have anything to say. She waited patiently, standing beside Christy while Andrew finished talking to Todd about where they would be staying and when they would be returning Sunday.

Andrew placed a kiss on the side of Shawna's head and looked her in the eyes as if searching for any hints of hesitation on her part. "Have a good time. Call us any time if you need us."

"I'll be fine." Shawna's tone was exactly the tone that any preteen would use with her caring parents when she wanted to be viewed as self-sufficient, brave, and independent.

Jacqueline hugged Shawna and gave her a big smile. Without looking back, Andrew and Jacqueline went out the front door, put their shoes back on, and left.

Christy glanced at Shawna, trying to read her expression. A glimmer of a tear seemed to be caught in the corner of her eye, but she was too brave to let it go.

Todd called out a final, "See you later" to Shawna's parents and closed the front door. He turned to Christy and Shawna and asked, "Do you want go down the beach? We have about twenty minutes before we need to get something to eat and head over to the Gathering."

"Wait." Christy put up her hand. "Before we do anything . . . Todd?" She pointed to his head and lifted both hands, palms up, waiting for an explanation as to why he was practically bald.

Todd rubbed his hand over the top of his head and grinned broadly. "I wanted to look respectable. I had an interview today."

"You did? For the teaching position?"

He nodded.

"And?"

"I don't know. If they hire me, the job starts in the middle of August."

Christy knew this wasn't the time to say anything about how she really would have liked to have known that he had his big interview today or at least have been given a chance to give some input into the haircut

decision. To her he looked more like somebody who lost a bet than a "respectable"
teacher. His permanent tan lines made it
clear that his hair used to be much longer.

Letting all that go, Christy turned to
Shawna. "So, what would you like to do?"

"If you don't mind, I'd like to unpack and
freshen up."

Christy and Todd exchanged surprised
looks at her mature response.

"Of course. I'll start dinner," Christy said.
"Is there anything you like or don't like? I
know we asked if you had any allergies and
your mom said you didn't."

"I don't have any food allergies, but I
don't care for nuts or bell peppers."

Christy spontaneously gave Shawna a
quick hug. "You and I are going to be good
friends."

Shawna stiffened and seemed nervous. In
a low voice she asked, "Did my birth mother
not like nuts or bell peppers, either?"

"I don't know, to be honest." Christy
placed her hand on her heart. "But, you see,
I don't like bell peppers at all. Or I should
say this baby of mine doesn't like them. And
when I was your age, I didn't like nuts on
anything either."

"Except Balboa Bars," Todd said.

Christy shook her head. "Actually, no. Not

even on Balboa Bars."

"Wait. What? Did I know that?"

Christy shrugged sweetly.

Todd's expression seemed to say that he would never understand the mysterious ways of a woman. "I'm going to cram in some more studying, then, since we're staying here. Let me know if you need any help with dinner."

The three of them went to their separate corners of the house. Shawna retreated to her guest room and closed the door. Todd went upstairs, and Christy went to work in the kitchen. Dinner was easy that night. She started out making quesadillas but ended up stuffing them with so many chopped-up garden vegetables that they turned out to be more like vegetable rolls on spinach tortillas.

They sat at the kitchen counter and ate quickly so they could get over to Trevor's house early for the Gathering. Christy put the brownies on a large platter covered with plastic wrap. She also had gathered together three big bags of popcorn, a jumbo serving bowl, plastic cups, napkins, and ten plastic bottles of drinks all ready to go in an ice chest by the back door.

Once they were loaded up in Gussie and backing out of the driveway, Christy turned

171

around to offer Shawna a comforting smile. Shawna seemed nervous. She had changed into jeans and a summer top, taken her hair out of the ponytail, and was wearing a noticeable amount of very shiny lip gloss.

"How many people usually go to this meeting?" Shawna asked.

"Around fifty."

"Are any of them my age?"

Christy was pretty sure the answer was no, but she said, "There might be." She didn't want to put Shawna in a panic mode, so she added, "I thought you could stay with me and help out with the food. That is, if you don't mind."

"I don't mind. But I'm fine on my own. I really am."

"Great." Christy glanced over at Todd. He shot her a quick look back that made it clear he was thinking about something that made him want to laugh aloud, but he was trying his best to hold it in. She had no idea what was so funny about asking Shawna to help with the refreshments.

Oh, Todd. You, you, you. You are as much of an enigma to me as I am to you.

TWELVE

"How will you introduce me tonight?" Shawna asked, as they walked toward the open garage where the Gathering met every Friday night.

"We'll say you're our friend," Todd said.

"Is there something specific you would like us to say or not say?" Christy asked.

"No." Shawna fell into step next to Todd. "Will there be anyone here who knows my birth parents?"

Todd slowed down his gait. "No, I don't think so."

"Shawna, we want to make sure you feel comfortable," Christy said. "If you'd rather not be here, tell us, okay? Because as soon as I set up the food, you and I could go back to our house, if you would like."

"No, I want to be here."

"Okay, good."

Todd gave Shawna a friendly nudge with his arm. "We want you to be here, too."

Shawna smiled up at him and then smiled at Christy. It made her feel as if they had somehow broken through to the more vulnerable side of Shawna, and she was no longer putting on a brave front in the midst of this new experience.

Some of the teens already had arrived and were setting up their beach chairs in the large space. Brennan came over and took one of the guitar cases Todd was carrying as well as the guitar stand. He gave Shawna a friendly grin. "Hey, how's it going?"

"I'm Shawna." She politely stretched out her hand to Brennan.

His hands were filled with gear so he replied with a chin-up nod. "Brennan. We heard you were coming."

"You did?" Shawna moved away from Todd's side and followed Brennan as if by magnetic force. "What did you hear?"

Brennan glanced at her over his shoulder. "Just that you were going to be here."

"Oh. Do you need help with setting up or anything?" Shawna's voice sounded like an average twelve-year-old for the first time. A twelve-year-old who was crushing on the cute high school surfer guy with the wind-whipped hair and long-sleeve T-shirt with sleeves pushed up over his elbows.

Christy set up the snacks and chatted with

some of the high school girls, all the while keeping a keen eye on Shawna. Todd, Brennan, and two other guys tuned their guitars and shuffled the stools around so they could make the most room for the beach blankets that a cluster of popular teen girls were spreading out at their feet.

Christy saw Shawna boldly ask the girls if she could sit with them. They exchanged surprised glances and looked her over before one of them shrugged and said, "Sure."

Now Christy was the one trying to swallow a smile, just as Todd had on the way over. *You are definitely Alissa's daughter. All you have to do is give your pretty little head a turn and you are "in." And you're only twelve! What are you going to be like when you're sixteen?*

The garage was packed that night. It seemed they had more teens than ever before. The worship time was reverent and meaningful, and Todd seemed to be caught up in the moment because he kept his eyes closed through each song and prayed especially long at the end.

Christy usually hung out on the side by the snack table or in the back. Some nights she stood the whole time because it allowed her to easily move around to wherever she might be needed. Tonight, though, her feet were sore, and she was tired. She settled in her chair and rested both her arms across her middle as if she were cradling her little one in her arms.

Todd started in on a time of teaching after the worship and said something that caught Christy off guard. "I know it's summer, but I want to sing my favorite Christmas carol to you tonight. Think of it as Christmas in July." He grinned as if he were the first one to ever coin that phrase. Closing his eyes, Todd sang "O Holy Night."

Christy hadn't realized that was his favorite Christmas carol.

His rich, deep voice filled the crowded garage. The students were all fixed on him. When Todd sang the line, " ' 'Til He appeared, and the soul felt its worth,' " he stood up and held out the last note on the word "worth." Instead of finishing the carol, he opened his eyes and looked around at the students, allowing a long pause to keep them riveted to his face and his sincere blue eyes.

"What do those words mean to you?"

No one spoke up.

"How does a soul, a living, breathing, human soul feel its worth? How do you place value on a soul?"

The teens at the Gathering were used to Todd's way of teaching by asking questions before diving into what he had to say. They knew that his questions were designed to make them tune into the topic. They also knew that when Todd paused it was to make them think and not because he was waiting for an answer.

Shawna didn't know that, though. Her mature-sounding voice broke into the silence. "It means that every human life has value. Every person should realize that God let you live for a reason."

All eyes were on Shawna.

"My birth mother considered ending my life before I was born, but Todd and Christy convinced her that my life had value. I was given a chance to live for a reason."

The crowd in the garage became still. No one moved. Their eyes shifted to Todd and then back to Christy and back to Todd.

What Christy saw on her husband's face just then was the most tender, fatherly look of compassion. He was looking at Shawna. Only Shawna. He seemed to be thinking or praying or both. She thought he looked as if he might cry.

"Shawna?" His voice was low and weighted with emotion. "Would you mind if I told everyone part of your story?"

"I don't mind." Shawna's voice was as steady and logical sounding as it had been when she made her earlier reply to the group.

Todd looked up and took in the gazes of everyone in the room. In that moment Christy was reminded of the passage in the Gospels when Jesus looked out over Jerusalem and was filled with compassion and said the people were like "sheep without a shepherd."

With his arms casually crossed in front of him, Todd started in. "When I was a teenager, my closest friend was a guy named Shawn. We did everything together. He was a brother to me, and I was a brother to him."

Todd's voice grew husky as he went on to share how an older guy started surfing with them and had told Shawn and Todd about Jesus. After several weeks of hearing what the Bible had to say, Todd chose to surrender his life to Christ, but Shawn didn't make the same decision.

"I was baptized in the ocean on July 27. It was an important day for me. It marked the beginning of my new life. I knew there would be no turning back to the old ways and the stuff I used to do."

Todd rubbed the back of his neck and shifted his position. "Shawn told me that day that he thought I was crazy. I told him to stick around and he would see that what happened in me, the transformation in my heart, was real.

"We hung out less and less. Shawn was mad that I wouldn't do the same old stuff with him. I kept pursuing him. By the next summer we moved in different circles, but I still tried to show up wherever he was."

Todd looked over at Christy with an expression of fondness. "I never thought of it until now, but that's how I met Christy. She was at the beach with a girl named Alissa, and Shawn wanted to be with Alissa so I went to where Shawn was." He smiled, as if the memory had engulfed him. "From the moment I first saw Christy I was drawn to her. She was unlike any other girl I'd ever met at Newport Beach."

Christy felt her face warming at his look and from his words. She just hoped he didn't tell everyone about how when he first went over to talk to her, it was because she had been wiped out by a wave and washed up on shore with seaweed tangled around her legs.

He didn't go that direction. His emphasis tonight was on Shawn and what happened to him. Christy had been there. She knew some of the details, but not all of them.

"After Shawn started going out with Alissa, he said he was going to a party. It had been a long time since I'd gone to a party like that, but I knew he would be there and Christy was there, too. She had stepped into a situation I was pretty sure she didn't mean to be part of so I asked if she wanted to leave, and we went down to the jetty to talk. Shawn and some of the other guys came down to where we were, and they decided to body surf. I tried to stop Shawn. He was so stoned that . . . he . . . we . . . we got in a fight. I couldn't convince him to stay out of the water."

Todd lowered himself onto the stool. He looked as if the telling of all this was taking a lot out of him. "Other guys were down there on the beach so I left, thinking they would hang with him. I wish I hadn't, but I walked away. Later that night I got a call that he was in the hospital. I went and sat by him all night, talking to him and praying for him. He wasn't conscious, as far as I know. But I wanted to believe that he could hear me. I begged him to surrender to Christ, to ask God to forgive him and take over his life. I also begged God to let him live."

Todd looked down. "That was one of the first times I felt what it was like when God doesn't answer your prayer the way you want Him to."

He drew in a deep breath. "Shawn passed away the next day. I want to believe that he made peace with God before he died, but I have no way of knowing until heaven."

Christy blinked back the tears. She had never heard Todd talk about Shawn's death in such a raw and vulnerable way. She looked around. Some of the girls were crying. Everyone in the room was riveted on Todd.

He cleared his throat and went on. "Alissa and Shawn had been together for only a short while that summer. He told me right after he met her that he really liked her and hoped she would stay in Newport Beach. But not long after Shawn died, Alissa went back East to live with her grandmother. She and Christy kept in touch because Christy reached out like a true friend and let Alissa know that she cared about her. A couple of months later Alissa told Christy that she was pregnant and it was Shawn's baby."

The attention on Todd awkwardly shifted to Shawna. Not directly, but with quick glances and side looks. Todd didn't have to say it. Everyone seemed to draw the same conclusion at the same moment. Alissa had every reason to choose not to have her life inconvenienced by this unwanted pregnancy.

Yet Shawna was given life. She had said it herself. Her life had value.

Christy wished she was sitting beside Shawna right then. She could only see the back of her head and couldn't tell if she was okay with all this.

Todd straightened his posture. "What Shawna said earlier is true. Alissa did consider terminating the pregnancy. But Christy and I both reached out to her and so did some women at a pregnancy center. I believe that's when Alissa's soul felt its worth. And she felt the worth of her baby's soul."

The air seemed to have grown very still, as if angels were surrounding the group, spreading their wings so that no sounds or any other forms of interference could break into what Christy felt was becoming a holy moment for the young hearts in the garage.

"I know it was difficult for Alissa to decide the next step because, as she told me more than once, she really loved her baby even before Shawna was born. Alissa wanted to give her what she felt was best for her. She decided to place Shawna into the arms of a loving couple for adoption."

Christy's throat hurt from swallowing her

tears. She wanted to be alone to cry for the hurt and pain Alissa must have gone through in giving up Shawna for adoption. Christy couldn't imagine giving birth to the child that was growing inside her right now and then letting that baby be raised by someone else. She knew now that she had been too young and lacked understanding to fully enter into what Alissa had gone through when she was a teenager.

Todd was the one who had written letters to Alissa and made phone calls and kept in contact with Shawna and her adoptive parents for the past decade. Christy loved her husband even more for the intentional way he had stayed in touch.

The room was still hushed except for a few sniffs camouflaged by coughs.

Todd squared his shoulders and looked at Shawna. "Thank you for letting me tell your story."

Shawna nodded.

Todd stood up and extended his hand to her. "Would you mind standing up? I'd like to bless you."

Shawna took his hand and rose. She stood facing him in front of the group. Todd placed his hand on her forehead in a pastoral fashion. He closed his eyes and lifted his face upward.

"Shawna, may the Lord bless you and keep you. May the Lord make His face to shine upon you and give you His peace. And may you always love Jesus first, above all else." Todd paused and added, "And may your soul always feel the immensity of its worth. Amen."

Shawna had kept her eyes open and stood perfectly still, as if she didn't quite know what she had agreed to when she stood up so Todd could bless her.

When Todd said, "amen," some of the teens in the group echoed the same.

Shawna turned to look at everyone as Todd removed his hand from her forehead. Her face reflected subdued amazement and curiosity.

Christy wanted to leap out of her folding chair and rush over to wrap her arms around both Todd and Shawna and bury her head between them so she could openly cry from the beauty of the moment.

She didn't move, though. She stayed seated and let her heart do all the leaping and rushing. Thankfully she found a tissue in the pocket of her jeans and used it to wipe her eyes. All of the words and actions of her husband during the past fifteen minutes had resonated in a deep place inside her. It was one of those moments when she truly felt as if she and Todd were united as one, and she could feel everything he was feeling. Their lives were knit together as a married couple, and both of them were intricately woven into Shawna's life.

Christy drew in a wobbly breath, and as she did, she felt a distinct fluttering inside. Her hand immediately went to her baby bump, and she pressed her palm against her shirt.

There it was again.

So faint, yet so distinct. A kick. A wiggle, as their baby moved inside her, and she felt it for the first time. It was like a butterfly flapping its eager, unfurled wings on the inside of her.

Christy pressed more firmly and breathed through her mouth, as if she were gasping for air. The movement stopped. The moment passed.

Shawna had sat down again. Todd had opened his Bible to Psalm 139 and was reading the chapter to the group.

Christy felt overwhelmed with wonder. She knew she would never forget the feeling of those two tiny wiggles. The first of many yet to come. The first tap-tap hellos from the inside. A very sacred reminder that she was carrying a child within her. A baby. Their baby.

As Todd read from Psalm 139, she kept her palm on her stomach and tapped her finger, as if trying to send a message back to her little one. Ever since Christy had gone searching for the "grains of sand" verse and read this Psalm aloud to their baby, she had gone back to it a number of times. She and Todd had read it together in various translations.

While he read it to the group now, Christy closed her eyes. Her thoughts reverberated as Todd's deep voice fill the room.

> Your works are miraculous, and my soul is
>   fully aware of this.
> Your eyes saw me when I was still an
>   unborn child.
> How precious are your thoughts concerning
>   me, O God!
> If I try to count them, there would be more
>   of them than there are grains of sand.

Christy opened her eyes and smiled softly as Todd finished reading to the group. She felt that something sacred had happened here tonight.

Certainly the group had been moved by hearing Shawna's story and the way Todd blessed her. It was more than that, though. For Christy, tonight was marked by the thought that she was carrying "a brand-new soul" inside of her.

She remembered how slowly the news had settled on her during the first weeks after the home pregnancy test. Hearing the heartbeat for the first time had been stunning. The sonogram image had been amazing. But the moment when she first felt the sensation of her baby fluttering inside felt sacred.

She was carrying human cargo. Human life had never seemed so eternal and valued as it did in this moment, in this garage, with Shawna and Todd and all the other souls that were beginning to feel their worth.

THIRTEEN

It took Christy a while to recover from all the emotions that had flowed through her and around her at the Gathering. As Todd, Shawna, and she were driving home, Christy tried to find a way to put the immense feelings into words.

Shawna, however, was already filling the time with her enthusiastic response to the evening. "I wish I lived here and could come with you guys every week. It was so fun, and everyone was really nice to me. I loved the singing. I've never been anyplace that had songs like that and where people were singing like that. I wanted it to go on all night. You are a really good singer, Todd. So are Brennan and Trevor. You guys should make an album. If you did, I'd buy it."

Todd looked at Shawna in the rearview mirror with an amused grin. He ignored her last comment. "Thanks for letting me share your story, Shawna. I'm glad you were there tonight."

"I liked the way you told it. My parents have always said that I was given life for a reason, and I believe that. But the way you said it all tonight felt really different."

"It was holy," Christy said. "A holy night."

"Like the Christmas carol!" Shawna said. "I loved it when you sang it, Todd. You could put that song on your album. Or maybe you guys could do a separate Christmas album. That would be cool. Do people here say 'cool'? My friend Lilly said that when she visited her cousin in California, her cousin still said 'cool.' Oh, and what does dawn patrol mean?"

"It means getting up early to go surfing when the sun comes up," Todd said.

"Oh. Because Brennan said he's going on dawn patrol tomorrow morning. He said you usually go with them, Todd. Are you going tomorrow?"

"I thought I might. It would be the first time I've been able to go all summer." Todd glanced at Christy. "What do you think?"

"Sure. I think you should go."

"Can anyone go?" Shawna asked. "Or is it only for guys?"

"Anyone can come." Todd glanced at Christy with the cutest look of youthful hope in his expression. "Why don't you both come?"

"Okay, sure." Christy immediately realized the sixteen-year-old in her had just given an immediate yes to the cute surfer guy with the buzzed haircut who was asking her to give up her Saturday morning sleep-in time.

The twenty-seven-year-old, five-month pregnant woman she now was inserted some second thoughts. Sleeping was her favorite thing to do lately. Now she needed to think about organizing everything tonight and adjusting the rest of tomorrow based on how long they would be at the beach. It was a good thing her parents and brother weren't coming up after all.

"Lilly won't believe I get to go surfing. I will get to go out in the water on a surfboard with you, won't I? Lilly told me that people don't really go surfing here. I mean, some people do, but not everyone."

Todd pulled into their narrow driveway and pushed the button to open the automatic garage door before parking Gussie safely inside. "We'll make sure you get out on a board tomorrow. You'll be able to tell Paula, I mean, Lilly, that you went surfing."

Todd glanced at Christy, and she knew exactly what he was thinking. When Christy first visited California, her friend Paula, back in Wisconsin, was the one who had advised her on what things would be like in Southern California, even though Paula had never been there. She even advised Christy on what bathing suit to buy, and it had been completely wrong. Christy thought it was cute that Shawna had a friend in Seattle who was advising her.

"This is going to be fun," Shawna said. "What should I bring? Will it be cold in the morning? How long will we be on the beach? I don't have a towel."

"I'll pack everything we need," Christy said. "Wear your bathing suit under your clothes and bring a sweatshirt."

Todd was grinning as he unpacked his guitar from the van and loaded several surfboards onto Gussie's roof. Shawna had scurried to her guest room, eager to have everything ready for her 5:30 a.m. wake-up call. Christy pulled beach towels out of one of the built-in closets in the garage next to the dryer. She then went through the house collecting sunscreen and an assortment of snacks that she stuffed into one of her jumbo beach bags. She set out a small, portable ice chest ready to fill in the morning and put two old blankets in the back of Gussie.

Christy was going to call out "good night" to Shawna, but her light was already turned

191

out behind her closed door. Christy headed upstairs and found Todd was ready for bed and setting his alarm. He looked up at her, still grinning.

"Can you believe how much Shawna has opened up already?" Christy asked. "When they arrived, I thought she was going to be the most quiet, studious little mouse. Now she's so talkative and excited about going to the beach with you guys in the morning. Are you really going to take her out on a board?"

"Sure, why not?"

"We need to be careful that she's safe. I'd feel awful if she got hurt."

"I'll keep an eye on her."

Christy was still thinking about everything that could go wrong when she crawled into bed next to Todd a few minutes later. "She seems to be more of a risk taker than I thought she would be. I don't know if it's a good idea for her to attempt surfing tomorrow. We don't even know if she's a strong swimmer. It could be dangerous if she's not used to the ocean."

Todd leaned in and kissed Christy's lips to silence her string of concerns. He cuddled up beside her. "I have a feeling she just wants to be with the surfers. She doesn't actually want to go out on a board. She's

192

just like you were."

Christy pulled back and looked at Todd. "I don't think she's very much like me at all. I see a lot of Alissa in her. Except she's surprising me with the way she's become so open and talkative."

"The way you were talkative with your aunt and uncle when you first came here."

"I don't think I was super talkative with them. I don't know. I don't remember."

Todd rolled on his back and placed his hands behind his head. "She's you, Christy. She's just like you were." He chuckled to himself.

"What's so funny?"

"You don't see it yet."

"See what?"

"She's you, and you're Aunt Marti."

Christy sat up and stared at Todd with a frown. "I am not Aunt Marti."

"Sure you are. You're worried about what she's going to eat while she's here. You tell her she can leave the Gathering with you if she's not comfortable. Now you're telling her what to wear tomorrow, and you're already worried she'll get hurt. Yeah, you're Aunt Marti."

Christy plopped back on her pillow and reached over to turn off the lamp on the nightstand. "I don't like your analogy," she muttered.

"You're just jealous because if you're Aunt Marti, then I get to be Uncle Bob, and you wish you could be the Uncle Bob."

Christy didn't answer. She was smiling in the dark, though. It was funny to think that she and Todd were old enough to play the part of Bob and Marti in their relationship with Shawna.

"Oh, hey, I almost forgot." Todd turned the light on.

Christy squinted at the brightness and watched Todd get out of bed.

"I bought a present for you." He went to the closet and pulled out a large, crumpled paper bag. He held it out to her. She sat up, and he stood next to the bed, waiting with a pleased look on his face.

Inside the bag was a thin, woven blanket that had blue, white, pink, and gray stripes and frayed tassels on both ends. She liked it but wasn't sure why Todd had bought it for her.

"It's for our son," he said. "Or daughter. That's why I got one that had both pink and blue in it. I know we haven't started work on the nursery yet, but a guy was selling those in the parking lot by the hardware store, and I wanted to get one for our baby."

Christy dismissed the fact that Todd had

bought what she would consider a beach blanket and not a baby blanket. She was used to his habit of buying things from street vendors and pawn shops. She didn't say anything to remind him that she already had planned the nursery around the theme of giraffes and was using yellows and greens instead of blues and pinks.

What she honed in on was that, for the first time, Todd had said, "our son or our daughter."

"Are you finally adjusting to the possibility that we might have a girl?"

Todd climbed back in bed and pointed at the blanket. "Do you like it?"

"Yes, I do. I like it a lot. Thank you. I'm sure we'll get lots of use out of it. We'll probably use it more at the beach than in the nursery, but it's really nice. And I love that you were thinking of our baby." Christy grinned at Todd and added, "Our baby, who could possibly be a girl."

"You know I'm just saying that so I'll appear open-minded. You and I both know he's going to be a boy."

Christy put down the blanket and reached for Todd's hand. She placed it over her baby bump. "I felt our baby move tonight when we were at the Gathering. Todd, it was so amazing. Not at all like I thought it would be. I think it's the first time I realized, I mean, deep-down realized, that I have a baby growing inside me."

"Is he moving now?" Todd looked hopeful.

"No. I thought he might kick again if he felt your hand covering his little cocoon."

"Hey," Todd said. "You said, 'he.' "

"I did, didn't I?"

They waited together for a moment, quietly poised with Christy propped up by her pillow and Todd's hand resting on her belly.

"Oh, well. Time for all of us to sleep, I guess." Christy reached over and turned off the lamp on the nightstand. She cuddled into Todd as he comfortably adjusted and wrapped his arms around her.

"I love you. Sweet dreams," Christy said.

Todd kissed the side of head. "I love you, too."

Christy was asleep in minutes.

It felt as if she had only slept for a few minutes when Todd's alarm went off. He rolled out of bed, and she pulled the covers up to her chin and moaned.

"Morning, Kilikina." Todd leaned over the bed and kissed her cheek.

She groaned again.

"You feeling okay?"

Christy rolled over and saw that Todd was already in his swim trunks and had on his Rancho Corona University hoodie.

"I'm fine. Just tired. I'll be down in a few minutes."

"Take your time. I set the alarm a little early."

"Don't tell me that. I'll fall back asleep. When do you want to leave?"

"About twenty minutes?"

"Okay." Christy stayed in bed as long as she dared before making herself get up. She went through the motions of washing her face, pulling her hair back, and putting on her bathing suit. She was so tired she could barely stuff her legs into her shorts and her arms into her Rancho Corona hoodie. Leaving the bed unmade and a cluster of dirty clothes on the floor, Christy went downstairs to find Shawna was up and chatting away with Todd.

An opened box of donuts sat on the kitchen counter, and Todd and Shawna were both eating one of the maple bars.

"When did you get those?" Christy asked.

"Just now. I bought you a buttermilk old-fashioned."

"They're really good," Shawna said. "We don't have donuts this good where I live. Well, maybe we do, but I've never had one like this at home. We don't usually buy a lot of donuts. I like this kind a lot."

"I was planning to make protein shakes for us this morning." Christy went through the motions of pulling out a container of almond milk and fresh strawberries that were washed, cut, and ready to put in the blender. "I have both chocolate and vanilla protein mix. And I have these individual insulated cups ready to go, so we can take them with us in the car."

Christy looked up and caught Todd's eye. He was munching on his donut, looking way too much like her good-natured uncle right now.

She froze in midmotion with a jar of Spirulina energy boost powder in her hand. Her eyes were fixed on Todd. The revelation was clear, and it stunned her.

"I am Aunt Marti, aren't I?"

Todd nodded. His grin was maddening.

"Help?" she said in a small voice.

"Put down the green stuff, Christy. Step away from the blender." Todd slid the donut box toward her. She could tell he was enjoying this way too much.

She took a lingering gander at the donuts. The old-fashioned one with the frosting dripping down the sides looked scrumptious. She lifted it from the box and took a dainty bite as Todd watched. It did taste yummy. A little too sweet, but very yummy.

"I'm still going to make a protein shake," she said.

He lifted his donut as if toasting her declaration. "Best of both worlds."

Shawna, who had no idea what was going on, excused herself to go brush her teeth.

Christy wrapped her arms around Todd and pressed her cheek against his chest. She could tell that he was still eating his donut, lifting it over her head and tilting his chin up so he could take a bite without getting the sticky frosting in her hair.

She pulled away and took two more bites of her donut. "Todd, how did we get this old?"

"By eating vegetables," he said with a wry expression.

With her donut between her teeth, Christy filled the blender with all the ingredients she had put out for their protein shakes. She secured the lid, pressed the button, and took another bite of her donut.

"I'll take one, too," Todd said. "If you don't mind mixing up another one of your concoctions."

"Me, too," Shawna peeped as she returned to the kitchen. "And if you don't mind, would it be okay to add a banana to mine?"

A few minutes later they were on their way to Huntington Beach with the box of donuts on the floor between the two front seats and their individual protein shakes in their cup holders. Christy felt content.

Shawna had lots to say about how well she slept in the guest bed and how nice it was to have her window open and be able to wake to the scent of salty air. It still surprised Christy the way Shawna was both articulate, polite, and mature for her age, but then in a flash she could sound like a giggly, impressionable young teen. This was not how she had pictured Shawna from their video calls.

"Brennan told me last night that you guys go to this beach and not the one right by your house because this beach has better waves in the morning. They're long, and you can ride them all the way to shore sometimes."

"That's right," Todd said. "I prefer the waves south of here, but Huntington is closer and works out better for everyone."

"How many guys usually come?" Christy asked.

Todd shrugged. "Hard to say. We're meeting up at a different spot this morning. Our usual place is where they're holding the Vans US Open this week."

Christy recognized that as one of the surfing competitions Todd often recorded on TV so he could watch it later.

"I know Brennan is going to be there," Shawna said pertly. "He told me he was coming. He said he almost always comes. Did you know that he goes to a Christian school? I wish I could go to a Christian school. I go to a private school. Lilly is my only friend there. Some of the students are so smart. All they do is study. It's a school for students who excel, but I'm not one of the really brainy ones. I'm more in the middle. Like Lilly. We're about the same IQ."

Christy had no idea what her IQ was and couldn't imagine comparing her IQ with her friends when she was in middle school. It made her wonder how much had changed in the world of education since when she was growing up. What would it be like for their child? Would he or she go to a public school? Private school? Would Christy homeschool the way Tracy did? Or would Todd get the job at South Coast Academy and stay there long enough as a teacher that they could enroll their child?

Todd pulled into the public parking area that lined the long stretch of beach at Huntington. The sky was cloudy, but the morning light was flooding the area with a stunning view of the vast blue ocean.

"Look!" Shawna called out. "There's Brennan with some other guys over there. Hi, Brennan! We brought donuts."

Christy glanced at Shawna's flushed expression and had a pretty good idea that this was not going to be a sit-on-the-beach-and-read sort of morning, even though she had brought two of her baby books with her. She had only one child to focus on. And it wasn't the one swimming around in her womb.

FOURTEEN

The first thing Shawna did when she walked over onto the beach was peel out of her oversized sweater, even though the air was chilly. Under her bulky sweater she wore a magenta-and-turquoise bikini top. Christy could tell it was thickly padded to make Shawna look like she had more on top than she really did.

The padding, the top's bright colors, and her hip-hugger shorts made her the center of attention for the five guys who had gathered down by the water.

"It's still pretty cold, don't you think?" Christy hoped Shawna would put her sweater back on. Not just for the chill factor but as a kindness to the guys who didn't need to have her parading her blossoming young body around in front of them.

"It doesn't feel cold to me," Shawna said. "The beaches in the Northwest where I live are much colder than this. I'm ready to go in the water." She unsnapped her shorts and shimmied out of them. The bottom of her bikini covered her in theory, but when she walked, she left very little to the imagination.

Christy tried to think fast.

Should I say something? I always felt so uncomfortable when it was up to me to say something to the girls in the youth group.

Todd was focused on untangling the ankle strap on his surfboard and hadn't noticed Shawna. The other guys seemed to be doing their best to not take in a full view of Shawna. Two of them were already heading toward the water.

"Are we all going in the water now?" Shawna asked. "Brennan, are you going surfing now?"

Brennan glanced at Christy with a look of *help*! He then looked back at his board, rubbing his thumb over the side as if trying to smooth out a ding. "Yeah, probably pretty soon." He sounded about as noncommittal as he could.

"How about if we let the guys go out by themselves now?" Christy suggested. "Then maybe Todd could take you out in a little while."

Shawna stood on the blanket with her legs slightly apart and her hands on her hips.

Her posture reminded Christy of cheerleading poses she had learned when she was trying out in high school. Shawna didn't look like a cheerleader, though. She was more of a female version of Peter Pan.

"I'm really looking forward to learning how to surf." Shawna's gaze was fixed on Brennan. "Whichever one of you guys wants to teach me is fine with me."

"Later." Todd grinned at Christy and headed for the water with his newest surfboard under his arm. It was his trademark color of orange.

Brennan quickly fell into step with Todd. The two of them hustled down to the water and dove right in. Christy knew that Todd liked to feel the water all at once whenever he got in the ocean, and that's why he went in headfirst and came bobbing up like a dolphin.

As Christy watched him, she felt a ruffle of sadness. When he popped up out of the water and gave his head his usual shake, his hair didn't spray a swivel of salty droplets the way it always had. He didn't have enough hair to shimmy. Christy decided then that she wasn't a fan of his haircut. She had to find a way to tell him to grow it out.

Shawna had resigned herself that the guys

didn't want to take her into the water with them. At least, not yet. She pulled her phone out of her bag and scooted over next to Christy on the large beach blanket. "Selfie!" She leaned up against Christy and clicked the camera before Christy realized what was going on.

"That wasn't very good. Let's try another one. Smile, Christy."

Christy smiled. Shawna clicked and clicked until she had one she liked. She then turned her attention to taking photos of the ocean and the lifeguard stations. She chattered as she texted them to Lilly.

Wedging her bare feet in the cool sand, Christy made herself comfortable and took in the beautiful view. The sun had risen behind them, and the clouds were floating away on a brisk morning breeze. A bank of thin clouds with a fluffed-up top layer rested on the horizon. The morning light turned the top edges of the ruffled clouds a soft shade of pink and made them look like a floating island made of cotton candy.

Christy reached for her phone and joined Shawna in capturing the California summer morning beauty. She was glad she had come. It had been a long time since she had paused like this and taken in the simple glories of the beach.

Christy and Shawna showed each other the photos they had taken, and Shawna said, "Yours are impressive. Are you a photographer?"

"No, but I have a really good camera my uncle gave me when I was in high school. I used to take pictures all the time. I studied how to get the best angles and let in the right amount of light."

"Why don't you still take pictures like that?"

"I don't know. I got busy with other things, I guess."

"I bet you'll take lots of pictures with your good camera when your baby comes." Shawna stopped scrolling on one of the images on Christy's phone. "This one of the ocean is so pretty! Can I send it to myself?"

"Sure."

Shawna tapped away. "I added my contact information to your address book. Now we can text each other." Her gaze fell on Christy's bare feet in the sand. "You like the sand, don't you?"

Christy nodded. "I love feeling the sand on my bare feet. It's been one of my favorite things ever since we moved to Newport Beach."

Shawna still wore her canvas shoes and had kept her feet on the blanket. While

Christy talked about how much she loved feeling the sand on her feet, Shawna slipped off her shoes and moved to the edge of the blanket so she could dip her bare feet into the sand.

"Right after I found out I was pregnant," Christy said, "I went down to the beach and sat for a long time with my feet in the sand. Do you remember the verse Todd read last night from Psalm 139?"

"Yes."

"When I was on the beach that day, I remembered the phrase in that chapter about how God's thoughts about us are more than the grains of sand." Christy lifted her toes and wiggled them, watching the shower of tiny grains of sand. "Can you imagine how much God loves us? More than all the grains of sand on all the beaches in the world."

"Let's take a picture." Shawna focused in on their matching feet and captured several shots. "Look how cute this one is." She turned her phone toward Christy. "I'm going to make this my screen saver. Sandy toes. It's so cute."

Christy thought the picture turned out sweet, but she wasn't sure why Shawna would want to make it her screen saver. Here Christy was trying to share a deep spiritual truth with her, and Shawna wanted to take pictures of their feet.

Shawna reached for Christy's phone. "I sent it to you. See?" Shawna tilted her head and squinted as she smiled at Christy. Her blonde hair was pulled up into a short ponytail that sprouted out of the top of her head like a tiny fountain. "Would it be okay if I made it your screen saver, too?"

Christy was caught off guard by the question. She nodded her agreement, thinking she could change it back easily enough after Shawna left.

"There. Look." Shawna held both phones next to each other. "Now we have matching screen savers of our sandy toes."

The gesture reminded Christy of the way she and Paula used to buy matching T-shirts when they were in elementary school. It was their symbol of being best friends. Perhaps matching screen savers were the equivalent with this generation.

"You have to keep this on your phone until your baby is born," Shawna said. "Then the first time you go to the beach with your baby, you have to take a picture of your baby's sandy toes and send it to me."

Christy put her arm around Shawna and gave her a hug. "Okay, I'll do that. Just for you. Oh my! You're freezing!"

"I'm not too cold yet. Here." She stood up and handed her phone to Christy. "Would you mind taking some pictures of me jumping? Have you done those before? You have to take the picture while I'm in the air."

Christy stood as well and followed Shawna out on the wide-open playground of sandy beach. She snapped dozens of photos of Shawna leaping in the air, doing cartwheels in the sand, and posing like a ballerina. In the midst of the fun, Christy realized how innocent Shawna was. She was uninhibited and comfortable in her agile body. She was a bit daring and definitely more athletic and coordinated than Christy had ever been.

It seemed that Shawna had no idea her figure was ideally proportioned or that her bikini was communicating something far more evocative than the thoughts that were going on in her head. Christy wasn't sure what to say before the guys came back or if she should say anything at all about Shawna's swimwear.

Her question was answered when Shawna did an impressive running cartwheel in the sand and came up holding on to the right side of her bikini top with both hands.

"It broke!" Shawna ran over to Christy and showed her where the thin strap had popped off from the padded triangle of fabric. "What am I going to do?"

"I think I have a travel sewing kit in my purse."

They returned to the beach blanket where Christy rummaged through a zippered pouch that contained an assortment of travel-sized items she had left in there ever since going to Katie's wedding in Kenya over two years ago. "Here it is. Put your sweater back on and then pull off your top. It will be easier for me to sew it than when you're wearing it."

Shawna slipped into her sweater and handed the top over to Christy. The sun was on their backs now, warming them and providing Christy with plenty of light to thread the needle.

"I hope you can fix it because it's not my bathing suit," Shawna said. "I borrowed it."

"Did you borrow it from Lilly?"

"Yes. How did you know?"

"Just a wild guess." Christy kept sewing and then asked a strategic question she hoped wouldn't alienate Shawna.

"Does your mom know this is what you're wearing this weekend while you're at the beach with us?"

Shawna shook her head. Her dark eyes showed the first bit of embarrassment

Christy had seen in her. "I have another bathing suit my mom bought for me that I'll wear when we're at the hotel pool the rest of this week. But Lilly gave me this one because she said that was the kind of bathing suit her cousin and all her friends in California wore at the beach. She said I'd get laughed at if I wore my one-piece."

Christy tried not to let her expression give away any of her thoughts. The memories of her first day on the beach were oh-so vivid.

"By any chance is your one-piece bathing suit green?"

"No, it's turquoise blue. That's my favorite color."

"I like turquoise, too."

Shawna was quiet for a few moments. "It's probably a good thing that the strap broke when it did. It would be a disaster if it had fallen off when I was out in the water with Brennan trying to surf!"

"Yes," Christy agreed. "That would have been embarrassing."

Shawna looked around. "Don't you think it would have been embarrassing if I wore my other bathing suit this morning?"

Christy grinned. "What do you think?"

"I think it wouldn't have been as embarrassing as I thought it would be, from what Lilly said."

"I think you're right." With quick stitches, Christy repaired the broken strap and then reinforced the strap on the other side as well. "I've seen a lot of girls on the beach over the years, and I've seen a lot of different bathing suits. I've worn a lot of different bathing suits. Here's what's amazing to me. The girls who end up getting the most respect from guys on the beach are the ones who are the most modest. They might not be the ones who get the most attention, but Todd has told me they are the ones who get the most respect. Does that make sense?"

Shawna nodded. She looked serious, as if Christy were telling her the secret of life and it was important that she take it all in.

"It's okay to stay covered up around the guys. It's actually better because you aren't sharing too much information, if you know what I mean."

"Yes, I know what you mean." The refined-Shawna voice had returned. "My mother says that cultured young women keep the personal parts of their bodies tastefully covered and not available for public viewing."

"Your mother is a wise woman."

"What about my birth mother? Was Alissa modest?"

Christy hesitated.

"She wasn't, was she?"

Christy tried to carefully choose her words. "Alissa had a really lovely, shapely body when she was a teenager. She still does, I'm sure. I just haven't seen her in a long time."

"She used her body to attract attention, didn't she?"

Again, Christy didn't want to answer. Her silence, though, provided all the information Shawna needed.

"My mother says that people should be attracted to you because of the beauty you develop on the inside."

"As I said, your mother is a wise woman." Christy felt relieved that she didn't need to say much more. She liked being the "cool" California Christy. She liked that she and Shawna had matching screen shots on their phones of their sandy toes. She didn't want Shawna to close her out.

"I brought my other bathing suit with me." Shawna pulled a swath of turquoise Lycra from her bag. "Do you think I should change into this now so when I go surfing I won't risk having another problem with Lilly's suit? She said it was expensive. I wouldn't want to ruin it."

"I think that's a great idea. I'll go with you to the restroom."

The wardrobe adjustment was accomplished without further discussion of modesty. The only problem was that as they strode through the sand back to the beach blanket, Christy noted that Shawna's figure was equally highlighted by the tight one-piece. At least the top wasn't padded so she looked her age and looked her natural size.

Clearly, though, Shawna was a lot like her birth mother. Christy remembered how Alissa could saunter through the sand on the beach and every head would turn. Her figure and her posture as well as the confident attitude she exuded made her irresistible to watch. Whatever Alissa had, it was in Shawna's DNA as well.

Todd had come in from the water and was going through the ice chest looking for a bottle of orange juice. When he found one, he took a long swig and then tipped the bottle in Shawna's direction. "You ready?"

"Yes!" She turned to Christy. "Are you coming, too?"

"No. I leave all the surfing to my husband."

"We'll start on the sand," Todd said. "I want you to get the feel of the board and learn how to stand." He placed one of his old boards flat in the sand. "Start by lying on your stomach, arms out to the sides because you have to paddle yourself out past where the waves break. That's it. Keep your feet together. Move up a little closer to the nose. There. That's good."

Christy watched as Todd patiently explained what he considered to be the easiest way to move from being on your belly to a standing position on the board. He showed Shawna where to stand and how to bend her knees.

In all the years they had been together, Christy never had asked him to teach her how to surf. He had gotten her out on a board with him, but she never asked for the step-by-step tutorial.

As she watched Shawna go through the steps and as she listened to Todd's calm instruction, she wished she would have had the confidence and the willingness to let Todd teach her how to surf when she was a teenager. In her opinion, five months pregnant was not the time to try to pick up a sport that required a lot of balance and strong core muscles.

And Christy wished that Todd would be hired for the teaching position. He was a great communicator and a skilled instructor. She knew that teaching the Bible made him happy. If he could be around teens and teach the Bible every day, she couldn't help but think that he would feel fulfilled.

She dearly wanted Todd to feel fulfilled. Ever since he stepped away from the difficult situation at the church where he had served as a youth pastor, Christy sensed that Todd felt like he was just "working." He didn't mind the work and he liked the people he worked with, but it never seemed that he was doing what he was created to do.

Shawna ran through the steps Todd had taught her, and he pronounced her ready to try it in the water.

"Will you take pictures, Christy?"

"Of course."

"Use my phone." Slender Shawna managed to hoist the big surfboard and hold it under her arm the way Todd did. Her strength was impressive. She looked over her shoulder and gave Christy a big, happy smile.

Christy snapped the shot and followed them down to the water's edge, anchoring her feet in the wet sand so the foamy, cool water washed over her and buried her up to her ankles. She loved all the sensations of this moment. The expansive view of the blue skies, now clear of any clouds. The fresh slap of the salty water on her bare legs. The faint scent of seaweed.

Most of all she loved the unimagined reality of what was happening right now. Her husband was paddling out into the beautiful Pacific, and beside him was the flesh-and-blood daughter of his old surfing pal whom he had lost all those years ago.

I have to tell Katie about this. About all of it. She'll understand what I'm feeling right now. She'll say this is a God-thing. A once-in-a-lifetime God-thing. And she'll know why every time I look at the picture of sandy toes on my phone, I'll stop and whisper a little prayer.

FIFTEEN

"And this one is of the first times I got up on the board." Shawna was seated next to Uncle Bob on the patio at Bob and Marti's house that evening at sunset. Uncle Bob was being Uncle Bob and was patiently showing interest in the many photos on Shawna's phone.

"I wasn't up for very long," Shawna added.

"But you got up a lot of times," Todd said. "You did great."

Shawna beamed. Partly from pride but mostly from sunburn.

The sun was setting, and the five of them were leaning back in their cushioned patio chairs. Their stomachs were full from Bob's grilled lemon chicken and the pasta salad. Marti had insisted they come over for dinner, and Christy gladly accepted the invitation at the end of their full day.

"Where did you go for lunch?" Marti

asked Christy. "Did you take Shawna to the salad place where you and I met for lunch?"

"No, we were at Huntington Beach until almost ten. Then we went home, took showers, and went over to Brennan's house."

Shawna added to the report. "After that we went to Balboa Island for Balboa Bars, and Christy showed me the gift shop where she used to work. She bought this shell necklace for me and got another one just like it for my best friend, Lilly."

"It's lovely." Marti removed her sunglasses now that the sky had softened to a primrose shade and the direct sunlight was no longer flooding the patio area. "Where did you say you went for lunch, Christy?"

"Brennan's house."

"Now, who is Brennan?"

Shawna listened attentively as Christy explained that Brennan was one of the teens from the Friday Night Gathering.

"He comes over a lot and plays guitars with Todd. His dad is the principal at South Coast Academy, and he asked Todd to stop by today. He wanted to talk about the interview Todd had yesterday for a teaching position at the school. We didn't mean to stay long, but we ended up having lunch there."

"Brennan's mother has a gourmet

kitchen." Shawna added her comment with the same composed air of maturity she had displayed when she first had arrived at Todd and Christy's with her parents. "She made pizza for us in her pizza oven. It was very good."

"What's the update on the job?" Bob asked.

"It's looking good," Todd said calmly.

Christy gave him a "go ahead" look. She had waited all through dinner for him to be the one to tell her aunt and uncle his big news.

"I'd start in August. I need to have the online course work done by September 15, and I need to have my lesson plans ready by, well . . ." Todd looked at Christy. "By yesterday, I guess."

"Are you saying you were hired?" Marti looked confused.

"Yeah, I have the position. There are some contingencies, but if I finish everything in time and pass the class, then, yeah. I'm going to be a Bible teacher."

Marti frowned. "You certainly don't seem too enthusiastic about it."

"I'm grateful more than anything."

"I think we're both still in shock," Christy said.

Todd leaned forward. He was sunburned,

too. The prominent red areas were on all the parts of his head that had formerly been shaded by his long hair. "I applied and nothing happened so I thought they had found someone else. Then they called yesterday, I went in for the interview, and now I have the job, if I want it."

"Do you want it?" Bob asked.

"Yes. Definitely."

Shawna's phone began to play a strain of classical music. She gracefully slid her chair back and in a quiet voice said, "Please excuse me. It's my dad." Shawna went into the house to take the call.

As soon as Shawna was inside, Marti said, "I am so impressed with her. Such a lovely young girl, with such refined manners. She's delightful."

"Yes, she is," Todd agreed.

"We love her," Christy added.

"I can see why you would." Marti turned to Uncle Bob. "If we had any good sense at all, Robert, you and I should have taken her in from the beginning."

No one responded to Marti's unexpected comment. Bob, Todd, and Christy all exchanged glances as if looking for clues as to what Marti meant. Undaunted, Marti spelled it out for them.

"The moment we heard that Alissa was

pregnant, we should have contacted her and told her that we would take her daughter. We should have been the ones to adopt Shawna."

Bob, Christy, and Todd were still exchanging glances. Did Marti realize what she was saying? At the time, she had nothing but disapproval for Alissa when she found out the teenager was pregnant.

Marti reached over and gave Christy's hand a squeeze. "She certainly appreciated the necklace you bought her."

Eager to keep the topic off Marti's comments about adopting Shawna, Christy said, "I appreciated the many gifts you gave me when I was her age. And all the gifts you still give me."

Marti seemed pleased to hear Christy's compliment.

Bob spoke up. "You know, Todd, it sounds like this teaching position is an answer to a prayer, but it's not what you thought you were praying for."

"I think you're right," Todd said. "I see it as God's provision for us. It's not something I even thought to ask for. And the idea of me being a teacher is loco." He gave Christy a half grin. "It makes me feel old."

Marti chuckled and leaned back. "Oh, the way you young people think these days.

You're both so young. You have your whole lives ahead of you. Having a baby and obtaining a stable job is only the beginning."

"I want to do what's right for Christy and for our child," Todd said.

"You know what, Christy?" Marti sat up straight, as if a brilliant idea had just occurred to her. "I would like to host a baby shower for you."

"That's kind of you, Aunt Marti, but you don't need to."

"Of course I do. As Bob mentioned earlier, we are ahead of schedule with the house now that we decided not to add the fourth bathroom or reconfigure the upstairs bedrooms. We'll be moved in by the first of September so the third Sunday in September would be ideal, don't you think?"

"Katie and Eli might be here by then."

"The theme, of course, will be difficult to determine since we don't know if you're having a boy or a girl . . ." Marti had a hopeful look in her expression, as she glanced at Christy and then at Todd. "It would make the planning so much simpler."

Christy wanted to laugh. She couldn't be sure if the idea of hosting a shower had suddenly dawned on Marti or if this was one of her aunt's clever ways of trying yet again to finagle her way to an early reveal.

"We'll all find out when the baby comes in November." Todd sounded as if his voice was on a recorded loop since he had repeated the same thing so many times.

Undeterred, Marti added, "I'm only suggesting that knowing would be much more accommodating for the guests and their gift selections."

"Martha." Bob's voice carried the hint of a growl.

Aunt Marti didn't look at Bob. Instead she turned her attention to Christy, who quickly swallowed her grin over her aunt's determination. "We'll have to settle with a generic theme, then. Whatever you like, Christy. You know best."

"That is really nice of you, Aunt Marti. Thank you."

"If you could possibly settle on a theme by this week, I'd like to arrange to have the invitations printed and mailed by the end of August."

Uncle Bob stood to clear the table. "That is my cue to fetch dessert for us. Party planning is not my specialty."

"Not mine, either." Todd gave Christy a kiss on the top of her head and stacked up the dinner plates.

Marti kept going with her shower plans. "If we could send the invitations out even sooner, that might help. I know this is shaping up to be a very busy fall. I'd like to get a commitment from the women in the Newport First Tuesday Club. They are all so frightfully overcommitted these days. I'm sure it will be the same for my book club and the board members of the Lido Isle Women's Association."

"How many people are you planning to invite?" Christy knew that her aunt was always going to meetings and organizing fund-raisers for the library, but Christy couldn't remember ever meeting more than one or two of the women from the groups.

"I anticipate at least fifty from my side."

"Fifty?" Christy repeated. "Five-zero? I thought you were talking about a baby shower for just family and close friends. That would be a dozen of us at the most."

"Oh, Christy, no. We'll have at least fifty with my friends. Then you, your mother, and possibly Katie, your work associates. Oh, and of course, it will only be fitting to invite Dr. Avery."

"Dr. Avery?"

"Yes. Isn't that the name of Todd's aunt? Dr. Linda Avery?"

Christy didn't remember ever mentioning the name of her OB to Aunt Marti. Maybe she had or maybe Todd had told her. Christy felt like she kept forgetting things ever since she became pregnant.

"Aunt Marti, I don't know think it's common practice to invite your doctor to your baby shower."

"We wouldn't need to tell anyone she's your doctor. I was planning to introduce her as Todd's aunt."

Christy wished she hadn't agreed to the shower so readily. It was beginning to seem as if her aunt were looking for a reason to show off her new house to all her friends in her social clubs, and Christy's baby shower was the ideal excuse. Why was Marti so determined to meet Todd's aunt that she had woven that piece into this extravaganza?

"You know what, Aunt Marti?" Christy could feel her face warming. "This doesn't feel right to me. The point of having a baby shower is not . . ."

"Not what?"

Christy wanted so badly to spew everything she was thinking and try to convince her aunt for once to see that the world didn't revolve around her and her way of doing things. There were other people to consider, and other ways of doing things that didn't have to be a big show.

Something inside her made Christy halt. She bit her lower lip and drew in a deep breath. It wasn't worth expending so much emotional energy when she was already exhausted from the long day and unwilling to get into a tiff with her aunt.

The screen door opened, and Shawna returned just then, gracefully taking her place again at the table. She was smiling, and her buoyant presence doused all of Christy's smoldering thoughts.

"My parents said to give you their best." Shawna filled the silence that had settled over Christy and her aunt.

"Are they having a good time?" Marti asked.

"I think so. They both said they're looking forward to the rest of our vacation starting on Monday."

"Do you have plans already?"

The two of them began an easy conversation, and Christy excused herself to go inside. She found Bob and Todd leaning against the kitchen counter, deep in a conversation about Todd's position at the school. Instead of entering in, Christy did something she hadn't done for some time. She quietly went upstairs and opened the door to the guest room that had been her domain for many visits over the years.

A swirl of memories greeted her as she entered the room that was now shadowed by the last dappled streaks of twilight coming through the open window.

So many conversations had happened here. So many prayers had been spoken here, including the one that burst from her heart the morning she knew that she wanted to turn her life over to God. She remembered the heart-to-heart discussion she and Katie had about Rick one dark night in this room. And how last January when Doug and Tracy needed the run of Christy and Todd's home after the twins were born, they had moved into this room for several weeks. She and Todd had slept together in this bed.

Christy lowered herself to the edge of the bed and smoothed her hand over the bedspread. So many memories.

In a few weeks Bob and Marti would move into their new house, and this house would become the memory-making place for someone else. The thought made her sigh. She stretched out on the bed, folding her hands over her stomach. When she did, she felt a flutter. The flutter.

Christy smiled and patted back. Her butterfly baby was tapping on the walls of its soft cocoon.

"I'm glad I got to bring you here, little one. Even if you can't see this room now, and maybe will never get to see it if they sell this house, I'm glad that when you and I were here together tonight that you did a little happy dance."

Christy closed her eyes and listened to the sound of the ocean. It was such a dear, familiar sound, and much more pronounced in this room than it was in their bedroom at home.

A clear realization came to Christy, covering her like gentle wave. Her aunt had prepared this room for her when she was a young teenager. Marti and Bob had made her feel welcomed at their home and let her know "her" room was always ready. It was not so unusual for Marti to want to prepare a nursery for Christy and Todd's baby. As Christy's mother had said, this was how Marti expressed her affection. She didn't say warm and comforting words. She didn't offer hugs and approving smiles. But she made rooms lovely and made them available, and that should count for something.

Okay, Aunt Marti. You win. You can invite as many people as you want to the shower, and you can tell them if it's a boy or a girl. I'll ask Dr. Avery to tell me at my visit on Tuesday. Then I will ask you to create a beautiful space for our son or daughter the way you created this wonderful room for me all those years ago.

SIXTEEN

That night, when they were home and about to slip into bed, Christy told Todd about her visit to the guest room and her plan to ask Dr. Avery to reveal to them if they were having a boy or a girl.

At first Todd didn't say anything.

"What?" Christy put her hand on her hip. She knew that look on his face. "What are you thinking?"

"I think you'll regret it."

"Why?" Christy thought she had explained clearly everything she had felt when she was in her old guest room at Bob and Marti's. She was surprised that Todd didn't immediately agree with her.

"The way I see it, you and I made a decision about this. It was our mutual decision. We felt confident about it then, and I'm confident about it now. We should stick with it."

"I thought you said it didn't matter to you

that much."

"I may have said something like that at the beginning. But now that we decided to wait, I think we should wait. Did you say anything to your aunt about this yet?"

"No."

"Good. Let's leave things the way they are."

Christy pulled the comforter up to her chin. She was too tired to talk about this anymore. It seemed best to sleep on it and start the discussion again in the morning.

Todd opened the baby app on his phone. "Did you know that our son is now the size of a small banana?"

"Mmm-hmm." Christy didn't open her eyes.

"It says here you have probably gained around ten pounds, and you need to make sure you're getting enough iron. You should eat more spinach and raisins."

"Fourteen," Christy mumbled.

"Fourteen what? You're supposed to eat fourteen raisins a day?"

"No. You said I should have gained ten pounds. I've gained fourteen."

"That's because you have a fourteen-pound banana in there."

"It's more like I have a one-pound banana

floating around in thirteen pounds of private ocean."

Todd placed his hand on Christy's baby bump. "Surf's up, dude!"

Christy chuckled. She was too tired to truly laugh so it came out sounding more like a string of weak coughs than a laugh.

Todd laughed at her laugh. "You're really tired, aren't you?"

"You have no idea." Christy rolled onto her side, which was now the most comfortable way for her to fall asleep. "I love you. Good night."

She didn't hear another sound the rest of the night. Nor did she hear Todd when he got up the next morning. She didn't know he had left until she hurried downstairs and saw the guest room door was open. A note was waiting for her on the kitchen counter.

Shawna and I went to early service with Bob. See you around eleven.

Christy couldn't believe she had slept until after nine. She felt as if she could sleep another five or six hours if she went back to bed. Opening the refrigerator door, she tried to decide what she was hungry for. Did she want some juice? Eggs? Just some tea? All she wanted was sleep. Lots more sleep.

"Come on, little banana." She placed her

hand on her stomach. "Let's go back to bed."

Christy had no trouble falling to sleep. She woke when she heard the garage door opening, followed by voices coming from the kitchen. Instead of going downstairs, she took a shower to wake up all the way and selected one of her roomiest summer dresses to wear. The last few days she had been having a hard time deciding what to put on because everything felt a little too snug, not only around her middle but across her bustline and especially around her hips.

For work, she had to wear all black. She had collected a variety of options over the past year. She was down to the stretchiest pants and the roomiest black tops, but she realized this morning that she needed to break down and buy some maternity clothes.

When she finally made her appearance in the kitchen, she found Shawna at the stove with a spatula in her hand and Todd emptying the dishwasher.

"Hi." She felt uncharacteristically shy about being around Shawna. "I guess I was pretty tired. How was church?"

"I enjoyed it very much," Shawna said. "It's quite different from the church my parents attend occasionally. Much less formal." She pointed to the creation in the frying pan on the stove. "Do you like frittatas? I added the spinach and mushrooms you had in the refrigerator along with some chopped tomatoes."

"Wow, I'm impressed!"

"Todd helped. I told him I usually make breakfast with my dad on Sundays, and he said we should make breakfast for you and to add spinach because the iron is good for you at this stage in your pregnancy."

Todd held up a loaf of bread. "I stopped and bought raisin bread. Thought I'd make some toast to go with the eggs."

Christy felt odd being the guest in her own kitchen. It was cute the way Shawna had found an apron and appeared in her element. Christy didn't want to step in and take over so she simply asked what she could do to help.

"You could pour beverages for us, if you like," Shawna said. "I'll have juice, thank you."

Christy poured three glasses of cranberry juice and put on the hot water for tea. Todd winked at her and put some bread in the toaster. He slid over to where she stood and gave her a morning kiss.

"How's our little banana doing?"

Christy rested her hands on her middle.

"Good. I think our little banana is still sleeping. I haven't felt any flutters lately."

"Can you feel the baby already?" Shawna stared at Christy's stomach. "What does it feel like?"

"It's faint. Like a tickle on the inside."

"That's so amazing. I wish I lived nearby so I could go to your baby shower and see the baby right after it's born. I'd be your favorite babysitter. I've already taken a first-aid class for babysitters, and I learned CPR."

"I wish you lived here, too," Christy said.

"You would be our favorite babysitter for sure." Todd held out a plate to Shawna, and she expertly flipped the frittata onto it before starting another one.

"I like your home," Shawna said. "It's alive."

"Alive?" Todd repeated.

Shawna looked up at him. "It's because of all the love that's here. Your house breathes. It breathes love in and out. I felt it the moment I stepped inside."

"That's beautifully said, Shawna," Christy said.

"Well, it's true." Shawna turned her attention back to her frying pan. It surprised Christy how comfortable the three of them worked together in the kitchen. It felt as if they had known each other all their lives. Christy also noticed how easily the conversation flowed as they sat around the small kitchen table and lingered over their group-effort brunch. The topic landed on what they should do with the afternoon. Todd suggested the two of them decide what they wanted to do, and he would join them for part of it, but first he needed to study for his online course.

"We could go shopping," Christy suggested. "Todd, you wouldn't have to come. What do you think, Shawna? Does shopping sound fun to you?"

"Sure, I like to shop."

"Good, because I need some maternity clothes."

The two of them took Christy's car, affectionately named "Clover" by Katie, who had sold it to Christy for a dollar when Katie went to Africa. They started their afternoon at the Irvine Spectrum shopping center and went on to two discount stores nearby.

Christy realized when she slipped the first flowing top over her head that her thoughts were centering on the baby more than ever. It seemed that the first few months all she thought about and read about was how to curb nausea and get enough sleep and exercise. In the last few weeks her focus had turned to what to eat mixed with a slew of regular life stuff, like her parent's upcoming decision about where to live and Todd's job possibility.

She turned to the side and looked at her profile in the full-length dressing room mirror. Smoothing the sleek, pale-green top over her midriff, it was clear that she was pregnant. That was an undeniable baby bump. At home she didn't have a full-length mirror, and her middle didn't show when she stood in front of the bathroom mirror. This was the first time she had stopped to take in the full side view of what was happening to her body.

"Do you like any of the tops?" Shawna asked from the dressing room next to Christy's.

"I haven't tried all of them yet."

"I don't like these jeans. I'm going to look for another pair."

Christy's sense of chaperone duty kicked in. "Wait just a minute. I'll go with you." She knew she might be overly cautious in wanting to have Shawna within view at all times. Shawna was a mature and capable young girl. But still, crazy things could happen to young girls, even in respected retail outlets.

Christy quickly tried two more tops and selected one of them because it seemed to have the most room for her to grow. Plus it was peach colored, and that had always been a favorite summertime color for her because it seemed to go well with her brown hair.

The two of them continued their hunt for maternity tops and stretchy black work pants for Christy and jeans for Shawna. Their efforts were rewarded at the third store when Christy found the kind of pants she was looking for along with three more tops. Two of them were black for work, and the other was a gauzy fabric with embroidery on the bodice, and it was free flowing all the way to almost midthigh.

"You could wear that one as a dress," Shawna said when Christy stepped out of the dressing room to get Shawna's approval.

"You might be able to wear this as a dress," Christy said. "I don't think I'd attempt such a feat. I like it as a maternity top. What do you think?"

"It's cute on you. I think you should get it."

"What about you? Find any treasures?"

"No. I mostly like trying different things to get an idea of what they look like on me.

I don't really need anything. I just like looking."

Christy had a feeling very few girls Shawna's age would say they didn't need any new clothes. Christy felt that way when Aunt Marti first took her shopping. But Christy couldn't remember ever saying she didn't need anything. Most of the time she had been willing to let her aunt spoil her.

"Are you getting hungry?" Christy asked, as they left the shopping center and merged onto the freeway. "We could stop for something to eat on the way home, if you like."

"Sure. What's your favorite place?"

"Well, it depends on what we're hungry for. Oh, I know. Let's go to Julie Ann's. It's my favorite café." Christy changed lanes on the freeway to exit onto 55 West, toward Newport Beach. "Although, I don't know if we'll have enough time before your parents show up."

"We can go back to your house," Shawna said. "I don't mind."

Christy made another lane change when a car swerved in front of them and moved two lanes over at a dangerous speed.

"What is that guy doing?" Christy gripped the steering wheel and eased up on the gas pedal. "He could have caused a terrible accident."

"That was scary," Shawna said.

"Are you okay?"

"Yes."

Christy quickly glanced at Shawna and then just as quickly returned her focus to the traffic on all sides of them. It sobered her to think what might have happened if they had been in an accident. Having Shawna with them this weekend felt natural and low stress. But now it struck Christy that they had taken on a serious responsibility when they had agreed to keep watch on Shawna's well-being and safety. Not to mention how terrified Christy would have felt if her baby had been harmed.

"You know those verses Todd read on Friday?" Shawna asked.

It took Christy a moment to remember. Her thoughts were still on the precious cargo she was carrying. Was she always going to feel the same way whenever she and their child were in a car? Or a plane? Or even walking across the street?

"It was in Psalm 139," Shawna said, as if trying to prompt Christy.

"Oh, yes. Right. Psalm 139."

"I marked that whole chapter and saved it on my phone."

"Good. I'm glad you did."

"It helped me to understand something,"

Shawna said.

"And what is that?"

"I wasn't an accident."

At first Christy thought Shawna had said they weren't in an accident when the car swerved toward them. Then she realized Shawna was saying that her birth wasn't an accident.

"Those verses say that God saw me and knew me before I was even born. My parents always helped me to understand that my life has value, but those verses made me feel like I was wanted before I was born. God wanted me."

Christy glanced at Shawna and wondered how so much mature insight could come from such a young girl. "You're absolutely right. God wanted you. He will always want you. I hope that you will keep drawing closer and closer to Him."

Shawna became quiet and gazed out the windshield. They were almost home when Shawna said, "Every time I look at our screen saver with our sandy toes, I'm going to think of that. I'm going to remember that God's thoughts about me are endless, like the grains of sand."

"Then I'm going to think the same thing, Shawna. And every time I do, I'm going to pray for you." Christy turned down the narrow street that led to their house and saw that Andrew and Jacqueline had just arrived and were getting out of their rental car.

"Good timing," Christy said as she parked Clover and reached for the shopping bags.

Shawna hurried to her parents to give them a big hug. "Do we need to leave right away?"

"Yes, we've made early dinner reservations at a special restaurant in downtown Los Angeles. It's going to take us a while to get there." Andrew looked at Christy. "I hope we're not cutting into any plans you made."

"No. We were just going to have something to eat and maybe go for a walk down to the water, if we had time."

Shawna's expression drooped, and her shoulders rounded forward, making her look the part of a sullen preteen. "We didn't get to make s'mores on the deck."

"I know. Todd told you we would do that, but I was too tired after we left Bob and Marti's last night."

"And we were going to ride bikes along the beach."

"Yes, we were going to do that this afternoon after shopping, weren't we?"

"Shawna." Jacqueline's soft voice was firm. Her look said, "Mind your manners."

Straightening her posture, Shawna returned to the polite version of herself. "I enjoyed everything about this weekend. Thank you very much, Christy."

"You're welcome. We loved having you." Christy gave Shawna a comforting look. "You'll have to come back sometime and stay longer. We'll ride bikes, walk along the beach, and make s'mores on your next visit. It will give us something to look forward to."

Shawna's face lit up. "I would love that. Thank you, Christy."

Jacqueline smoothed her hand over Shawna's wind-tossed hair. It was the gesture of a nurturing mother.

"Let's go in and pick up your luggage," Andrew suggested.

The four of them went inside and found Todd seated at the kitchen counter with his laptop open and a stack of big books open around him. He got up as soon as he saw them.

"It can't be time for you to leave already," Todd said.

Shawna went to him and gave him a long hug. She turned to Christy and gave her an even bigger hug.

"Thank you both for everything." Her voice was wobbly and sounded as if she might burst into tears. Christy knew that if

Shawna cried, she would cry, too.

"Of course." Todd folded his arms across his chest. He looked choked up.

With a courageous smile, Christy said, "I told Shawna she'll have to come stay with us again."

Todd nodded. "Absolutely. Any time. We mean that."

"Thank you," Jacqueline said. "This has meant a lot to all of us."

They all nodded and smiled. The sweetness of affection floated in the air between them. Andrew followed Shawna to the guest room and got her suitcase, which she already had packed, being the responsible young woman that she was.

They headed for the front door, none of them saying anything.

"Oh, wait!" Christy dashed to the guest room, calling over her shoulder, "I almost forgot."

She came out with the throw pillow with the S on it. "This is for you. I made it, and I want you to take it with you."

Shawna and her parents looked surprised and touched by Christy's gesture. Shawna took the pillow and traced her finger over the S that Christy had cut out of bright-pink floral material and appliquéd on the front.

Christy broke the silence by saying, "Now that I know turquoise is your favorite color, I'll make another pillow for you the next time you come. I'll make the S on that one out of turquoise fabric."

Shawna looked up with tears in her eyes. "Could you make it a C instead of an S?"

"Okay." She wasn't sure why Shawna would ask for a C.

Her expression must have reflected her question because Shawna went to Christy and wrapped her arms around her middle, squeezing her tightly. Christy felt the pillow tap gently against her side.

"I would like a C because that one will be for my middle name." Shawna looked up at Christy. "It's the name my birth mother gave me. You know what it is, don't you?"

An old memory rushed over Christy of a phone call she had with Alissa right after Shawna was born. Alissa hadn't yet decided if she would keep her daughter or give her up for adoption. But she had chosen the name for her baby girl and sounded convinced it was exactly what she wanted her child to be named.

Christy smiled down at Shawna. The tears now glistened in her eyes, too.

"Yes," Christy answered in a choked voice. "I know your middle name. It's Christy."

SEVENTEEN

As soon as Shawna and her parents drove away and Christy and Todd stopped waving from their driveway, Christy curled herself into her husband's broad chest and let loose with the tears she had been holding in.

Todd held her close and murmured, "What is it, Kilikina?"

Christy pulled back and looked at him. Her thoughts were jumbled the way her emotions had been for months, and it felt overwhelming. She was flooded with memories of Alissa and felt the sadness of Shawna's good-bye hugs and tears. At the same time she was remembering the deep panic she had felt when the car swerved in front of her and then the fear that had coursed through her as she realized the responsibility that came with the care of another person — Shawna and Christy's unborn baby.

On the top of all that, she suddenly didn't

know how to process that she had gained so much weight already and that her body was set on a course to radically change. The side view in the dressing room's full-length mirror had left a vivid image in her mind. She tried to picture how she would look in a few months when she was about ready to burst with this small banana baby who would grow into a plump human, God willing. Christy carried clear memories of how petite Tracy looked when she was carrying the twins a year ago. She couldn't imagine her body looking like that.

The onslaught of so many emotions at once was too much. All she could do was cry.

"What is it?" Todd looked concerned.

"Life," Christy said. "All of it. I feel overwhelmed."

He kissed her twice. "Let's walk down to the water."

It was one of his statements. Not a question. Not a suggestion. Not up for discussion. It was a call to action.

Christy willingly agreed. She went inside for her sunglasses and decided to take the new pink-and-blue-striped baby beach blanket with them over her arm. Todd locked up the house and held her hand all the way to the water.

Neither of them spoke. They exchanged three hand squeezes as their secret code of "I-love-you." As they strolled barefoot through the sand, Christy drew in a deep breath and felt her heart and mind reset. This place always did that for her. Getting her toes in the sand replaced her mentally crowded screen with a blank one.

They went to the water's edge and walked side by side, hand in hand along the firm, wet sand at the shore, weaving in between the late Sunday afternoon crowds of beach-goers. Todd stopped and looked out at the waves. He put his arm around Christy's shoulders and drew her close.

"Do you want to sit for a while?" he asked.

"Sure." She spread out the blanket for them up on the dry sand, and they sat close together with Todd's arm around her shoulders once again. Christy loved the way it felt as if he were sheltering her and their baby. All her panicky feelings had disappeared. This was home. Here, with Todd, on this beach, on a summer afternoon. She knew where she was. She knew who she was. Her heart felt willing to receive whatever God had next for them, including Todd's new job.

"You doing okay?" Todd asked.

"Yes." Christy burrowed her bare feet in

the sand and pulled them up, smiling at the sight of her sandy toes. A sweetness rested on her as she remembered the screen savers and her promise to pray for Shawna. In a few months she would replace the photo with an image of her baby's sandy toes.

"Being here on the beach anchors me," Christy said. "I'm glad we came."

"Whenever we do this," Todd said, "I always wonder why we don't do it more often."

"I know. It's terrible that we don't come down here all the time. People save up for years to be on the beach for a one-week vacation. Yet we rarely stop to enjoy the beauty."

"I wonder if that will change when we start bringing our kid down here."

Christy looked at Todd and smiled. "You didn't say 'son.' You said 'kid.' "

"Did I? I must be slipping." He grinned at Christy. She leaned in and kissed his cheek, right on his dimple.

Todd kissed her back. His was a lingering kiss, and when he drew away slowly, Christy leaned in even farther and kissed him back with equal tenderness.

"I love you," she whispered as they pulled apart.

Todd's strong arm drew her even closer.

"I love you, Kilikina." His free hand went to her belly. "And I love you, kid."

Christy chuckled. She placed her hand on Todd's and said, "Are you still set on the name Cole Bryan if it's a boy?"

"Absolutely."

"What if it's a girl? We should come up with a few options, just in case your prediction is wrong."

Todd pulled back with a mock expression of shock, as if his being wrong was not possible. "Okay, you go first. What have you come up with?"

"Not much. I don't have any family names that I'd like to carry on. I've thought of incorporating a friend's name as maybe the middle name, but nothing strikes me as sounding just right. At least not yet."

"What names have you considered?"

"Well, Shawna, after being with her all weekend. And Katie, of course. Or Tracy, since I know she's already praying for our child and has been for a long time."

"What about Juliet?" Todd asked.

"That's my middle name."

"I know."

Christy hadn't considered pulling an option from her own name. She had only run through the old-fashioned names of her mom and aunt and wasn't crazy about Margaret or Martha.

"I'm not sure," Christy said. "Juliet seems to work better as a middle name. I want the first name to be short. I've always liked short names. That's why I like Cole. I want something short for a girl."

"Julie?"

Christy considered it for a moment. It reminded her of Julie Ann's café. She loved Julie Ann's Café. But it didn't strike her as the name for their baby. Their girl. If they were having a girl.

She and Todd tossed a dozen more names back and forth, but none struck both of them the same way at the same time.

"Didn't we come up with some names for our kids when we were at Rancho? Before we were even engaged?"

Christy vaguely remembered a few whispered conversations with Todd when they dreamed together about their future. She hadn't written down the name suggestions, and none of them were coming back to her now.

"I think we came up with a couple of Hawaiian names," Todd said. "Do you remember any of them?"

"I don't. I wish I did. I have a book of baby names at home," Christy said. "Tracy left it for me. Next time we're sitting around, let's go through the book and make a list."

Todd looked doubtful. His doubt seemed tied to Christy's line about "next time we're sitting around," as if he couldn't picture that happening a lot in the near future. "I really should get back at it with the class. I'm behind and need to have the next lesson done by tomorrow morning."

Todd stood and offered her a hand. "I'm going to tell Zane about the job tomorrow. I don't know how he'll take it. I keep thinking the orders will slow down, but we received another order last week for ten benches from a shopping center in North Carolina."

"You guys have been so successful in such a short time."

"It's because of Bones. He's supplying us with all the old boards. He hardly charges us anything for them. That means we can keep our prices down, and we can blow away the competition. Not that we have a lot of it."

"What do you think will happen when you run out of boards?"

"That'll take a while. Bones has hundreds of retired boards in the shed at his place in San Clemente. Maybe thousands. You were there with me. You saw what he has."

"I never went into the 'graveyard' with you. You told me about it, though."

"I keep telling Bones he should charge us more, and he keeps saying we're doing him a favor by clearing them out." Todd had picked up their pace as they held hands and were retracing their path along the shoreline. "Did I tell you that the article I wrote about Bones is coming out in the September issue of the surfing magazine Sierra's husband sells photos to? What's his name?"

"Jordan."

"We should have them come stay with us some weekend."

"I'd love that." Christy cautiously added, "But when?"

"Not this month. And not next month. October maybe. Or November."

"As in, November when the baby comes?"

Todd stopped walking and looked at Christy. He ran his palm over the top of his fuzzy head. "Oh, wow."

"Did you forget there for a moment that we're having a baby?"

"Maybe. But only for a second."

"Well, I'm starting to think about the baby all the time. I want to start doing things, like getting the nursery ready and signing up for a birthing class."

Todd looked confused. "Why do you have

to take a class to learn how to give birth? I thought it all happened naturally. I heard you talking about that with Tracy on the phone a while ago. Natural childbirth. Doesn't that mean you just let the baby come?"

"Not exactly, Todd." Christy explained what natural childbirth meant and the options for different classes that would prepare them, based on their birthing plan. "There's also an introduction meeting on the first Saturday of each month at the hospital. I think it's too late to sign up for the August class, but we should sign up now for September. They'll take us on a tour, tell us what to expect, and show us the labor and delivery rooms."

"Us?"

"Yes, us. You need to take the tour with me. I need you to be there when the baby comes, coaching me, the way Doug told you he coached Tracy."

Todd had started walking again at a fast pace. "We need a main calendar." He sounded nervous. "We need to schedule everything. I don't know my class schedule yet. I'll find out on Friday when I go in for the teacher's orientation day."

"Friday? That's when we go back to see Dr. Avery."

"I don't know if I'll be able to go with you this time. I'll find out. What did you decide? You're not going to have her tell you if we're having a boy or a girl, are you?"

"No. I thought about it a lot, and I think you're right. We made a mutual decision. Let's stick by that decision."

"Okay. Good." He seemed to be mentally checking things off a list as they covered the last few yards of sandy beach and hit the sidewalk. "What about your parents? What's happening with them? Do you think your dad could help with the nursery? Or maybe your aunt? Because I'm not sure when I can do the painting and everything."

Christy couldn't remember seeing Todd this anxious for a long time. Their leisurely sunset stroll on the beach had evened out her emotions but seemed to have put Todd in a schedule frenzy.

"Don't worry. I can work on all that and get some help. I was going to call my mom tonight to see if she has any news about Dad's job. We don't have to start on the nursery right now. I was only saying that I'm feeling like I want to start taking steps to prepare for the baby. Time is going a lot faster than I thought."

As soon as they were back in the house, Todd was at the kitchen counter, diving into

working on his online class. He was concen-
trating so intently, Christy decided to grab
her phone from her purse and take it upstairs to call her mom. She saw that she had
missed three calls. Two were from her mom,
and one was from Tracy. Both of them had
left messages.

Tracy's message was short and sweet, like
Tracy. "Just checking in. I wanted to see
how you're doing. Call me back when you
have time. No rush. Love you."

Her mom's message was simply to call her
back, which Christy did as soon as she was
comfortably settled in her snuggle chair by
the open window. The breeze was perfect,
and the temperature of their bedroom felt
just right. Christy loved this corner spot.

"I wanted to let you know that we'll be up
your way tomorrow," Christy's mom said
almost as soon as she answered.

"Tomorrow? How long will you be here? I
have to work until five."

"We're only coming for the morning. Your
father has an interview."

Christy sat up straight. "An interview?"

"It's for a manager of a small apartment
complex in Costa Mesa." She sounded quite
proud of herself. "I found the posting online
and I think it will be ideal. Your father will
take care of the grounds and maintenance

of all the units, and we'll have our own apartment at no charge. It means we'll be close to you, Christy."

"Mom, it sounds perfect! I'm so excited for you guys. Could you come by the spa afterward and tell me how the interview went?"

"I'll ask your father. He has to get back to the dairy because he only took half a day off. Please pray about this, Christy. I hope this is the answer for us."

The next morning while she was at work, Christy prayed for her parents several times. She kept checking her phone to see if her mom had left a message. Finally, when Christy was at lunch, a call came through from her mom.

"I think the job and the housing would work out nicely for us," her mom said. "There are only twelve units. The grounds are in good condition, and the unit we would live in is a downstairs apartment with two bedrooms and an updated kitchen."

"When will Dad find out if he got the position?"

"Hopefully he'll know by later this week. We're on our way back to Escondido now. We didn't have time to come see you."

"That's okay. I'm glad to hear the update. This is such good news, Mom."

"I know. It is. Now all we can do is wait."

As soon as her mom hung up, Christy texted Katie to see if she was available for a quick call. It had been far too quiet on Katie's side of the globe, and she hadn't given a peep of a hint as to when they were coming to California. Christy realized the time difference made it unlikely Katie was awake, but maybe Christy would catch her up doing something in the middle of her night and ready for a chat.

When Katie didn't reply, Christy decided to use the last fifteen minutes of her lunch break to tap out a quick e-mail to Alissa. All the endearing moments she had spent with Shawna were still fresh in her thoughts, and she wanted to share a few of them with Alissa before the days steamrolled the great memories.

Christy chose her words carefully. She told Alissa how adorable Shawna was as well as smart and mature. Attaching a couple of photos from their morning at Huntington Beach, Christy told Alissa about how Shawna had a tender heart.

Two days later Alissa replied to Christy's e-mail.

"Your words were like honey to me, Christy. I love that you and Todd were able to spend that time with Shawna. Her parents are exceptional, and I'm so grateful that they care for her deeply. What will make the difference in her teen years, though, will be people like you and Todd who show her God's love in a pure way, the way you both showed it to me when I was a teen. I pray for her all the time.

"Can I tell you something? Some days I wonder what it would have been like if I'd found a way to keep her. Now that Brad and I have two girls that we adopted, I feel like I understand the depths of joy and sorrow on both sides of adoption.

"I loved the photos you sent of her. Do you have any more? Tracy and I were talking the other day about how great it would be if you guys could come up after the baby is born. Next Easter vacation, maybe?

"Sending lots of love from all of us here in Glenbrooke, Alissa."

Christy did a little dreaming about going to Oregon next Easter. She tried to picture her and Todd traveling with a baby. Would they fly? Drive Gussie? What would it be like to see their friends again, now that they were young parents, too?

Her daydreaming made Christy wonder what was happening with Eli and Katie. She still hadn't heard anything about their plans to come to California. Were they waiting for approval from the board of directors of the ministry?

She sent her friend another text and received a short reply. I'LL CALL WHEN I CAN. BUSY WEEK. NO UPDATES YET. BIG HUGS. HOW'S THE BABY?

Christy wrote back that the baby was fine and that she missed Katie a lot. She also told her that Todd had settled things with Zane and let him know Todd had taken the teaching position.

Katie texted back COOL.

But to Christy it didn't feel very "cool." For the next two nights Todd didn't come home until well after midnight and then sat up several more hours working on his homework for his class. Even though Christy knew this transition was temporary, it was rough on both of them.

She decided to stop waiting for Todd to be available to help her on projects around the house and dove into the task of cleaning out the room that would become the nursery. The next project was the addition of a large, framed calendar on the wall in the kitchen near the door that led to the garage. She wrote in all the important information on the dates she knew of between August first and the end of the year. She affixed a cup to the wall and filled it with fine-point marking pens so Todd could add anything he wanted to the calendar.

On Friday, Christy went to the doctor's appointment without Todd and had only a brief exam because Dr. Avery had been called out for a delivery. The new nurse practitioner took over for Dr. Avery and told Christy everything looked good and to come back in a month.

For all the ways the week felt disconnected with her husband in conversation and physical attention, it felt productive. Christy had done a lot and had managed to sleep extra. She also worked full days at the spa yet managed to keep her husband fed and in clean clothes at the same time. That, she decided, was a significant number of accomplishments.

As Christy and Todd rushed out the door to the Friday Night Gathering, her mom called.

"Your father got the job. The owner called this afternoon and would like us to move in the end of August. We are so pleased. This is an answer to prayer."

"Hooray! That's wonderful!" Christy looked over at Todd who was backing Gussie out of the garage. "My parents are moving to Costa Mesa."

"Tell them I'm stoked to hear that."

Christy repeated Todd's message, and her mom said, "Have you talked to Marti today?"

"No."

"You might want to call her before she calls you."

"Okay. Why? Is something wrong?"

Christy's mom paused before saying, "It would be best if you heard it from her."

As much as Christy admired and appreciated her mother's integrity in such things, it was torture for her to go through the whole night at the Gathering without knowing what was going on with Bob and Marti. Her imagination came up with dozens of scenarios, and none of them were cheerful.

EIGHTEEN

The first thing Christy did Saturday morning was send a text message to her aunt, asking if she could stop by her house. Marti replied, I HAVE A LUNCHEON AT NOON. I'LL STOP BY YOUR PLACE ON MY WAY HOME.

The next thing Christy did was go downstairs where Todd was already up, sitting at the counter, working on lesson plans.

"I have to go into work at noon," he said. "Zane may have found a guy to take my place. He's going to interview him today."

"What are your feelings about all that? About not working with Zane anymore?"

Todd gave her a muddled look as if the word "feelings" hadn't been part of any his choices about this job change. "It's good. It's all working out." He returned his attention to the laptop.

She realized how differently she processed things. Todd seemed content, though, and

264

that gave her a sense of peace about their future.

Christy dearly wanted to take a nap once Todd left, but this was her chance to keep going on the household projects she had scheduled for that morning. By the time Marti arrived, the nursery was cleared, and the room cleaned top to bottom. Christy had finished the laundry, scrubbed the bathrooms, and vacuumed the floors.

"Would you like something to drink?" Christy asked as she and Marti stood near the front door. Christy would have felt more comfortable sitting in the living room, but Marti appeared to be in her woman-on-a-mission mode.

"No, I can't stay long. What I need to tell you is simple and to the point. Your uncle has informed me that we are not able to keep two rental houses once we move into the new house. I'm quite upset. He had a terrible financial reversal with one of his commercial properties recently, and all I can say is that it's a good thing your father didn't take the custodial position Robert suggested to him several months ago. Norman would be out of a job already."

"Oh." Christy assumed that Marti had heard her dad had been hired to manage the apartment complex in Costa Mesa. "I'm glad he didn't take the job from Uncle Bob, then."

"Yes, well, that's behind us. We are now faced with a bigger decision. Ultimately, it's your uncle's decision, but since it involves you and Todd, I'm sure he would like to hear your thoughts before we move forward."

"Move forward on what, exactly?" Christy still wasn't certain what her aunt was saying.

"Move forward on selling this house, dear. Weren't you listening?"

"Selling this house?" Christy couldn't move. She could barely breathe.

"We need to sell either this house or our house, and I couldn't bear to let our beach house go. We have far too many memories in that house. I told Robert we needed to find a reliable renter, and of course, you and Todd are the only logical choice now that your parents are content to move into a tiny apartment."

Christy felt the baby do a flip, and her hands went to her midriff as if to comfort her little one from the rush of adrenalin it must have just shared with her. The movement was definitely not a flutter or a kick. It was a loop-de-loo and prompted Christy to go to the couch and sit down.

"What are you saying, Aunt Marti?"

Marti gave in and joined Christy on the other end of the couch. "What makes the most sense is for us to sell this house, and for you and Todd to move into our house when we go to the new house. Your rent would go up, of course, but wouldn't you love raising your child in a more spacious home?"

"How much would the rent be?" Christy's voice cracked as she asked the all-important question.

Marti gave her the amount, and Christy's eyes grew wide.

"That's almost twice what we pay here."

"Yes, but it's half the going rate for a house on the beach," Marti said. "It's much larger than this little cottage. It has all modern upgrades, an ocean view, and of course we would leave the furniture so it would come fully furnished."

"Yes, but, Aunt Marti . . ."

"If the rent is an issue, you could consider subletting the downstairs guest room to a respectable friend of yours and let them share the expense with you. You allowed Doug and Tracy and all their children to stay here for months and months last year without charging them rent. Certainly you could bring yourselves to charge someone if you moved into our home."

Christy's shock turned to anger. She knew that as their landlord, Marti had the right to do whatever she needed to. But Christy didn't want to move. Even though she tried to shut down her intense emotions, her eyes filled with tears.

Feeling wobbly, Christy stood and said, "I'll talk with Todd about this, and we'll let you know."

Marti stood and looked at Christy quizzically. "Are you feeling all right, Christy?"

"No, I'm not."

"I'll let you rest, then." Marti headed to the front door. She turned around with a pleasant smile. "I love the thought of you and Todd living in our house. It's just about perfect, isn't it?"

No! It's not perfect.

Christy wasn't able to reply. She couldn't tell in her circus of emotions if this was, in fact, a big blessing, or if she was being railroaded. Were her hormones out of whack again, and that's why this unforeseen conversation felt so overwhelming? Or was it Marti's delivery of the information?

"And do me a favor, will you?" Marti stood by the open front door, about to exit. "Don't mention any of this to your uncle. He's been quite distracted by this financial reversal and has been looking into a long list of options to put his business aright again. I've thought this through, and selling this place is what makes the most sense. It will put everything right again. And it will take all this stress off your uncle. I trust you can understand."

Christy nodded, even though she didn't want to understand. She cared deeply for her uncle, and of course she didn't want to see him struggle with a setback in his real-estate business. But this was Todd's and her home. It was the place they wanted to live. This was where he had grown up and where she wanted to bring up their child.

She lowered herself to the couch again as soon as Marti was out the door. Both her arms were around her middle, cradling her baby. "I'm sorry," she whispered. "I didn't mean to send that big rush of emotions to you. Everything is going to be okay. God will take care of us. He always does. He is our dwelling place."

Silent tears fell on her forearms as Christy looked down and blinked. She couldn't help but think that she would have been more objective about this if Todd had been here or if Uncle Bob had been the one to pre-sent the options to them.

She felt like a helpless renter. Christy

knew that her parents had struggled with that underdog feeling ever since they had moved to California more than a decade ago. They had never been able to pull together the funds for a down payment to buy a house. Christy suspected it would be the same for Todd and her for a long time, too.

Why did Aunt Marti have to be so abrupt about it all?

Christy thought about how during her pregnancy more than once Aunt Marti had been abrasive and unsympathetic.

Is this some strange sort of jealousy or passive-aggressive attack on me? Marti is doing all the normal "aunt" things like hosting a big shower and saying it will be better for us and our baby to live in their house. But there's no love in it. I haven't felt as if she's been truly happy for me that I'm having a baby.

Stretching out on the comfy sofa, Christy closed her eyes. The cooling ocean breeze was rolling in from the opened sliding glass door. This was a place of peace. She loved this house, this room, and all the memories that had soaked themselves into these floors and these walls. She didn't want to move.

What was it Shawna said about our house? It's alive. It breathes.

All the thoughts on her heart tumbled out

in a prayer. "Father, I know You have a plan for us. You know what's best for us and our baby. You also know how much I love it here. Right here. Thank You for taking care of us. As Katie always tells me, You will accomplish Your purpose for us. I believe that, Lord. Please just help me to be open and understanding and willing to receive whatever it is You have for us."

Christy felt her baby move again. This time it was more of a tap, a tiny foot thumping against the lining of her womb. She tapped back three distinct taps with her fingers and whispered, "I love you, little one."

Christy decided she would wait until Todd had finished his online course before divulging Marti's plan. However, even after the class was completed and the next few days rushed by, she never found a convenient time to tell him. Neither Bob nor Marti contacted them about it. So Christy decided to wait.

She found she was continually thinking about her baby. She had transitioned into only wearing her flowing tops and stretchy pants or one of her two loose sundresses. The fluttering movements came often now and Christy enjoyed reading everything she could to find out which organs were devel-

271

oping at this point and how much their little one could hear, sense, or see. The wonder of it all was stunning.

In every way, she felt pregnant. She felt it when she tried to bend over, but her middle didn't bend the way it used to. She felt it when she had to get up in the middle of the night and go to the bathroom. She felt tired all the time. Too tired after work on Friday to go to the Gathering. Christy readied the snacks and loaded them in a laundry basket for easy carrying.

Todd dashed in just twenty minutes before the Gathering was supposed to start. The first thing Christy noticed was that he had a relieved look on his face.

"I just heard from South Coast," Todd said. "I've been officially hired. I passed the online course, and my initial lesson plans were approved. I start full-time a week from Monday."

Christy went to her happy man and gave him a big hug and a kiss. "That's wonderful!"

Todd noticed that she was still in her work uniform. "Are you ready to go?"

"I need to stay home tonight. I'm really tired. I got the snacks ready for you, though."

Todd looked at her more closely. It was

the first time in over a week that he seemed to have locked in on her and not been distracted. "You okay?"

She forced a smile and nodded. Carrying the weight of her aunt's distressing announcement was wearing her down, and she knew it. She needed to talk everything through with Todd. But not now. He needed to rush out the door, once again. All she said was, "We need to talk sometime. Soon."

"I agree." Todd kissed her again. "Let's spend tomorrow morning together. I won't go surfing. I'll tell Zane I can't come in till later. I'm sorry I've been neglecting you, Christy."

"It's okay. It's been crazy. I understand. I really do." Once again, her emotions were right on the surface, and she could feel her eyes filling with tears. "I hope it goes well tonight. I'll be praying for you. I love you."

"I love you, too." Todd's kiss was brief. He grabbed the laundry basket filled with snacks and headed out with a glance over his shoulder.

"Don't forget to bring the laundry basket back. We need it here." Christy kept smiling until he was out the door. As soon as she knew he was gone, she went to the refrigerator. Once again, she was starving. Her appetite had been crazy this past week. About every two hours she felt as if she hadn't eaten for days. She would dig into one of the healthy combinations she had been faithfully preparing only to find that after six or seven large bites, she couldn't eat any more. That is, until two hours later.

Regular spa clients could tell now that she was expecting, and all of them expressed their surprise when they found out how far along she was. Every one of them made it a point to say kind and supportive things about how good she looked or how happy they were for her. Several suggested that she wear stretchy, tight tops so that her baby bump wouldn't be hidden under the spacious tops.

Christy, however, didn't feel comfortable demonstrating for the world exactly how round her belly was. She wanted to wear what she wanted to wear, eat what she wanted to eat, and prepare for the birth the way she wanted to prepare. Even so, everyone, including complete strangers in the grocery store, seemed to offer advice.

Tonight, she didn't want anyone's advice. She wanted ice cream. And something else. Not pickles, like the combination some people had joked about at work. She wanted something salty, though. Christy riffled through all the vegetables and stacked containers of fresh watermelon and cantaloupe that she had cut up the day before. She moved around all the bags of veggie burgers and frozen blueberries in the freezer. No frozen chocolate chip cookies were hiding out from a previous Friday Night Gathering. No smashed-up pints of Chunky Monkey ice cream were sequestered in a far corner the way they had been when Doug lived with them.

She didn't want any of the nutritious and healthy items she had stocked their house with. She didn't want to go to the store. She didn't want to call for a pizza.

Christy didn't know what to do. Take a shower and go to bed?

No. She knew it was time to cash in on a "phone a friend" invitation that had been offered long ago. Christy went for her phone, pressed the button, and waited.

"Hi, Uncle Bob? Could I ask you to do me a huge favor?"

"Of course, Bright Eyes. Anything. Name it."

"I need some ice cream. And something salty."

Her uncle chuckled but didn't question her request. "Salty, huh? Are you thinking pretzels?"

"No. Wait! I know. I want barbecue potato

chips. The kind that make your fingers turn all red and dry out your lips."

"Got it. I know just the kind. What about the ice cream?"

Christy thought hard. Too hard for such a simple question.

"Are you still there?"

"Yes. Sorry. I'd like extra creamy vanilla bean. Nothing low fat or low sugar."

"Right."

"And then could you also get a pint of whipping cream and a dark chocolate candy bar? The good kind. Like the ones from Switzerland, or the big ones that have 80 percent cacao. I want to make my own hot fudge to go on the vanilla ice cream."

There was only a slight pause before Uncle Bob said, "You know what, Christy? You and I are related. There is no doubt about it. We are cut from the same cloth. We may not share the same DNA, but we are united by something deep and unbreakable."

Christy laughed. "And what exactly is that? Cravings for sugar, salt, and fat?"

"Call it what you will, Bright Eyes. I see it as our sacred bond. Get out the bowls and spoons. I'll be there in a jiffy. And, by the way, you do know that the expected payment for such delivery services is in having the honor of sharing this delightful repast with you."

"I was hoping you'd say that. I wouldn't want it any other way. Thank you, Uncle Bob."

"Well, you know I don't want it to be said that I didn't do my part in helping introduce your child to the finer things in life at a very early age."

Christy laughed.

Right before her uncle hung up, he said, "I'm saving the joy of introducing my specialty waffles to your child for a later date."

"I look forward to that day." Christy was still smiling when she hung up. She could picture their daughter — in this imaginary scenario it was definitely a girl — sitting at the counter at Bob and Marti's kitchen. Uncle Bob was sliding a plate with a steaming waffle across the marble counter. It rested in front of a toddler who was wearing a pink leotard and frilly tutu. Uncle Bob was showing her how to get the butter to melt in all the small squares.

Aloud, Christy said, "Bob and Marti can't leave that house. They just can't. We're not supposed to live there. They are."

There was no one to hear Christy's declaration. She wasn't sure why she said it. The words felt more like a prayer than a plea.

All she knew was that she loved her life just the way it was. Now that Todd had a steady job doing something he loved and her parents were moving only ten minutes away, she felt blessed to overflowing.

She knew it wasn't her place to speak into the difficult financial decisions her aunt and uncle needed to make. But if by any chance one of them did ask her opinion, Christy would tell them about the simple epiphany she just had. She would tell them that she wanted her child, boy or girl, to sit at the same kitchen counter where she had sat hundreds of times and she wanted it to still be Uncle Bob's kitchen and Uncle Bob's waffle maker and Uncle Bob's merry eyes that watched her child take a big bite and grin broadly.

NINETEEN

"Are you telling me you and your uncle put away the whole bag of chips and most of the ice cream?" Todd was seated across from Christy with a breakfast menu in his hands. As a surprise, he had taken her to a beautiful restaurant in Laguna Beach that overlooked the ocean. Todd told her he wanted to celebrate his new job and have some time for just the two of them on what had turned into a perfect Southern California summer morning.

Christy had eagerly agreed to the fun plans. It wasn't until they were seated by the window and she read the menu items that she felt a little queasy. Salmon Eggs Benedict, crab cakes with blue cheese and capers, and the house specialty, huevos rancheros. None of it sounded good to her, and she knew she needed to tell Todd why.

"I see that they have Scottish oatmeal with currents and macadamia nuts," Christy said. "I think that's what I'll get but maybe without the nuts."

"Wait a minute." Todd reached across the table and rested his rough hand on her wrist. "You can't dodge my question like that. Did you and Bob really eat all that last night while I was gone?"

Christy nodded.

A half grin spread across his unshaven jaw. "You never cease to amaze me, Kilikina."

"I hope you mean that in a good way." She put down her menu.

"Yeah, I mean it in a good way." Todd pulled back his hand and took a final look at his menu before he set it down. "So, what did you and Bob talk about?"

Christy decided this might be the best time to bring up the topic that had troubled her all week. She told him about Marti's visit a week ago, her bold declaration and simple solution of Christy and Todd moving into their house.

"You knew all that and didn't bring it up to me earlier?" Todd asked.

Christy nodded. "You had a lot going on. I didn't want to load you up with anything else."

Todd leaned forward and reached for both her hands this time. "Christy, I knew all this a week ago Friday. I didn't say anything to you because I didn't want you to be stressed about it."

"How did you find out?"

"Bob came to see me at work. He explained the situation and asked how I'd feel about moving into their house. I told him that on my new salary we wouldn't be able to afford the rent. I also told him that we're at home where we are now, and neither of us would want to move."

"What did Bob say?"

Todd pulled his hands back. "He said that was the end of it. He'd look into other options, and he told me not to worry about it. That's why I didn't say anything to you. I wish Marti hadn't come at you the way she did. That wasn't fair. I don't like when she drives wedges between people in your family."

"In our family," Christy corrected him. They had agreed when they were first married that all the relatives on both sides would be viewed as "our" family and that they wouldn't allow any division of "your side" and "my side."

"You're right. Sorry. It is our family. I'll say something to Marti. For now, I don't think you and I need to worry about being evicted."

Christy agreed. "That's the way Uncle

Bob sounded last night. He said he was working on some other projects, and he wanted what was best for us and our family."

"Maybe you and I should talk to them together. I mean, we want what's best for them, too, right?"

Christy nodded. The waiter arrived, and they placed their order. Christy's phone chimed, and she glanced at it to see if by any chance Katie was texting her since she'd been waiting to hear an update from her. She scrolled though the message and smiled.

"Good news?" Todd asked.

Christy held up her phone for him to see. "It's from Shawna. She's been sending me these cute pictures of her doing silly things. I may have encouraged her too much after the first one she sent of her and Lilly giving themselves facials with some bright-pink goop." She scrolled back and showed the photo to Todd.

He shook his head. "Did you and Katie do stuff like that?"

"Of course." Christy scrolled back to the photo Shawna had just sent of herself holding up a gooey donut. She showed it to Todd. "Your donut influence apparently stuck with her. Shawna wrote, 'My dad and

I found a new Saturday morning hangout. Want to join us?' "

"Tell her I said there's no way a Seattle donut can be better than the ones I get at my secret place."

"So, now it's your secret place, huh?" Christy loved feeling like she and Todd were back in sync.

The rest of their breakfast date Christy and Todd talked about the baby and everything they had on the calendar in the upcoming months. There was an ease to their conversation that had been missing for many weeks. Christy had tucked the book of baby names in her purse just in case they wanted to dream about some good names for a baby girl.

Before they got to the dreaming part, Christy's phone chimed again with a distinct tone she had set up for whenever a video call came in. That meant the call could be from only one person. Katie.

"Hey, *jambo*!" Christy tried to keep her voice low so the people at the table right behind them weren't privy to the conversation. "Todd and I are having breakfast in Laguna Beach." Christy turned the phone so Katie could see Todd and then did a quick pan of the view out the window.

"Wow. Nice," Katie said. "Great view.

Here's my view. The cement walls and barred windows of our monkey-proof mansion. All 520 square feet of it." She did a blurry spin around the living room.

Christy knew something was wrong. Katie's expression and tone made it clear. She pulled her phone earbuds from her purse and plugged them in so they could have a semiprivate conversation. Christy looked at Todd with an expression meant to say, "Is this okay?"

He gave her a nod and started in on the plate of huevos rancheros the waiter had just delivered.

"Katie, what's wrong?"

"How did you know something was wrong?" Katie's green eyes looked bloodshot.

"Because I know you. Tell me. What's happening?"

"We're not coming to California. All the plans have changed."

"Oh, Katie, no."

"I kept putting off calling or writing you because everything was on hold, and then they let us know today that the funds aren't there. So we aren't coming."

"I'm so sad."

"I know. Me, too. It's complicated because some people in leadership here have been fighting for us to go since the whole point is for us to raise support for the ministry and pull together the volunteers who will come next spring and summer to do the work of digging the wells in the villages."

"How will they raise funds and get volunteers, then?"

Katie shrugged. "I don't know. The whole ministry here is in a season of change. We've hit some political barriers in the country that we didn't have before. Visas are being easily granted to volunteers who are coming from Canada and Great Britain, but they're cutting back on the number of visas issued to people from the U.S."

"Does that mean you might have to go to Canada or England to raise funds and find teams to help?"

"We might. Probably not. I don't know. I just want to cry my eyes out, Christy."

"Then that's probably what you should do. I wish I could be there with you, Katie."

"I wish I could be there with you." Katie had let the tears flow and was wiping them with the back of her hand. "It was all too perfect, wasn't it? My being there when your first baby was born, just like we always said we wanted."

Christy bit her lower lip. She couldn't say anything that sounded trite like, "God is in control" or "There's a purpose in this that's greater than what we can see right now." She understood those truths to be real and not just platitudes because she had seen them play out in her life many times over the years. Christy knew that Katie had seen her fair share of God-things and would agree that something was going on that they didn't understand. It was just that those kinds of statements didn't soothe an aching heart at a moment like this.

"I love you, Katie," Christy said softly. Her eyes were squinting as she looked into the camera on her phone. "I appreciate your letting me know right away."

Katie nodded. "I think I'll go do the ugly cry now before Eli comes back from the cafeteria. There's a large group here at the conference center this week, and we're short staffed. Both of us have been working twelve-hour days. I'll probably fall asleep before I even make it to my bed. I love you, Christy. I promise I'll call again as soon as I can."

Katie disconnected the call before Christy could say anything else. She pulled the earbuds out and looked up to meet Todd's concerned gaze.

"They're not coming." Christy repeated what Katie had said and stirred her oatmeal.

Todd ate slowly, taking in all the details.

"I know it's probably for the best for them right now but I really, really wanted to see her. More than that, I was dreaming up fun things we could do together. It would have been so nice to be in each other's everyday lives again."

"Maybe it will still happen."

"Maybe. But she sounded pretty definite about it." Christy kept talking, spilling her thoughts and feelings to Todd in a big lump. It was a luxury she hadn't enjoyed for a while. She concluded her diatribe with, "So much is happening right now, with my parents moving to Costa Mesa and Bob and Marti about to move into their new house, too. It's like the summer is already over."

"Yeah. We've hardly used our patio fire pit. We should have some people over and make s'mores."

Christy pushed the bowl of oatmeal to the side. Her appetite was gone. "Do you miss Doug and Tracy?"

"Yeah, I miss Doug a lot on Friday nights. I would have had him fill in for me last night."

Christy told Todd about her idea last spring to take a leisurely summer vacation driving up the coast in Gussie and going all the way to Glenbrooke in Oregon to Doug and Tracy as well as Alissa and her husband, Brad.

"That would have been nice." Todd sounded bummed. "Or I guess I should say that would have been awesome, since the trip would have included seeing Doug. I wish we could have done it, but there's no way."

"I know. But when Alissa wrote me back she said we should come up next year for Easter vacation."

"Good idea. Let's do that." Todd finished off his Mexican-style eggs. Christy could smell the spicy peppers from across the table. If even a twinge of appetite had remained, it was gone now.

"Our lives have changed, haven't they?" Todd said. "Being responsible stinks sometimes."

Christy felt the baby move just then and instinctively placed her hand on her stomach.

Todd's expression lifted. "Is he kicking?"

Christy grinned and nodded. "It gets stronger each time. It won't be long before you'll be able to feel it on the outside."

Todd looked at Christy with undying affection in his clear blue eyes. "Thank you, Kilikina."

"For what?"

"For carrying our child. For letting your body be turned into an internal boxing ring. For everything you've gone through and will still go through to bring our baby into this world. You're doing something I can't do. Not even angels can do what you're doing. You're such a womanly woman. You're even more beautiful pregnant. I'm pretty much in awe of you right now."

Christy's heart melted. Outwardly, though, she made a joke and asked Todd what the restaurant had put in his spicy breakfast selection.

"Truth serum." Todd paid the check and held Christy's hand as they exited the restaurant. The street they were on was lined with lots of boutiques and shops that featured well-known local Laguna artists. Instead of leading Christy directly to the parking lot across the street, Todd suggested they go shopping.

"I want to buy something for you," he said.

"Like what?"

"Whatever you want. Would you like a necklace? A new book? I just want to get you a present."

They strolled through several shops, holding hands and commenting on different trinkets as well as beautiful oil paintings.

Christy couldn't remember ever having a shopping trip like this with Todd. He didn't like to shop. Plus they never felt like they could spend money on anything extra. The way he was acting and the things he was saying made Christy feel as if he had just fallen in love with her and was trying to express that love in her love language.

It was sweet and sort of strange at the same time. Christy knew that Todd was a good man and that he would make a good husband and a good father. She had just never experienced him lavishing so much attention on her before.

In one of the shops Christy spotted a small picture of a baby giraffe, and she was immediately drawn to it. She didn't know if that was because of the call with Katie. Or that when they had traveled to Kenya for Katie and Eli's wedding several years ago, they had seen giraffes in the wild and Christy had treasured the moment. Or perhaps because she was thinking a lot about the nursery and was still set on using giraffes as part of the décor.

"You like that, don't you?" Todd asked.

"I love it. Look at that little face. Those eyes. That is one adorable baby giraffe."

Todd motioned for the sales clerk that they wanted to purchase the framed picture.

She came over and removed it from the wall. Christy was nervous that it might be more expensive than they could afford. It was reasonably priced, and she knew it gave Todd a lot of pleasure to buy it for her.

That afternoon while Todd was at work, Christy walked around the empty nursery, holding up paint chips in one hand and the picture of the baby giraffe in the other. She decided where the crib would go, the changing table, and the corner where she wanted to put a glider rocking chair along with a corner table and lamp. The new picture, she decided, would go on the wall behind the rocking chair. The color she was drawn to for the walls was a buttery shade called "vanilla crème." She liked the idea of the walls being a soft, warm, neutral shade so she could mix and match all kinds of fun colors everywhere else in the room. It made her heart happy to visualize what the room would look like.

The next morning she and Todd were up and ready for the early service at church. They had agreed to pick up Uncle Bob as long as he didn't mind stopping at the hardware store on the way home so Christy could buy the paint.

Todd was in a great mood and had the stereo in Gussie playing one of his recorded worship songs as they backed out of the garage and drove to Bob and Marti's house.

"Do you ever think of how many times you've taken this route over the years?" Christy asked.

"Do you mean how many times I've driven over to your aunt and uncle's house?"

"Yes. Think of all the times you came to see me when I stayed there."

"Or how many times I drove away after you threw a shoe at me."

Christy laughed. "I only did that once. And you have to agree that it was for a good reason."

Todd leaned toward her slightly and directed his voice toward Christy's baby bubble. "Did you hear that? Your mother thinks it's okay to throw shoes if she has a good reason. Beware, my child. Learn to duck early, and you just might survive."

"Don't listen to your daddy." Christy rubbed her belly. "I would never throw a shoe at you. You don't have to be afraid of me."

Todd rounded the corner to Bob and Marti's street and slowed as they pulled up in front of the house that held a thousand memories for both of them. Their smiles disappeared.

In the front of the house was a For Sale
sign.

TWENTY

Uncle Bob trotted out to Gussie and opened the side door. He climbed in and greeted Christy and Todd with his usual cheery, "Morning!"

"You put your house up for sale." Christy's statement sounded as stunned as she felt, a reaction to the sight of the For Sale sign.

"Best option for all of us." He closed the door and put on his seat belt, as if this were a typical Sunday morning.

"Is Aunt Marti home?" Christy asked.

"She's in bed. With a migraine."

Todd slowly pulled away from the curb, driving as if he was in shock, too.

"Wait," Christy said. "Stop. I'm going to talk to Marti."

"I wouldn't advise it," Bob said.

Christy already had opened her door. She gave Todd a look that said, "Trust me on this."

Todd nodded. She climbed out. "You guys

go ahead. Come back for me after church."

"Do you want us to pick up the paint?" Todd asked.

"Yes. Come get me after you buy the paint." Christy strode past the For Sale sign and used the key she kept on her key chain to open the front door. She stepped inside and called out, "Aunt Marti? It's Christy. I'm coming upstairs. But first I'm going to get something to drink."

Going on nothing but sheer instinct, Christy went to the kitchen and opened the cupboard where Marti kept her fine stemware. She took two of the elegant fluted crystal glasses and placed them on a tray. In the refrigerator she found a bottle of sparkling water, which she poured into both glasses. She cut two thin slices from the lime in the fruit bowl on the counter and let them float in the bubbly water.

Carrying the tray upstairs with care, Christy called out again. "It's me, Aunt Marti." Christy balanced the tray in one hand and tapped on the closed master bedroom door. Trying the handle, she found it was unlocked. She opened it and stepped into Marti's sanctuary.

Marti was in bed with a frilly, decorative ice pack covering her eyes. She lifted one side and glared at Christy like a disgruntled pirate. "I'm not well," Marti moaned.

"I know. Here, you told me once that sparkling water sometimes helped your migraines." Christy waited for Marti to prop herself up enough to take the fluted glass without it spilling.

She sipped slowly before handing the stemware back to Christy. "The lime should have been added to the rim for garnish, not used as a floating life raft on top of the beverage."

Christy grinned. Even in her diminished state, with a lavender and lace eye patch, Marti managed to share her opinions. Christy sat at the foot of Marti's bed and lifted her glass in a toast to her aunt.

With a sigh, Marti leaned back against her luxurious pillows. "Christy, what are you doing?"

Since her first few daring steps had met with relative success, Christy continued her bold approach. "Aunt Marti, you love this house, don't you?"

"Of course I do."

"You don't want to sell it, do you?"

Marti removed the eye patch and placed it on the nightstand. She lifted the glass and took another long sip. After an unhappy pause she said, "We have no choice, Christina. I don't expect you to understand."

"Have you considered all the options?" Christy asked cautiously. "I mean, other than Todd and me trying to find a way to rent this house so you can sell the house we're in."

"Robert said he would never sell the house you're in as long and you and Todd want to live there. He was terribly upset at me for suggesting it."

"I don't mean to overstep my place here, Aunt Marti. I really don't. But wasn't the original plan for you guys to fix up the new house and sell it at a profit? I mean, wouldn't that help with cash flow?"

Marti gave Christy a piercing look. "Yes, that was the plan before we decided to live there. It was also the plan before I mailed sixty-seven invitations for your baby shower listing the new house as our address. I refuse to send out another sixty-seven embossed invitations changing the location to this house. Besides, I simply can't entertain that many people in this house."

Christy knew it was unlikely that all of Marti's socialite friends would come to the shower. She also knew how much the invitations had cost, and she agreed it would be a waste of money to send out a corrected invitation. But it seemed ridiculous to move into an expensive house during a personal financial downturn based on a bunch of invitations.

"Are you saying that if you weren't hosting my shower at the new house you would be open to selling that house instead of this house?"

Marti looked peeved. "You know that we weren't able to do the upstairs renovations."

"Do you mean the fourth bathroom you were going to add upstairs?"

"It wasn't just the bathroom. We were going to open up the wall between the two ocean-facing bedrooms and create a master suite and bath. When Robert's hideous commercial investment failed and set us back so severely, we had to halt all changes to the house and leave the upstairs as is." Marti's lower lip drooped. "I hate the floor plan. The master is on the main level next to the kitchen. Can you imagine such poor planning?"

Christy knew how much Aunt Marti relied on her beautiful upstairs hideaway bedroom and private balcony. This was her retreat.

Without realizing it, Christy must have taken on a serious expression because Marti frowned at her. "You look disturbed. What are you thinking?"

"I know you said that you don't expect me to understand, but Aunt Marti, it doesn't make sense to move into a house with a floor plan you don't even like. And it's absurd to use the invitations to my baby shower as an excuse."

Marti blinked. She looked like someone who had just been snapped back to the present after being hypnotized. "Did your uncle tell you to come up here and talk to me this way?"

"No, it was my idea."

Marti adjusted her pillows. "You certainly have become brash. And don't blame it on your pregnancy."

Christy softened her expression. "I had a sort of vision."

"What sort of vision?"

"I imagined being in your kitchen in this house. Uncle Bob was making waffles, and my daughter was seated at the counter waiting to have one."

"Your daughter?" Marti's interest was piqued.

"She was wearing a pink tutu."

"Are you saying you know you're having a daughter?" Marti looked ready to spring into action.

"No. I don't know if we're having a boy or a girl. I just know that I felt deeply glad thinking about my child making some of the same memories in this house that I have because of your generosity to me over the years."

Marti looked out the opened French doors that led to her beautiful, private balcony. She smoothed her hand over the comforter on her bed. "So you think that we should stay here and sell the big house."

"Yes, I do. I think you should live in the house you love and enjoy this beautiful bedroom. This is your home. A home is different than a house."

Marti's expression started to cloud over again. "It's not that simple, Christy."

They sat in silence for a few minutes, both of them sipping the last of their sparkling water.

"What if?" Christy asked cautiously. "You could host the shower at the new house and tell people it's for sale at the same time? One of your friends might want to buy it."

"That's ridiculous."

"Why?"

"It's simply not done that way. It's tacky."

"Okay, so don't tell anyone the house is for sale. Go ahead and host the shower at the new house and then put up a For Sale sign the next day."

"What would I use for furniture? I cancelled all the orders I placed for new furniture and resigned myself to moving in with the furniture we have here. However, I can't move this furniture out while we're trying to make a good showing of this house so it will sell quickly."

"You could have the new house staged the way they do on the TV shows. Don't houses sell faster when they're staged?"

Marti's expression brightened. "You know, that could work, Christy. Why didn't I think of that? It would solve everything."

Christy was pretty sure she would never fully understand the way her aunt's mind worked. All she knew was that the light had broken through, and Marti was now alive with ideas. She exclaimed that she knew just the right person to do the staging and needed to call her right away. She tossed back the plush comforter, scurried to the master bathroom, and closed the door behind her.

"You're welcome?" Christy said under her breath. She picked up the emptied glasses, placed them on the tray, and exited the bedroom, closing the door behind her.

She thought about what an odd morning this had been as she rinsed out the glasses and placed them on a dishtowel to dry. The baby was doing its usual midmorning tumbling routine, and Christy had the urge to walk home and help herself to the rest of the watermelon in her refrigerator.

She sent Todd a text, telling him she was walking home. Then she went back upstairs to let Marti know she was leaving. Christy knocked on the door. She could hear her aunt's muffled voice and took a chance by opening the door and sliding back into Marti's haven.

Her aunt was on the balcony, stretched out on a padded lounge chair, carrying on a vibrant conversation with someone. "No, we'll use the mahogany pieces," Marti said. "We'll need at least one additional couch. Two, if you can fit them along the same wall. That means we'll need additional throw pillows as well."

Christy caught Marti's attention and motioned that she was leaving. Marti paused her conversation on the phone and blew a kiss in Christy's direction. "You're an angel. You know that, don't you? Thank you, Christy dear. Thank you."

"I'll see you later." Christy grinned and gave her aunt a wave.

Marti appeared to have recovered from her migraine. She was back at the helm, reveling in the joys that came from being the captain of her own life.

The walk back home invigorated Christy. She couldn't remember the last time she had made this trek by foot along the long stretch of sidewalk that separated blocks and blocks of beachfront houses from the sand. Lots of people were out that morning, strolling, biking, skating, and pushing strollers. She thought about what it would be like in a few months to make this jaunt to Bob and Marti's while pushing a stroller with her precious cargo onboard.

Several times Marti had urged Christy to register for more baby items online. She had signed up at three different sites so Marti could list them on the shower invitation. Then Christy had gone in and clicked half-a-dozen simple items she thought she could use, such as a cute fabric cover for the car seat and a set of crib sheets that had baby giraffes on them. What she hadn't listed were any larger items like a car seat, crib, stroller, or high chair. Marti assured Christy that her friends would want to bless Todd and Christy with all the high-end essentials, but Christy needed to add her preferences to the list.

When she arrived back home, Christy pulled out the container of cut-up watermelon and took it over to the couch. She put up her feet, put on her favorite music, and opened her phone to one of the online sites where she was registered. For the next hour she merrily clicked on every baby item that caught her eye, and bite by drippy bite, she made the watermelon disappear.

After she finished registering, she checked her e-mail and saw one from Katie waiting in the inbox. Christy scrolled through the message, reading slowly and hearing a few unspoken thoughts between the lines. Katie's disappointment in not coming to California had hit her harder than she expected. She said she was depressed and that she didn't remember feeling this lost and lonely since she was ten years old.

Christy tried to figure out why Katie was depressed when she was ten. She never had heard Katie say that before. But she did know Katie's home life had been oppressive. Maybe as a ten-year-old Katie had figured out that other kids had parents who truly cared about them and that made her realize her situation wasn't normal or healthy.

Christy came to that conclusion because of the last few lines in Katie's e-mail. She seemed to doubt for the first time since she had become a Christian in high school whether God truly was looking out for her best interest.

After a few more lines recounting the challenges of being so far away from all that had been familiar to her before moving to Kenya and marrying Eli, Katie wrote:

> I know it's terrible to say these things, but Eli says it's better if I get them out and be honest with what's going on in my heart rather than act as if everything is a-okay.
>
> I love it here. You know how much I love it here. But ever since our plans were shut down, I feel an overwhelming need to go to Escondido. I have this fear that my parents are going to die before I see them again.
>
> There. I said it. I need to see my dad one more time. I don't want to. I don't think it's going to change anything, but I feel as if I need to do it. And now I can't. I thought God had worked out the perfect way for the much needed visit to happen.

Christy thought carefully about how to respond to Katie. It was awkward because, like Marti, Katie had more to work with than she realized. At least, that's the way Christy saw it.

When Katie was in college, she had inherited a lot of money from her great-aunt. Even though Christy had no idea how much Katie still had of the inheritance, she guessed it was enough to buy a plane ticket.

She could fly home if she needed to see her parents.

Christy wrote back and suggested that Katie consider making the trek and staying for a week or two.

> I'm sure Eli would understand if you explained to him how you're feeling. I know you guys have been working very hard, pouring yourselves out for others. It's okay if you need to do this one thing for yourself, Katie.
>
> Think about it. Pray about it. I support you whatever you decide. I'll be praying with you.

She hit send and heard the garage door open. Todd was home.

"Hey, how are you doing?" He rested a gallon of paint on the kitchen counter and came over to join Christy in the living room.

"I'm good." She put down her phone and rested her hands on her protruding middle.

Todd eyed the bowl full of watermelon rinds. "Did you eat the whole watermelon?"

"Yes, I did." Christy patted her belly and giggled. "Can't you tell? Oh, Todd, quick. Put your hand right here."

He leaned in and placed his large palm flat against her shirt.

"Over this way. Right there. Do you feel that?" Christy put her hand on top of his and pressed it down more firmly than he seemed willing to press. She looked up at him expectantly.

Todd's eyes widened. His mouth opened. In a choked whisper he said, "Is that him?"

Christy nodded. "Say hello."

"Can he hear me?"

"According to all the info in the baby books, our baby can hear us and is even able to distinguish our voices."

Todd lifted Christy's top and placed his cheek against her belly. "Hey, this is your dad. I . . ."

It seemed that Todd was going to say, "I love you," but he started crying and couldn't finish his sentence. His tears fell on Christy's baby bump, showering their child's protective cocoon with his unspoken love.

Christy smiled and stroked Todd's fuzzy head. She never dreamed how sweet and rich this time of pregnancy would be for them.

"I love you, baby," Todd managed to say. "I can't wait to hold you. But not yet. Don't get any crazy ideas. You just keep growing in there, okay? Take your vitamins and grow big and strong, okay?"

Todd kissed Christy's belly and looked up at her. She was grinning and couldn't help but repeat the line that made her want to laugh. "Take your vitamins?"

Todd sat up and shrugged. His dimpled smile made it clear he realized how silly that had sounded. "I didn't know what to say," he whispered.

Christy chuckled. "He can still hear you."

"Not if I whisper."

"Oh, Todd, you are going to be the funniest dad."

His expression immediately turned somber. "Do you really think so?"

Christy nodded. "I know so."

"Did you want me to start painting the nursery today? You can catch a nap down here while I work on it. I don't think it's good for you to be around the paint fumes."

"It's your only day off," Christy said.

"I know. But I can at least start. I want to do something for you. And for the baby."

Christy took the advice she had just written to Katie and did something for herself. She stretched out on the couch while Todd went upstairs with the paint. He was whistling as he climbed the stairs. Christy rolled onto her side and cradled her "watermelon belly," quietly humming the song Todd had been whistling. She didn't know what vitamins were in watermelons, but she was confident their little one had gotten more than his daily dose.

TWENTY-ONE

The sun-filled days that lined up on Christy's new wall calendar seemed like neat rows of determined soldiers. They marched through the final weeks of August and into September with a rapid, steady gait, relentlessly heading toward her due date.

On the kitchen counter Christy kept a new notepad. Daily she added to the "to do's" and checked off the "done's." The nursery was a permanent item at the top of the list. Aside from the striped beach blanket and a collection of books stacked in the corner, the nursery was bare. Todd had painted the small room, and together they had hung the baby giraffe picture. It was a sweet time for them and ended up being about the only few stolen hours the two of them had shared during the entire month of August.

Todd was at full speed turning over the business at Zane's and prepping for South

Coast Academy. He was in his zone. He was also tired all the time, when Christy did see him, but he was happy with the new position. Christy decided that was the part of this big life change that she would focus on.

At the spa the days remained full, and Christy managed to keep up with her forty-hour week even though it was starting to wear on her to be on her feet all day. The plan was for her to work until the second week of November. Christy had read enough to know that her many trips to the restroom would only increase in the weeks ahead. Her indigestion and being woken in the middle of the night by a big kick would only intensify. Some days she wasn't sure how she would be able to show up for work, but she was determined to hang in there.

The biggest change for Christy was that her parents moved the last weekend of August. The Casitas Linda complex was an aging but peaceful cluster of two-story apartments. The units were spacious and were built in the adobe Spanish-style that had been popular in Costa Mesa during the 1960s and 1970s. Christy's mom said she liked the red-tile roofs and that most of the tenants were close to their age.

Christy had a good feeling about them being there. She could tell that her parents were pleased with their new home and position as managers of the complex. They were only a ten-minute drive from South Coast Academy and a fifteen-minute drive from Todd and Christy's home in the other direction.

The mature garden landscaping that wove throughout the large, square complex seemed like it would require much of her dad's time each week since he had signed on to do gardening as well as maintenance of the units. He couldn't be happier about that arrangement and had bought himself a wide-billed gardener's hat that had funny-looking flaps hanging down the back to protect his neck.

Aunt Marti found her rhythm again once she and Bob settled between them that they were going to stay in their current house. All her efforts were funneled toward the baby shower. The soldier days of September marched right up to the third Sunday, the day of the shower, and according to a text Marti sent Christy early that morning, everything was ready.

At Marti's insistence, Christy and her mom arrived an hour early for the shower. It was the first time either of them had seen the inside of the grand, modern house. The style was completely different from Bob and

Marti's current home. The angles were straight, and the many windows were either tall and narrow, or in some rooms the windows took up most of the walls.

"Wow," was the only word both Christy and her mom could manage to say as they stood on the white marble floor of the grand entryway and looked up at the high ceilings. A wide, curved staircase led to the upstairs.

"There is no denying it. This house is a showstopper." Marti was wearing one of her new favorites — a flowing silk top with billowing sleeves that added a distinct flair when she motioned one direction or another with her graceful arm fully extended.

"I should tell you both that I've decided to make flyers available after all. They're here, in case you should happen to fall upon the topic of the house being available during a conversation with one of the guests today."

Marti floated over to an entry piece made of a beautiful, deep-colored wood with beveled glass in the top cabinet. She pulled open the top drawer and revealed a stack of full-color flyers that highlighted key features of the house. It was all very high-end, and Christy could finally understand the torment her aunt had been in over this house. To live here would certainly give the impression to all of Marti's socially-elevated friends that she had "arrived."

Christy wondered how it would go today and if her aunt would change her mind and conclude that she did, in fact, need to be surrounded by this sort of modern elegance every day. This house made their current home look like a vintage beach cottage. It made Christy and Todd's home look like a last-century bungalow.

"This was Christy's idea, you know." Marti lowered her chin and her voice. She spoke to her sister as if Christy weren't standing next to them. "If Christy hadn't come over that day and done her tough-love intervention, I'd still be a tangle of nerves over this house. I'm keeping only positive thoughts that it will sell quickly, and we can all move past this exhausting experience.

"And of course," Marti added as she closed the drawer, hiding the flyers. "All discretion is expected. I'm telling you only so you can be aware and graciously offer the information, should it be appropriate."

Marti led them down the wide hall to the right, pointing out the guest bathroom with a fluff of her billowing sleeve and leading them on into the master bedroom. It surprised Christy how small and dark the bedroom was compared to what they had seen of the rest of the house. No wonder Marti didn't like it. The view that was visible from the top six inches of the shaded window was of the neighbor's garage.

They gave their appropriate oohs and ahhs in the master bath as Marti pointed out the jetted tub, the rain showerhead, and heated tile floors. Christy wanted to stop her aunt and tell her they weren't potential buyers so she didn't have to try so hard to impress them.

Instead, she rested her hands on her bulbous belly and finished the tour. Marti led them through the stunning gourmet kitchen where two caterers were preparing their refreshments. Christy thanked both of them personally and continued on through the dining area with the beautifully decorated table and then on into the spacious main living space. The contrasting dark wood and the plush ivory furniture were accented by colorful pops of an elegant, beachy shade of aqua in the pillows and the large oil painting of a gorgeous ocean sunset that hung over the white marble fireplace.

In the center of the room was a crib, already filled with presents. Beside the crib was a stuffed giraffe. Its long neck stretched a full two feet above the crib and was positioned so that it appeared to be looking down at the abundance of gifts.

"Aunt Marti!"

"That's the one you wanted, isn't it? The crib, I mean. I had your uncle set it up to display the gifts. He assured me it's easy to dismantle to get it over to your house and up those narrow stairs to the nursery."

"I love it. Thank you." Christy tried to give her aunt a hug, but Marti offered only her perfectly made-up cheek so Christy could give her an air kiss an inch away from her skin.

"There are so many presents."

"They have been arriving all week."

"Who sent them?" Christy could understand half-dozen or so gifts arriving from a few relatives in Wisconsin, but it looked like there were at least forty gifts filling the crib and stacked up in front. She hoped her aunt hadn't gone a little crazy and overbought for the baby.

Instead of answering Christy's question, Marti changed the topic and pointed out the chandelier she had custom designed at the beginning of the renovation, before their finances took a downturn.

"My designer said I may have come up with a new style." Marti motioned at the high ceilings and sparkling chandelier that was accented by dangling diamonds of glass in the same soft blues, greens, and sunset pink colors of sea glass. "She said instead of Shabby Chic, I've created Beachy Posh. What do you think?"

"It's beautiful," Christy's mom said. "Elegant but at the same time very inviting."

"That's it exactly. Elegant but inviting. That's how I will describe my design style from now on. Would you like something to drink?"

"Not yet, thank you." Christy pointed at the crib again. "I would like to know, though, why there are so many gifts. Did people send them to you instead of bringing them to the shower?"

Marti turned her attention to the delicate hem of her butterfly sleeve, as if trying to hunt down a loose thread. "Well, Christy, since you insist on knowing, we received more regrets than I had expected. It seems this is a full weekend for many of my friends. And, of course, you had so few names to give me of your friends. None of Margaret's friends was willing or able to make the journey from Escondido. So . . ."

Christy glanced at her mother, who remained calm at her sister's comments.

"However," Marti continued when she

didn't get a response out of either of them. "As you noticed, the invitees have been generous. You'll also see a number of cards in the gift basket there by the giraffe. I'm sure you'll find quite a bounty of gift cards in those envelopes. But please don't open them until you get home. I've always found it tawdry to call out the names of those who couldn't make the effort to at least send a gift."

Christy's mom asked, "How many people do you think will be here?"

"Oh, I would say, at least ten." Marti looked up, a pleasant expression fixed on her face. Evidently she took it as a personal insult that out of sixty-seven invitations, so few were coming. But she refused to reveal that to her sister and niece.

Christy felt embarrassed. She knew the low attendance wasn't her fault. She had invited all the women she worked with, but Eva was the only one who said she was coming. Christy didn't have any close friends nearby. Her focus in this season of life had been on work and spending time with the teen girls who went to the Gathering. She hadn't invited any of the teens, and she didn't feel close enough to any friends from church to invite. When she did have free time, she wanted to spend it with Todd. She knew she shouldn't feel bad about the turnout, but she did.

"The house is breathtaking." Christy's mom seemed to know how to redirect a conversation with her sister in precarious moments like this. "I've never seen anything like it."

Seeming relieved at the change of topic, Marti drew a quick breath. "I'll give you a tour of the upstairs later. I must attend to a few details. Please excuse me."

Talk about an elephant in the room! Or should I say a giraffe in the room. Poor Aunt Marti. She made such mammoth efforts to have the shower at this house to accommodate the masses she was expecting.

Marti turned as if she had had another thought. Glaring at Christy's ankles, she added, "Do have a seat, Christy. Elevate your feet, if you can. You look fatigued already."

Christy knew her ankles were swollen. So were her face, her hands, and especially her thighs, which seemed to have decided to expand in equal proportion to her middle. In an e-mail to Katie, she had referred to her thighs as the "Solidarity Sisters" and said she hoped they would stop showing their sympathetic expansion in response to her big, round belly.

She looked awkwardly, uncomfortably pregnant, and she knew it.

It still felt odd to Christy that she had gone from no one knowing or even guessing that she was pregnant for the first four or five months to now looking like she was ready to pop any minute, and yet she still had nine weeks to go. She couldn't imagine what her body would look like then. She already felt self-conscious.

Lowering herself to the luxurious sofa, Christy seemed to sink into the corner. "I don't think I'll be able to get up," she told her mom.

"I'll lend you a hand, if you get stuck. But I doubt you will. You're very agile, Christy. And you look lovely. I like your hair down like that. It's pretty."

Her mom's smile and comforting words did wonders for Christy. For a moment she felt like it was okay to be who she was and nothing more. She didn't have to pretend this house was her natural habitat, the way Marti was. She didn't need to apologize for the low attendance. Nor did she need to feel embarrassed for the way her body was choosing to shelter and harbor this new life that was growing exactly as it should inside her.

Christy reminded herself of what Dr.

Avery had said four days ago at her checkup. All the routine weighing, measuring, and listening revealed that everything was just as it should be. The baby was healthy, and that's what mattered. The due date was still estimated to be November 20, and Dr. Avery had even complimented Christy on how good her blood pressure was.

She also thanked Christy for the invitation to the baby shower and said she was looking forward to coming. Christy had been surprised that Dr. Avery had accepted the invitation and hoped that turned out to be a good idea, especially now that she was one of the meager number of guests.

"You know what? I think I'll use the restroom before anyone arrives." Christy pushed against the armrest and shifted her hips to the side, navigating her way to a standing position without her mom's assistance.

"See?" her mom said. "You don't need help getting up."

As Christy made her way to the bathroom, she felt her mother's gaze on her backside. She knew that part of her had expanded as well. She had avoided looking in the wraparound mirror in the dressing room two weeks ago when she had bought another pair of black pants for work. That pair was two sizes larger than the ones she had because she didn't want to have to buy still another pair before the baby came. The jumbo pants were not so jumbo anymore.

Christy lingered in the downstairs bathroom trying to give herself a pep talk before going back to the living room. How could she best prepare herself to meet ten of Marti's "dearest" friends, knowing that all of them would be evaluating her?

She realized that the best part of this already-uncomfortable party was that her mom was with her. Over the past few weeks she had spent more time with her mother than she had over the past six months. It was easy to swing by after work and convenient for her mom to drop by Christy's house on her way to the grocery store. Being with her mom was the highlight of this shower for Christy, and she suspected having her mother nearby would be the highlight of her life in the years to come.

She and her mom had somehow crossed a bridge that brought them into the land of mother-daughter friendship. It was an unexpected gift. It was also Christy's favorite gift out of all the presents she opened that day at her baby shower.

Late that night, after all the presents had been transported to Christy and Todd's living room and Todd had prepared everything he needed for classes in the morning, Christy made herself comfortable in the chair in the living room. She then called Katie on her laptop at the time they had set up more than a week ago for their big catch-up call.

"Christy!" Katie's exuberant greeting on their video call prompted Christy to turn down the volume, just in case her sleeping husband could hear them all the way upstairs. "Look at you! Stand up. I have to get the full view."

Christy shook her head. "Maybe later. I'm too comfortable. I love you, Katie, but I'm not standing for anybody right now."

"At least let me say hi to the baby. Turn the camera. Oh, there you go. Hi, little monkey. Are you being nice to your mommy? Look how big you are!"

"I know. I'm huge."

"I didn't mean it to sound that way, Chris."

"I know. But it's true. My cells are expanding by the minute. I never would have believed my skin could stretch like this."

"You look good. You really do."

"Thank you, darling, wonderful, kind, and sweet Katie girl. I love you, too, and I will say all the same things to you when you get to be a jumbo mama someday."

"And I will look forward to that day. So, tell me about the shower."

Christy panned around the room at all the gifts. "It was ridiculous, Katie. All I did was sit there for an hour and open all these presents from people I've never met in front of five people I didn't know and keep trying to act surprised and thankful. I mean, I was thankful, but it was so strange."

"Wait. Did you say five people?"

"Yes. Well, actually, ten. Five of them I didn't know because they were my aunt's friends. The other five were my mom, my aunt, my OB — who happens to be Todd's aunt — and me. Oh, and the caterer. She came in the living room and had dessert with us."

"Wow, that is crazy. So, are you calling your OB 'Aunt Linda' now?"

"Yes. I'll still call her Dr. Avery at her office, but she was definitely Aunt Linda at the shower. Since there were so few people, my mom and I had a chance to talk with her a lot and get to know her. She's really great. She kind of choked up when she said how much she appreciated reconnecting with Todd."

"That's cool. So what are you going to do with the loot? The nursery isn't big enough to hold all that."

"I know. My mom is going to come over this week, and we're going to take our time going through everything and keeping only what works." Christy zoomed in on a framed piece of calligraphy. "This is one of my favorite gifts. It's from Shawna and her mom. They had it made for me. They're verses from Psalm 139. Isn't it pretty?"

"Definitely a keeper."

"And did you see the giraffe?" Christy tilted the camera.

"Adorable. And huge. You'll have to name her Daisy."

"Daisy?"

"Yes, like the famous giraffe here at the Kenyan giraffe park."

Christy laughed. "I thought you were saying we should name our daughter Daisy."

"Daughter?" Katie's face moved in closer to the camera. "You found out you're having a girl, didn't you? Aunt Linda spilled the beans at the shower, didn't she? Go ahead. You can tell me."

Christy felt her face warming. "Well . . ."

"Yes? Yes? Don't keep me in suspense! Are you having a boy or a girl?"

TWENTY-TWO

"I don't know if it's a girl or a boy," Christy told her eager best friend, who had leaned in closer to the video camera.

"Honest?" Katie squinted and crossed her arms, giving Christy her best tough-chick expression.

"Yes, honest. We still don't know what we're having. I was just having fun teasing you."

"You're mean." Katie kept her arms crossed.

Christy grinned mischievously. "I was kind of mean at the shower, too."

"You were? Christy! What's happening to my sweet, innocent, eternally compassionate friend? You've turned into a crazed pregger woman."

"That's probably truer than you realize. I couldn't resist playing a little trick on Aunt Marti when I opened the gift from Aunt Linda."

326

"Because Dr. Linda is the only one who knows if you're having a boy or a girl," Katie surmised.

"Right. So when I opened Aunt Linda's present, I could see several outfits inside. The first one I pulled out was the cutest, tiny pink bathing suit, and of course, Marti went a little crazy."

"What else was in the box?"

"A pair of little blue swim trunks and a yellow-and-green, floppy, baby-sized beach hat. Aunt Linda covered all the color options with her gift. It wasn't a big reveal."

"You are cruel. Remind me not to trust anything you do or say until after you pop that baby out and get your nice Christy personality back."

Christy grinned. "Okay. Enough about me and how mean I am these days. Tell me about you."

Katie leaned back and nodded. "Well, I'm good. We're good. It's good here. I know you must have been wondering after that one e-mail I sent when I was certain that God didn't love me anymore. But I'm okay with not knowing what He's up to. At least right now. I don't have a lot to report. Just that I'm content. I really am. That's all."

Christy studied the image of her dearest friend on the computer screen. She could tell that Katie was telling the truth. "That's good to hear, Katie."

Katie nodded.

"No other updates?"

"Well . . ." Katie put her finger on her chin and looked at the ceiling as if trying to remember something. "There is one small bit of news."

"Ooh!" Christy was suddenly distracted. She had been balancing the laptop on her belly, and it suddenly rolled to the side, and she had to catch it. "That's the baby! You're getting your own little hello from the land of wibbles and wobbles."

"Let me see."

Christy smoothed down her shirt and turned the camera so it could hopefully catch the next roll.

"I don't see anything. Show me your belly."

"Katie, I don't want to show you my belly."

"I'd do it for you, if I was the one with the acrobat baby and we were separated by thousands of miles and you wanted to see your future niece or nephew do a somersault."

"Okay." Christy reluctantly lifted her shirt, adjusted her posture so her stomach was protruding as much as possible, and held the laptop directly over her exposed midriff. As if on cue, her tumbler performed an act of skin-stretching amazement that made it clear a heel or an elbow had pressed as hard as it could on the inside and provided an easily visible surge across Christy's taut skin.

"Did you see that?" Christy turned the laptop back toward her face and saw both Eli and Katie were pressed together, watching the show. "Eli!"

"That was cool," he said calmly. "Can't wait to see him on the outside when we come in a few months."

"What!? You're coming?" Christy immediately forgot her embarrassment. "Your plans are back on?"

The view on her laptop screen turned into what looked like an old-time Punch and Judy puppet show Christy had seen on an old classic movie. Katie was elbowing Eli, he was holding up his hand to block any more exuberant blows, and all the while Katie was squawking that it was supposed to be a surprise, and he had just ruined everything. She bopped him on the top of his head.

Christy couldn't help laughing at them even though she wanted them to stop their playful fight so she could hear the details. "Hello! I'm still here. Tell me what's happening, you guys!"

Christy looked up and saw her sleepy-eyed husband coming down the stairs. He stopped halfway and squinted at Christy. "You okay? I thought we were getting burglarized."

"No, it's just Katie and Eli. I'm watching them have a fight. But apparently they're coming here in a few months."

"Oh, okay. Later." Todd turned and went back to bed.

Christy laughed. She realized in that moment what a crazy, wonderful, filled-with-unexpected-surprises sort of life she had. She laughed so hard she had to yell at Eli and Katie who were still squabbling. "I have to go. E-mail me, Katie. Tell me everything."

"Wait, I'll tell you now."

"No. I have to go. I mean really go. Bye."

"Oh! That kind of go. Okay. I'll e-mail you. Mwaah." Katie blew a kiss at the camera and ended the transmission.

Christy barely made it to the bathroom in time. She implemented a system Katie had used several years ago with her ongoing "Note to self" reminders.

Note to self. Always go to the bathroom before calling Katie.

In the weeks ahead, Christy found she needed to alter that "Note to self" to

"Always go to the bathroom before doing anything or going anywhere."

She was glad to see that Katie's e-mail with the updates of their travel plans was in her in-box when she woke up the next morning. Katie said she had thought about Christy's advice to use her financial resources to come to California and see her parents. Then Katie added a piece of information Christy hadn't heard before.

Eli and I made a decision a few months ago to donate most of what I had left of the inheritance money. We split it between the clean-water ministry we work with and another ministry here that provides food to refugees. I didn't feel right having so much money sitting in the bank when I see so much need here. We both know it was the right thing to do, and we're glad we did it.

The only thing is that now we don't have a lot of resources to draw from when it comes to things like expensive airline tickets. We think we have enough for two tickets, if we wait for the prices to go down during our rainy season. Eli thinks we'll be there by Thanksgiving. I'm already dreaming of turkey, stuffing, and pumpkin pie, just in case you are planning your menu early this year. Only the real stuff, by the way. With lots of butter. None of this to-furky or gluten-free stuffing. When we get there, I'm going to be all about the gravy. And the mashed potatoes. And that green-bean casserole with those little fried onion bits on top.

Over the next few weeks Katie's stream of e-mails continued with the theme of all the foods she was looking forward to eating when she and Eli got to California. Christy kept a list. She thought it would be fun to go through the list and make sure she personally prepared or had on hand every-thing on Katie's wish list. That included the random request for orange Otter Pops. Christy didn't know if they even made Ot-ter Pops anymore, but she was determined to have a box waiting in her freezer, if pos-sible.

By the middle of October, Christy ran out of steam. She was five weeks away from her due date when she called into work and said she needed to take a personal day off.

"Do you need to talk with HR about go-ing on maternity leave sooner than you expected?" Eva asked. She had been sup-portive all along but even more so after at-tending Christy's baby shower.

"No, I think I'll be fine. I just need to stay

home and make fingernails today."

"Make what?"

Christy was so tired, and it took her a moment to realize what she had said. She had been reading the baby app on her phone right before deciding she couldn't make it to work and had felt slightly overwhelmed that her body was contributing at this very moment to the formation of itty-bitty kidneys and fingernails as well as her child's central nervous system. No wonder she was wiped out.

"I meant to say I'm exhausted. If I can sleep today, I think I should be okay to come in tomorrow."

"It's not a problem, Christy. You take care of yourself and that little one. And if you do need to start your leave early, we can work around it."

Christy went back to bed and slept nearly all day. That is, except for the four or five times she had to go to the bathroom. Every night was the same way, and that was part of the reason for her sleep deprivation.

Tracy had told her it was God's way of preparing all new moms for the demands that would soon be made on them in the middle of the night when the baby is ready to be fed or needs to be changed. If that bit of insight was supposed to make Christy feel grateful or something, it wasn't working.

For the next three days, Christy stayed home from work. Each day she insisted she would be back at work, but each new day she felt even less energy. The third day she missed was a Friday, which meant she had the weekend to rest up. She spent the day on the couch and used her phone so much she had to recharge it before noon. She sent numerous text messages, read long articles on the Internet about what she needed to know and do as she was entering the last few weeks of her pregnancy.

The day wore on, and Christy couldn't get comfortable no matter what position she tried. She texted Todd numerous times, but he never replied. She called him twice and left messages. He didn't call her back. He had left so early that morning, she doubted that he knew she hadn't gone to work yet again.

A wave of sadness washed over Christy as the late-afternoon sun came through the sliding glass door and spilled a wide streak of buttery light across the floor. She knew Todd would be busy with his new job. She had been super supportive and gone out of her way to do whatever she could to help him be ready to walk out the door each morning. On the outside she continually said it was fine. It was important that he do what he needed to do.

But during this melancholy golden hour when she felt so weary physically and emotionally and so alone in their quiet house, Christy decided that her husband had abandoned her during the second half of the pregnancy.

He had promised he would be there for her and go through this with her, but where had he been at her last two doctor's appointments? Where was he a week ago when she went on the tour of the maternity wing of Hoag Memorial Hospital by herself? Why was it that her mother had been the one to help finish up the nursery?

He doesn't know how hard this is. He doesn't really care. Not really. Am I going to end up raising this child by myself, too?

She checked her phone messages again and saw that she had an e-mail from Katie. It was short, and it was not sweet.

I hate that I have to tell you this. We aren't coming this fall. We've tried every possibility, and we just can't make it work. We kept watching the airfares, but they never dropped the way we hoped. We've prayed about it a lot, and we both know this is what we're supposed to do. With all the changes in the ministry leadership, Eli has been given a ton more responsibilities and that means he can't be gone right now.

I guess you're going to have to have that baby without me. Writing those words breaks my heart. I know we're supposed to be grown up and mature enough to be flexible when we don't get everything we want. But I'll just say it. I like it better when God spoils me and gives me everything I ask Him for. I just do.

So, we'll set up a lot of video calls, okay? Save that list of all the food. I will come and eat all of it one day. I just don't know when.

Todd bounded in the door just as she finished reading the e-mail, and Christy tried to pull herself together.

"Hey, how are you doing?" He looked around, taking in the facts. Christy was on the sofa in lounge-around clothes. She hadn't prepared anything for dinner. Nor had she made snacks for the Gathering.

"I texted you a bunch of times," Christy said.

"I didn't get any texts from you."

"I asked if you could bring home some dinner for both of us and also pick up food for the Gathering. There's no way I can go tonight."

Todd pulled out his phone. He looked frustrated and went over to show her the screen on his phone. "No phone messages and no texts. You sure you sent them? I have to leave in like ten minutes."

Christy took a closer look at the icons at the top of the screen. "Todd, you have your phone on airplane mode."

His frustration turned to a look of anger as he took his phone off airplane mode and a continual series of pings sounded as all his missed messages loaded.

"Don't be mad at me," she said under her breath.

Todd frowned as he clicked through his messages.

Christy stood to head to the bathroom again and pressed her hands into the small of her back to stretch before shuffling away. Todd looked over at her, and she realized he was gaping at her rotund belly as if he hadn't even noticed she was pregnant until this very minute. Her posture and the position of the baby certainly must have made her look outrageously large, but she wasn't prepared for his comment.

"You're huge."

It was one of his statements. A declaration

of the obvious.

And it devastated Christy.

She plopped back on the couch as if she had been struck in the head by a flying basketball. Her arms instinctively wrapped around her middle, and she burst into tears.

Todd immediately recognized his blunder but appeared stunned at her intense response. He tried to comfort Christy, but she was too emotionally charged to do anything but flail her arms at him, as if she were trying to protect herself and her baby from a wild bear that had lumbered out of the woods into their private garden.

"Just go!" Christy yelled. "Leave me alone!"

"No. I want to stay here with you and make sure you're okay."

"I'm not okay. I'm not going to be okay for many, many weeks. Just leave us alone and come back in December!"

"I'm not leaving," Todd said firmly.

His tone came out too firm for Christy's heightened sensitivity, and all she could do was wail as if she were a spoiled child who had been told she couldn't have ice cream.

Through the bizarre explosion of hormones, emotions, and exhaustion, Christy felt as if her real self were still reclining on the sofa and what she was watching was simply a terrible drama on a low-end cable station.

"Go!" she yelled again. "Just go!"

Through Christy's bleary eyes she could tell that her husband had no idea what to do. More than fifty students were waiting for him at the Gathering. He had no one he could call to fill in for him. Her scrambled brain told her over and over that he needed to get out the door. Once he left she knew she would calm down, as she had many times during the past few months.

"I'm going to ask your mom to come over." Todd pushed a button on his phone.

That solution seemed to ignite another cinder cone in Christy, and she tried to grab the phone from him. "No!"

He hung up and looked at her with desperation in his eyes. "Christy?" He tried to reach for her shoulder to anchor her. "Christy, breathe. It's okay. Tell me what you want. Whatever it is, I'll do it."

This time she didn't knock him away. She breathed in short gasps and felt the tears dripping off her chin. She couldn't move. The tornado had passed, leaving broken pieces of their relationship strewn all over the space between her and her terrified husband.

"Breathe," Todd said in a calmer voice.

"That's it. Just breathe. It's okay. You're okay."

Christy felt a blanket of shame cover her as she reached for a tissue from the box on the coffee table. Her breathing was still erratic. She drew in a long breath and blinked away the last tear. "I'm sorry," she whispered.

"It's okay." Todd sat beside her and slipped his hand in hers.

She couldn't believe what had just happened. Where did those intense emotions come from? Had she been harboring anger toward him all these weeks and months for being too busy to spend time with her? Or was this the way her heart needed to explode at the news of Katie not coming and not being there with her during the huge life moment of having a baby?

She blew her nose and slowly rested her head on Todd's strong shoulder. "I'm sorry," she whispered again.

"Shhh." Todd rested his cheek gently on the top of her head. He started to hum and then began singing to Christy in a low voice,

Close your eyes
Rest on me
Angels watch over
While you sleep

He hummed some more the way he always did when he was composing a new song and trying to figure out what should come next.

Christy pulled away and reached for another tissue. She felt nearly normal. "You need to go to the Gathering," she said in a calm and controlled voice. "I'm sorry for the meltdown. I'm fine now. You should go."

Todd placed his open palm on the side of her face. "I'm sorry, Kilikina. I'm so sorry. I didn't mean to say anything to hurt you."

"I know."

"Please forgive me."

"I forgive you." She did her best to muster a small upturning of her lips. "Please forgive me for going ballistic."

He shook his head. "There's nothing to forgive. I'm the one who blew it." Todd leaned in and kissed her on the end of her nose. "You sure you're okay?"

Christy nodded. "I'll be fine. Could you leave your phone on, though, just in case I need you?"

"Of course." He held up his screen to her so she could see that airplane mode was off. "I'll stop at the grocery store on the way home. Text me if there's anything you want."

"Something with coconut in it," she said.

Todd's expression lifted from worried to

slightly amused. "Okay. Anything particular?"

"I don't care. I've been craving coconut all day."

"Okay." Todd took Christy's hand and gave it one more assuring squeeze. "I'll bring you a Phil. 1-7 special when I come home."

Christy had no idea what he was talking about, but it didn't matter because he was out the door, still wearing his teaching clothes, and she was alone again in the quiet house.

She heard Gussie's motor sputtering as Todd backed out of the garage, and then she made her way to the bathroom. She had padded to the middle of the kitchen when the Phil. 1-7 reference dawned on her.

Coconut.

Way back in their high school days, Todd had mailed her a coconut from Hawaii when he was there surfing. On the side of the coconut he had written the reference for Philippians 1:7 in what Katie had once called "Bible code." The verse was, "I hold you in my heart." It had become the banner verse for their relationship during their high school and college years.

Christy trotted quickly back to the bathroom and said aloud in the open space,

"Well, I hope you're holding on with all your might, Todd Spencer, because I'm afraid I am no longer the timid little skinny girl you mailed that coconut to a decade ago. You and I might need a new banner verse for this season of life. Something like, 'Love is patient.' "

Then, because the coconut reminded her of Katie and that brought back the depressing news from Katie's e-mail, Christy felt more alone than ever. She closed the bathroom door and locked it even though she was the only one home.

She had no tears left to squeeze out. She only had sadness. Sadness and a fleeting thought about how her body was busy making fingernails, tiny kidneys, and most importantly, a complex central nervous system.

"Love is patient," she whispered, patting her large midriff. "I'm sorry. I hope I didn't short circuit your nervous system. I love you. Grace on us. And peace."

TWENTY-THREE

Later that night Christy held an opened greeting card in her hand and stared at Todd in disbelief. "Where did you get this?"

"At the grocery store. Why?"

Christy closed the card and looked at the front again. The photo was of two tall palm trees with a gorgeous sunset in the background. The two palms were bent toward each other, and in between them was a baby-sized palm tree. The small palm tree stood tall and straight with its floppy palm fronds shooting out the top.

The words printed inside of the card were *Love is patient*

Under that line Todd had written *I love you, Kilikina. Forever.*

"Do you like it?" Todd appeared apprehensive, as if he wasn't sure if another tidal wave of emotion was building inside of Christy and was about to come his way again. "I looked for carnations, but they didn't have any. I saw the card and thought it was like a mama palm tree and daddy palm tree with a baby palm tree."

"Todd, I love it!" Christy explained how, when he left, she had said aloud that they needed a new verse for this season of life, something like "Love is patient."

"You said that?"

Christy nodded, still feeling amazed at the consequence.

"Sounds like something Katie would call a God-thing."

"I know." Christy felt a cloud rolling over her expression. "I didn't tell you, but I heard from Katie, and they're not coming."

"Not at all?"

"Not in the near future, apparently. They just can't. I understand, but I also am really, really sad."

"I'm sorry to hear that. I was looking forward to their coming, too."

Christy looked at the front of the card again and knew she had to frame it and find a special spot for it in the nursery.

"Thank you, Todd. This card means a lot to me."

"You're welcome." Todd went back to unloading the groceries. "I hope you're as happy with what I bought you for your special request for coconut." He pulled a small glass bottle from the bag and held it out to her with a proud smile.

"Coconut water?" Christy scrunched up her nose at his creative choice but then tried to adjust her expression before he saw it. Too late.

"Not what you had in mind? How 'bout this?" Todd pulled a container of coconut macaroons from the bag.

Christy's expression lit up.

"Or this?" His third coconut item was a pint of a frozen dessert labeled "Coconut Bliss."

Now Christy was really interested.

"As a final option." Todd pulled out a large plastic bag of shredded coconut that he undoubtedly found in the baking aisle. "You can add shredded coconut to your pizza, your frozen eggplant lasagna, or even your scrambled eggs, if you want."

She toddled to the other side of the kitchen island and gave him a big-baby-belly-between-us hug. "You're wonderful. Thank you."

They shared a quick, sweet kiss, and Christy glanced at the clock. It was almost eleven. Usually she would be asleep by now. All the naps on the couch over the past three days along with all the kicks from the baby and trips to the bathroom meant that her sleeping rhythm was jumbled.

"You know what?" Christy opened the refrigerator. "When you said scrambled eggs, I suddenly got hungry. Do scrambled eggs sound good to you right now?"

"Sure. You want me to make them?"

"I can do it."

Todd looked as if he had been struck by sudden inspiration. "How about if I start a fire in the pit on the deck, and we eat outside?"

Christy agreed without hesitation. She knew it was a silly thing they were doing, but to her it was also the most romantic thing she and Todd had done in weeks. They wrapped a big blanket around both of them and sat as close together as they could on the funky bench Todd had made out of the backseat of his old VW bus, "Gus," and his old orange surfboard that he called "Naranja" as the back.

For so many years Christy had rolled her eyes whenever anyone commented on Narangus, which she considered an eyesore on their deck. Tonight, though, Narangus ministered to her in a way none of the other beds, chairs, or couches in the house had been able to. Narangus was the perfect height for her swollen legs. The padding in the old car seat was just the right density, and the firmness of the surfboard felt good against her sore back.

"I can't believe I'm saying this." Christy swallowed her last bite. "I'm more comfortable sitting here than I have been anywhere for weeks. Could you clean this ol' buddy of yours up and bring him inside?"

Todd laughed.

"I'm serious!"

"Okay, I'll do it." He tenderly placed his palm on Christy's rounded bulge. "Did you hear that, son? Your mother says Narangus gets to come back inside. It's all because of you, buddy. I owe you one."

"This is a temporary situation," Christy said. "Narangus told me he likes it out here on the deck, and this is where he would rather be."

"Oh, he told you that, did he?"

Christy felt a big kick and placed her hand on top of her stomach. Todd slid his hand across her midriff, following the trail of movement. "Whoa! He's all over the place."

"I know. It's been like this for days. Every time this little one tries to get comfortable, I get more uncomfortable. I know there can't be much room left in there." Christy slid her hand across the top of her belly and pressed down gently, trying to get a deeper breath. "I have a feeling our baby is about to drop. I've been reading about what's next, and it's just about time."

"We better come up with a girl's name then," Todd said.

Christy slipped her feet out of her fuzzy slippers and lifted them up to the fire one at a time to get the soles of her feet nice and toasty. "Are you thinking now that it could actually be a girl?"

"I don't have an instinct going one way or the other. Do you?"

"Not really. I have been thinking about girl names, though."

"Me, too."

Christy turned to him. "Okay, you go first. What did you come up with?"

"I still like Juliet for a middle name. What about Emily for a first name? Emily Juliet Spencer."

Christy considered if for a moment before saying, "I like the name Emily, but it reminds me of the Gilmore Girls."

"Who are the Gilmore Girls? Do they come to the Gathering on Friday nights?"

Christy laughed. And, of course, that meant she had to go to the bathroom. She slipped her feet back into her slippers and pulled herself up as gracefully as she could. "I'll be right back. Keep thinking of more girl names. And no, the Gilmore Girls don't come to the Gathering."

The discussion for a girl's name became an ongoing game for them over the next few weeks. They texted each other options during the day and vetoed suggestions in bed at night. Todd wrote names on the calendar before he went to school in the morning. Christy wrote names on the bathroom mirror with toothpaste.

Their suggestions were all over the place. Hawaiian names, Hebrew names from Old Testament lessons Todd was teaching, made-up names that brought up nothing when they searched online, and every family name they could think of.

They went through two books of baby names and scanned numerous websites. Yet they couldn't agree on a single name. Except Juliet as a middle name.

Todd was able to join Christy for her doctor's appointment the second week of November because they had taken the last slot of the day. Christy was officially on maternity leave and didn't feel safe driving because she had to move the seat back so far. Todd had been especially attentive lately and insisted on doing all the driving and all the grocery shopping.

As they walked through the parking lot hand in hand, Christy said, "I was thinking maybe we should go ahead and ask Aunt Linda to tell us today if it's a boy or a girl."

Todd stopped walking and looked at Christy with an expression she had seen on him more often. It was the sort of look a teacher gives as a nonverbal warning to a student who is acting up. "Christy . . ."

"What? I just thought if we knew it might help us to come up with a name for a girl."

Todd was still shaking his head. "Nope, not a chance. No way. Not now. We've waited this long. We can stay in suspense a few more weeks."

Christy wasn't convinced.

"I'm serious, Christina." Todd's voice was firm.

She couldn't remember him ever calling her Christina before. This was apparently very important to him.

"Okay," Christy said as they resumed their walk up to the front door of the medical building. "We'll wait."

"Yes, we will," Todd said decisively.

Visits to see Dr. Avery had become a friendly, warm time with hugs along with all the routine, professional steps. She checked Christy's chart and gave her a warm grin. "You're almost there. The baby has dropped nicely. You're in a good position. There's a chance you might deliver before the due date. Do you have everything ready, just in case?"

"I think so." Christy glanced at Todd, and he nodded.

The two of them had worked together over the last few weeks to pack their bag for the hospital and to have everything ready to bring the baby home. The car seat was installed in Clover, and Todd had loaded his phone with a list of all the people he was supposed to call so, in case he got flustered, he wouldn't forget anyone. Christy had attended four birthing classes: three of them with Todd, and one with her mom. They had selected their pediatrician and had met him by chance when Todd and Christy attended a second tour of the hospital so Todd would have all the information Christy had received when she went by herself the first time.

Dr. Avery discussed Christy's birth plan that she had written out and had added it to Christy's file. Christy asked some final questions. Most of them had to do with what symptoms she should watch for since she had been having Braxton Hicks contractions for more than a week.

"You have my number," Dr. Avery said. "Please don't hesitate to call me if you have any questions, or if you're concerned about anything."

"There is one thing," Christy said slowly.

Todd gave her his "teacher" look, as if she were going to ask Dr. Avery to reveal the sex.

"No, not that, Todd. Don't worry. What I want to ask about is my weight." She felt funny saying it aloud. At every visit she had watched the assistant log the number from the scale, and every visit Christy had felt a sickening thump in the pit of her squashed little stomach. She had passed the ideal weight gain listed on all the websites and was still gaining.

"I've been eating healthy almost the whole pregnancy. I've tried to do all the things they say about exercising and sleeping. I just feel awful that I've gained so much. I'm worried that it's not healthy for the baby."

"I've been keeping an eye on it," Dr. Avery said. "You're okay. You are over the average total weight gain, but you don't show signs of any of the dangers from it. I think you have a big baby in there. At least eight pounds. And I have a feeling you'll be one of those women who loses all her pregnancy weight and more once the baby comes and you start to nurse."

Christy felt a twinge of relief. The hopeful thoughts kept her buoyant over the next week, as she watched the scale at home and saw that she had gained another two pounds. She kept saying to herself, "Don't stress about it. Everything is okay. The baby is fine."

What made it difficult to keep up the internal pep talk was that she felt so uncomfortable. So exhausted. So ready for this baby to be born. All she wanted to do was eat fruit popsicles and mashed potatoes.

Aunt Marti called her on a Thursday morning, a week before Thanksgiving. She had been calling every day to check in and started each call with, "How are you doing today, Christy darling?"

Christy appreciated the chance to vent about her latest ache and then go on to listen to whatever Marti had on her mind to chat about that day. Christy especially appreciated that Marti had not once said any of the things other people were saying such as, "Have you had the baby yet?" or "Do you think today's the day?" or "How much longer?" Those questions drove Christy crazy. Her replies to such questions in text messages and comments on her social media pages were as short and as sweet as her fatigued brain could make them.

The one person she didn't mind answering with more detailed information was

Shawna. She had started texting Christy several times a day. Shawna's texts included lots of emojis and an occasional photo of her new puppy or selfies of her with her best friend, Lilly. Shawna's notes always made Christy smile, and she didn't mind the awkward questions such as, "Do you feel like your body has been taken over by an alien? Lilly wanted me to ask you that."

Marti's morning phone call on the Thursday before Thanksgiving was different than her usual check-in. She asked Christy, "Would you and Todd pray for us about something?"

"Yes, of course." Christy couldn't remember her aunt ever asking her to pray about anything.

"Would the two of you pray that we sell the house quickly? The expenses are adding up, and we would like some help from God on this."

Christy's uncle had trusted his life to the Lord a number of years ago after a frightening accident with a fire on his old barbecue grill. His faith was real, and his trust in the Lord was deep. Christy guessed her uncle had been praying for months about their financial situation. She was glad to join them in praying, especially since Aunt Marti was the one asking.

"Todd and I will pray about that with you guys, Aunt Marti."

"I appreciate that, Christy. God seems to listen to you and Todd more than He does to me."

Christy wasn't sure how to reply to her aunt's comment.

Marti didn't seem to want a reply. She moved on to the next topic. "Now, I know you have been uncomfortable, especially these last few days. I wondered if it would take your mind off things if you got out of the house for a short while."

Christy was still in her roomy pj's and cautiously asked what her aunt had in mind.

"Your mother is coming for lunch today, and I thought it would be nice if the three of us could meet at my house. What do you think?"

"I'd love to come, Aunt Marti."

"Wonderful. I've already sent Robert to pick up salads for us. I sent him to that place where you and I met for lunch several months ago. That organic place. Ollie's. Do you know what you would like to order?"

"Yes, I like the 808 salad with no feta, and I'd love a Sweet Peaches smoothie. It's number four on their menu. I've actually been craving one for weeks now."

"I'll make the call. You get yourself ready,

and your chauffeur will be there in half an hour or less."

Christy took the stairs faster than usual, cradling her heavy belly as she climbed up to her room. She rushed to take a shower and put on the freshest, roomiest dress she had. With the hair dryer set on high, she dried the crown of her head and then brushed her long, damp hair and twisted it up in a tight knot on top of her head the way she had been wearing it for weeks. She couldn't stand the weight of her hair or the way it stuck to her neck. Two weeks ago she had considered cutting it short. But she didn't want to do it and then regret her impulsive choice later. The spun knot on top of her head had been the answer.

Christy slathered her bare arms and legs with her favorite tropical-scented lotion. The bathroom filled with the tantalizing fragrance of coconut and mango. She dabbed on a little makeup and headed downstairs with care. When she was skimming comments that morning on one of the baby blogs she had been following, she had read about a woman who fell on her way to the hospital when she was going into labor. The baby was fine, but the mother broke her foot. Christy took it as a cautionary tale and made sure she was doing her best to see over her belly and watch where her footsteps landed.

Christy retrieved her phone, made sure the house was locked up, and blotted her forehead with a paper towel because all the dashing around had caused her to perspire like crazy. She took a slow drink of cold water and still felt slightly light-headed.

Maybe I shouldn't go.

Uncle Bob's car pulled up in front of the house just then, and through the small kitchen window Christy could see that he had hopped out and was hustling to the front door so she wouldn't have to waddle out to the car unassisted.

Too late now.

Christy met Uncle Bob at the door with a breathless smile. A familiar Braxton Hicks contraction was coming on, and what she really wanted to do was sit for a moment, close her eyes, and breathe through it.

Instead, she took his arm as he said, "Your chariot awaits, my dear."

Christy tried to step as lightly and securely as she could, using her free arm to undergird her middle. The clenching sensation heightened, and she had to stop walking. Her legs felt unreliable.

"Hang on," she whispered. A wave of nausea came over her, and she was sure she had overdone it by rushing to get ready. Certainly she had used more adrenaline in the last twenty minutes than she had in the last two weeks.

"Take it easy," Uncle Bob said calmly. "We're in no hurry."

Christy could feel her heartbeat quickening as the contraction increased. She clung to Uncle Bob's arm and tried to let out a long breath through her mouth. The tightening eased, and she opened her eyes.

"Are you all right?"

Christy nodded, determined not to be any more dramatic than she knew she must have already appeared to be. Uncle Bob took a slow step forward with Christy on his arm and then another. On the third step, Christy felt a warm fluid sensation that she realized she had no control over. She stopped, mortified.

First she glanced at Uncle Bob, and then she quickly looked down at the walkway beneath her damp shoes. She couldn't move. She couldn't speak.

"Well, how 'bout that?" Uncle Bob was staring at the small puddle Christy was standing in. His expression made it clear that he knew what had just happened. So did she.

Without a hint of rush or panic, Uncle

Bob said, "How about if I drive you to the hospital today instead of to lunch?"

Christy nodded. She couldn't speak. She couldn't think.

She was about to have a baby.

Twenty-Four

Christy slowly crunched on ice chips as the low beeps sounded on the monitors in her hospital room. Her water broke seven-and-a-half hours ago. At the moment, all she could think about was the Sweet Peaches smoothie she had missed out on for lunch. She would love to have something to eat right now, but she couldn't imagine anything staying down.

It was strange. All of it. This was not what she thought being in labor would be like. She had intense moments followed by lulls where she actually fell asleep for a few minutes until the next muted contraction came over her. She was both at ease and miserable at the same time. The pain she felt could be described more as intense pressure and great discomfort than actual pain. It had been this way to a lesser degree for several days off and on, but now the contractions were regular and powerful, and she knew there was much more to come.

Todd had arrived at the hospital within twenty minutes of when Bob brought Christy in and she was ushered to the maternity wing in a wheelchair. Her mom and Marti had gone to Christy's house to fetch the overnight bag before they dashed to the hospital. Even Christy's dad had come. He didn't want to come into the room, but Christy knew he was sitting in the waiting area and had been there all day.

Dr. Avery had checked on Christy twice. The labor and delivery nurse, Kelly, had been kind and attentive, and Christy felt more at ease every time Kelly came in the room. On her last visit she had reported that Christy was dilated to seven and everything looked great.

"Any idea how much longer?"

Kelly gave Christy a sympathetic look. "It's hard to tell with the first baby. You're making good progress."

"It feels like it's taking so long."

"I know. It can seem that way. But you're doing great. You really are. The baby is coming, and it's not in any distress. How's your pain level?"

"It's okay. I'm so tired, though."

Christy was rethinking her choice to have a traditional hospital birth. She kept thinking of the videos she had watched of women her age laboring in bathtubs or walking around and even rolling on big rubber balls. As least they were doing something. She felt like she was just sitting and waiting, breathing through the continual discomfort and trying not to tangle the tubes in her arms on the rail of the elevated bed.

Todd went over to the side of the bed and stroked Christy's cheek. "Do you want anything?"

She handed him the empty cup. "More ice, I guess. What about you? Do you need to take a break and find something to eat with everyone else?"

"No, I'm good. I'm not leaving." He held up the cup. "Well, except to get ice."

He left, and Christy was alone in the room for the first time. She prayed a simple prayer asking for a safe and healthy delivery of their baby. In the silence she told the Lord that she was afraid. Afraid of what was about to happen. Afraid of what was going to be asked of her body. Everything in her wanted this to be over. She wanted to get this baby out of her. She was tired, so tired of being pregnant. At that moment, in the middle of her honest confession, Christy started to cry because she had an irrational fear that she was going to be pregnant and in labor for the rest of her life.

Todd returned to find her sobbing.

"What happened? Are you okay?" He pressed the button for the nurse.

"Did you just call the nurse?" Christy asked.

"Yeah."

"Why did you do that?" She let out a cry as a strong contraction overtook her.

Todd grabbed her hand. "Breathe. Just breathe."

He was squeezing her hand so tightly and she was so mad at him for ringing for the nurse when all she was doing was feeling sorry for herself, that she pulled away and yelled, "Don't do that!"

Todd looked stunned, and Christy wondered if her voice had come out as abrasive as it sounded to her over the pounding in her ears. She felt hot. Too hot. Beads of perspiration dripped down the back of her neck. Every part of her body ached. Her legs felt wobbly, and her feet were cold.

"I need my socks!"

Todd quickly went to the overnight bag and pulled out the fuzzy anklets Christy had packed. He pulled back the sheet and cautiously slipped them on her feet. "How's that?"

Christy couldn't reply. Another huge

contraction overwhelmed her. She leaned back, panting as Kelly came in.

The contraction digressed, and Christy started to cry again. "Is my mom still here?"

"I'm sure she is," Todd said. "Do you want her to come in?"

Christy nodded. She couldn't open her eyes. She had a fuzzy recollection of writing on her birth plan that she only wanted Todd to be in the room when the baby came. Now everything felt so intensified in her body and in her pounding head, all she wanted was to feel her mother's cool hand on her forehead.

Todd slipped out of the room, and Christy heard Kelly checking the monitor. Her voice was close as she said, "You're in transition, Christy. This should go quickly for you. Focus on your breathing. I know you feel irritable. That's normal. Try to stay relaxed."

Christy nodded as the next contraction came on, and she closed herself into her own dark world and breathed as steadily as she could.

"Christy, honey, I'm here."

Christy felt her mom's cool hand on her forehead, just as she had wanted. It reminded her of when she was young and had the chicken pox. Her mother had stayed with her all through the night, comforting her.

"I don't want to have a baby," Christy mumbled through her tears. "I can't do this."

"Yes you can, honey. You're doing so well. I'm here. Todd is here. We're not going to leave unless you want us to."

"No! Don't leave." Christy groped for Todd's hand as the next contraction came on with force. She leaned her head back and cried out.

She lost any concept of time as she focused on breathing through each increasingly strong contraction. She felt like throwing up twice but had nothing in her stomach to bring up. Her ears were ringing, and her lower back was killing her.

After some time she heard Dr. Avery's voice followed by a reply from Kelly. Perspiration was streaming down Christy's forehead. Her mother stepped in with a cool washcloth for her.

"Well done, Christy." Dr. Avery's voice was strong and confident. "Your baby is about ready to make an appearance. We're going to prep the area. You keep breathing. We're here. We're going to take care of you and your little one."

Christy went back to focusing on breathing, only breathing. She knew her mom was on her right side and Todd was on her left. Her legs felt as if they were quivering uncontrollably and an intense pressure in the small of her back seemed to override all the other pain that coursed through her abdomen and hips.

She paid little attention to all the adjusting of the bed and the ways the nurse was positioning the lower part of her body. For the first time in her life, she felt no sense of modesty, nor did she care if any part of her was covered. All she wanted was to get that baby out!

As excruciating as it was, Christy complied with the directions Kelly gave her on where to put her feet and how to move. Christy felt as if all her muscles were in a torrent of first turning to cement and then reverting to wobbly noodles.

She tried to remember everything she had read, everything they had covered in the birthing classes. She couldn't remember any of it. It seemed impossible to concentrate on anything but the overwhelming force of what her body was doing. She felt out of control. Her body was going to keep at this intense labor with or without her participation.

She heard Todd's voice and felt his strong

hands supporting her left leg. Her mother supported her on the right side. Kelly began what at first felt like an invasive stretching of her numb skin in the most sensitive part of her body. However, the cooling gel and the change in the pressure of the baby's position came as an odd relief in the middle of another long, painful contraction.

"Okay, Christy. This is it," Dr. Avery's calm voice came from the end of the bed. "On the next contraction I want you to give a nice, gentle push. Can you do that for me?"

This is it! The baby is coming. I'm having a baby! Okay. Okay. Now. Push!

"That's good. Nice and easy. Okay. Deep breath. That's it. Just like that on the next contraction. You're doing great."

In the short interval on the downside of the contraction, Christy opened her eyes and looked at Todd. Tears streamed down his face. He gripped her hand.

"I love you, Kilikina. I love you so much."

She had no time to respond. The next wave was cresting, and she felt desperate to push again. The pattern repeated itself for what felt like hours. She had no idea where the fortitude came from to push again each time Kelly said to push, and Todd counted so Christy would know how long to hold the push before breathing again.

At one point, Christy opened her eyes and saw her mother's steady gaze fixed on her. "Hi, Mom," Christy said as calmly as if she were a little girl who had woken from a nap and found her mother at her bedside, watching over her.

In a voice filled with wonder, Christy's mom said, "Hi, honey. You're doing such a good job."

Dr. Avery coaxed Christy into the next contraction and happily announced, "That's it! Your baby has crowned. Now I want you to use all your strength on the next contraction. Todd is going to count to ten, and you hold on till he gets to ten before you let your breath out. Okay? Are you ready?"

Bolstered with the possibility that she would see her little one in only a few minutes, Christy gave the next push all she had, holding on until Todd counted to ten. She flopped back into the pillows, panting and numb all over.

"All right," Dr. Avery said. "Good. Almost there. Here you go. Now! One more."

The next contraction dominated her whole body. She pushed, stopped to gasp for air, and pushed again.

Gripping Todd's hand with strength from an unimagined source, Christy let out a wail as she pushed with all that was within her. An intense sensation of release catapulted through her body, and she knew she had done it.

"It's a girl!" Todd shouted wildly. "A girl!" He leaned down and kissed Christy as the tears flowed down his face.

Christy tried to let the declaration sink in. *A girl? We have a girl!*

She had no strength left to raise her head, but a moment later she felt the weight of her newborn daughter on her chest. Christy tried to focus through her tear-filled eyes. A tiny, pink face squinted back at her.

"Oh," was all Christy could say. "Oh. Oh. Oh."

A pair of hands was wiping off their daughter's head and tucking a soft blanket around her as Christy focused on her baby instead of on the swift procedure Dr. Avery was completing as the umbilical cord was cut and tied.

Todd stroked Christy's cheek. "We have a baby girl. Thank you." Todd squeezed his eyes closed. "Thank You, Father God." He slid his finger next to their daughter's hand, and her tiny fingers grasped his finger, holding tight. The connection seemed to overwhelm Todd. Through his tears he spoke softly, "It's me. Your daddy."

Christy smiled up at Todd. The look on his face made it clear that he had no regrets that they had a girl and not the son he was so sure they would have. Todd pressed his forehead against hers. "You're amazing."

Kelly was by her side with a cup of cold water. "Here you go. Try to take a few sips. She's beautiful, Christy."

"I need you to bear down for me," Dr. Avery said. "That's it. A little more."

"I can't stop shaking," Christy said.

"You're almost done." Kelly offered her another sip of water.

A secondary sensation of release came over Christy followed by Dr. Avery saying, "Great. Well done. I'm going to give you a few sutures now. You'll feel the tug. It'll be over in a couple of minutes."

Before Christy could concentrate on what it meant to be getting sutures and thinking about where those stitches were being placed, Kelly had returned to the bedside and distracted Christy by covering her with a warm blanket to ease her quivering.

Christy was overcome with every emotion and every sensation she could imagine. Their daughter squinted her eyes shut and gave a little cry that sounded like a kitten. That's when Christy noticed her mom, who had quietly and steadily been there beside her through all of it and was now standing back at the foot of the bed. Christy motioned for her to come closer. She took her mom's hand and smiled.

"She's beautiful." Her mom gave Christy's hand a long squeeze. "Do you want me to go to the waiting room and tell the others?"

"Yes. Thanks, Mom. I love you."

Her mom leaned in and kissed Christy tenderly. "I love you, too."

Christy was so glad her mother had been there. It was an instinctual wish that she hadn't expected to feel. She knew what an extraordinary blessing it was that the two of them could share the experience.

The next few moments were a blur as Christy felt herself relax. The stitching went quickly. Her daughter rested calmly on her chest. Todd stroked Christy's damp hair, and Christy tried to memorize every detail of their daughter's sweet face. Both Todd and Christy were enraptured with the fresh, new soul cradled in Christy's arms.

Somewhere in the calming-down moments, Kelly had carefully lifted their little one and took her only a few steps away to a warming station where she was cleaned up, weighed, and measured.

"Eight pounds, fifteen ounces and twenty-one inches." Kelly reported. "She's precious.

What's her name?"

Christy and Todd looked at each other, and their joyous expressions faded.

"We . . . um." Todd struggled to find the right words. "We are . . ."

On top of every other feeling Christy was inundated with, she felt embarrassed that she and Todd hadn't agreed on a name for a girl yet. They had nine months to come up with a name, and here they were with their baby in their arms and no name for her.

We are already the worst parents in the world, and we haven't even had the job for ten minutes. Why did we wait so long to settle on a name?

"I'm sure you'll know her name soon." Kelly seemed to have guessed what the problem was. "Sometimes all it takes is for the parents to look into their baby's eyes, and the name seems to come to them."

Christy looked at their daughter whose eyes were closed. She appeared to be as exhausted by the journey into this world as Christy was in assisting her arrival. Christy leaned forward. Everything in her ached as she pressed the first kiss on her daughter's forehead.

"First kiss," she whispered. The first of what Christy knew would be a lifetime of thousands of kisses.

"Let me hold her." Todd scooped his hands under their swaddled baby and carefully drew her close. He studied her face, touched her button nose, and pressed his kiss to her forehead.

"You know what she smells like?" Todd asked.

Christy remembered how Doug had commented after their son Daniel was born that he had that "new car smell." She really hoped Todd wasn't in a stupid-joke mood. She didn't want anything irreverent to ruin this perfectly sacred moment.

Todd grinned at Christy. "She smells like Hana after it rains."

Christy was pretty sure he was catching a whiff of the tropical coconut and mango lotion she had slathered on herself earlier that day. She undoubtedly had perspired the fragrance all over the sheets as well as their daughter when she held her. Christy didn't mention the lotion, though. She liked that Todd had chosen to compare their baby's scent to one of their favorite shared memories of being on the rainy side of Maui many years ago.

Both of them had overcome significant fears on that trip. They were in an open Jeep as they left the remote Hawaiian town of

Hana. It had just rained, and Christy told Todd she never in her life had smelled anything as heartbreakingly beautiful as the fragrances in Hana after it rained. Todd told her that she would never forget the scent, and she hadn't. Neither had Todd.

Todd drew their daughter close and whispered to her in an endearing daddy voice. "That's what you smell like, Hana . . ." Todd stopped midsentence. He looked at Christy with an expression of pure joy in his screaming silver-blue eyes.

The sunrise moment of inspiration dawned on Christy, too. "Hana," she echoed.

Todd nodded. "Hana."

With a huge smile Christy said, "Yes! Hana. Hana Juliet. It's perfect."

"Did you hear that?" Todd kissed his baby's forehead again, and she opened her eyes just a sliver. "Welcome to the world, Hana Juliet Spencer. We already love you more than you will ever know. More than you will ever ask."

TWENTY-FIVE

The weeks that followed Hana Juliet's arrival were laced together with all the anticipated super highs and super lows that come with being new parents. Sleep deprivation was an ongoing issue. Working out a routine with diapers, laundry, and meals was a challenge.

Fortunately, nursing wasn't one of the difficulties Christy had to overcome as a new mother. She had heard lots from moms who had struggled with nursing and mastitis. She had read about remedies ahead of time and saved articles encouraging young mothers not to feel guilty if they needed to supplement or pump or use formula. With so many bloggers talking about it, Christy had prepared herself for that hurdle.

When it turned out that nursing was about the easiest, most routine part of her first few months as a mother, Christy found herself hunting for something to read that would help her to feel less guilty whenever she let other young moms know that she hadn't had any difficulties. She even had success pumping, and when she offered Hana a bottle, the baby took it without hesitation.

"It's kind of a miracle," Tracy told her on the phone. "Enjoy it!"

"I am. I'm so happy, Tracy. I never imagined how full my heart would feel. She's so sweet."

"How are you holding up?" Tracy asked. "Are you healing quickly?"

"I don't know if it's quickly, but I'm following all the advice, and so far I'm okay."

"Good. Make sure you eat enough."

"I'm eating plenty, trust me."

Christy loved being home all day and tending to her little family without the pressure of going back to work right away. None of the ongoing diapers and spit up seemed to bother Christy or Todd. But Christy noted plenty of times when Todd handed off Hana and declared that she was hungry and Christy needed to feed her, when all Hana needed was a diaper change.

What was unmistakable, though, was that from the very first moments, Todd was smitten with Hana. He was mesmerized by her. Uncle Bob said that Todd wasn't the only one whom Hana had wrapped around her little finger. Uncle Bob took special joy in rocking Hana to sleep. Even Christy's dad seemed reluctant to hand her over after he had been holding her.

Christy's mom kept commenting on what a pretty baby Hana was. She had delicate features and a button nose. Her eyes were a light blue and seemed to be staying that color. She had a bit of downy hair covering her perfectly round head like the fuzz on a baby chick. Her hair appeared blonde some days and more of an auburn shade other days. Christy's dad let it be known that he was hoping Hana's hair would take on the ginger shade that ran through his side of the family.

Christy had fun preparing to send out the baby announcements with the giraffe on them. She filled in all the information starting with the birth date of November 17 and writing out the full name, Hana Juliet Spencer. There was a space to add the meaning of the name, which Christy hadn't noticed when she bought the announcements. She had to look it up. When she found the meaning of Hana Juliet, she told Todd, and they agreed it was perfect.

Gracious Youthful One.

Christy sent an announcement to Todd's

mom. It was returned, and someone had written on the envelope, "No longer at this address." When Christy showed it to Todd, he said little. The sorrow he had felt over his mother choosing to have no contact with him had been eclipsed by the joy of being a father and pouring out endless affection and attention on his own child.

Christy and Katie managed to squeeze in a fair number of video calls, including one during which Hana cried the whole time. Katie refused to end the call because she said it was killing her not to be there in person. The crying and watching Christy walk back and forth rocking Hana were as close to a real-time experience as Katie could get.

"So, what was it like? Birth, I mean," Katie asked on one of their calls. "How does it feel to have a miniature human come out of your body? It freaks me out sometimes when I think about it. Was it terrible, or did you like parts of it?"

"My favorite part was when it was over," Christy said with a deadpan expression.

"I think I'm going to be the same way," Katie said. "I don't really get these women here who say that childbirth is such a sacred experience."

"No, they're right, too. It is a sacred

experience! It definitely is like nothing I've ever done. I felt like I had no control over what was happening, and I needed to call out to God for strength. I felt like He was there with me. I can't explain how. At the time, it wasn't as if I was looking around the room for guardian angels and spotted one. The realization came afterward, when I tried to remember everything that had happened. I recalled how close the Lord felt through it all. It was like He was one of the people in the room."

"And so was your husband and your mother. That's pretty much a holy union of support right there. Not every woman gets to experience that."

Christy read a tinge of sadness in Katie's expression. "How are your mom and dad?"

"About the same, as far as I know. I thought about them a lot when I planned on going to California. Now I feel like I'll see them again whenever I see them. It's strange. I know that God is mapping all this out, as far as our plans to make the trip. I just can't say I have any idea what He's doing. All I know is that He hasn't forgotten about us."

Christy was talking to Katie in the nursery while Hana was lying on a mat on the rug, staring at a mobile with dangling giraffes, elephants, and monkeys. She was kicking her little legs and making sweet squeaky sounds.

Christy glanced up at the framed gift Shawna had given her of Psalm 139. It had been hung over the changing table next to the baby giraffe picture she and Todd had bought in Laguna and next to the three palm trees card she had framed.

"No, He hasn't," she said. "God is thinking about you all the time, Katie."

"That's pretty comforting on a morning like this. We received reports yesterday of more political unrest in an area where some of our teams are working. Everyone is okay, but it reminds me that there are no guarantees in this messed-up world. All we really get for sure is God. Only God. He's with us no matter what."

Christy thought about Katie's words over the next few weeks as everything around her was headed toward a joyful Christmas Day celebration at their home. A Christmas card arrived from Alissa and Brad with a photo of them and their two darling girls. The printed card had the word "Immanuel" on the front with a beautiful design of red poinsettias. On the inside the words were, "God is with us." At the bottom was printed the Scripture reference from Isaiah 7.

It was Christy's favorite card that year. She punched a hole through it and hung it on their Christmas tree with red ribbon. She wanted to be reminded that God was with them. He had been with them all along. He knew them before they were born, and His thoughts toward them were more than the grains of sand. That theme had repeated itself in Christy's heart and life throughout the year. Now that it was Christmas and Hana was safely in their arms, Christy wanted to remember the promise again. "God is with us."

Christmas morning dawned with brilliant sunshine. Hana was full of coos, and Todd was determined to get the music just right through all the speakers downstairs so they could be serenaded with Christmas carols all day long.

Christy dressed Hana in a fussy red-velvet dress that was one of at least two dozen outfits Marti had given to Hana since she was born. Every time Marti came over she showed up with an adorable new little outfit and Christy could tell that it was a healing and joyous thing for Marti to pamper the newborn. Christy didn't even try to curb the attention Marti lavished on Hana. Instead, Christy made sure Marti knew how much she appreciated Marti's version of love and caring.

The new house hadn't sold yet. Marti reminded Christy nearly every day that she was counting on Christy to pray. Christy prayed every day. She prayed for more than just the sale of the expensive house. She prayed for her aunt like never before. It was, as it had long been, Christy's deep desire that Marti would fully comprehend and believe that God was with her and that He wanted an open and ongoing relationship with her.

Christy and Hana went downstairs just as the doorbell rang and their first Christmas morning guest appeared at eight o'clock, right on the dot. It was Aunt Linda and her arms were full of gifts, including a bagful of scrumptious bakery items as her contribution to the brunch.

Todd jokingly asked if she was moving in.

"I couldn't help myself. It was so fun buying for a little one. I'll warn you, though," she said. "I might need to leave if one of my patients goes into labor. It's happened on Christmas before."

"Like on the first Christmas," Todd said.

It took Aunt Linda a moment to catch his meaning. "Right. Yes. Well, what can I do to help?"

Christy handed Hana to Aunt Linda. "You

can get your cuddles in now before the baby hogs arrive. And by that, I mean my uncle and my dad."

Christy had kept the breakfast plans simple. Her mom was bringing an egg casserole that had been a family tradition since Christy's childhood. Uncle Bob wanted to bring bacon and sausages. Neither Todd nor Christy's dad complained about that. Christy had prepared slices of fruit and had everything set out for people to make their own coffee or tea as well as pour juice for themselves. She added Aunt Linda's pastries to the counter.

Bob and Marti arrived just then, bringing in way more gifts and food than was necessary. The red ribbons on the gifts and fabulous smells from Bob's selection of breakfast meats elevated the festive feelings.

A few minutes later Christy's parents and her brother arrived. Christy hugged her "baby" brother and introduced him to Aunt Linda. David went right to the corner chair where he lowered his tall body and opened his arms, inviting Linda to hand over the baby. Christy watched, astounded to see her handsome, grown brother turn into an uncle before her eyes.

"Make that three baby hogs in this family," Linda said as she and Christy moved into the kitchen.

"Four, actually. Todd takes her every chance he gets. He loves to sing to her. He's completely taken with her. I love seeing them together."

Linda smiled. "You know what? Todd deserves you."

Christy felt warmed by Linda's remark.

"You have a wonderfully supportive family, Christy. I'm happy for Todd. It's nice to meet your brother, too. He certainly resembles your father."

Christy agreed. David resembled their dad in many ways, but the biggest difference was that David had a wide smile and had fully embraced his extroverted personality from the time he was about sixteen. He had grown up in a house full of introverts and now seemed to spend more of his free time and holidays with his wide circle of friends. Christy was glad that Hana seemed to be the enticement that convinced her man-child brother to spend Christmas Day with them.

Petite Marti planted herself in the center of all the activity and asked to have everyone's attention. "I have a special Christmas gift for all of you. Since we're all together and that doesn't happen often, my gift this year is a family photo shoot on the beach!"

With that, Marti turned toward the front door. "The photographer is on the sand waiting for us now. Shall we go?"

A flurry of questions followed Marti as the group scrambled to head down to the beach. Christy took Hana from David and wrapped her in a hand-crocheted blanket that was draped over the back of the sofa. She knew Marti always had to take the reins to organize Christmas for all of them. This year the control was disguised as a special gift.

The morning air was brisk, but the friendly California sun was out, warming them as they made their way to the sand. Christy had bundled up Hana so that when Todd carried her to the beach almost all that was visible was her button nose popping up.

"Trust me," Marti called over her shoulder. "All of you will thank me later when you see the pictures."

Fortunately, the photographer and his assistant were set up at the end of the sand so the group didn't have to tromp down to the shoreline. He instructed them to slip out of their shoes, and the assistant directed them where to stand and how to turn. After several snaps of the camera, he had them sit in the sand and look natural, a bigger feat than he must have anticipated because he quickly moved on to taking shots of smaller family groupings, starting with Christy, Todd, and Hana seated in the sand.

Christy wiggled her bare toes into the cool, golden sand and smiled. She hated to admit it, but Marti was right. They would treasure these Christmas photos for years to come. She especially liked the way Linda had been so comfortably enfolded into their family.

Hana didn't cry until the very end of the short family photo shoot. Christy knew it was almost time for her to eat. The photographer assured them that he took plenty of good shots and they could all return to the house.

Christy walked over to the photographer and his assistant and said, "Thank you. Merry Christmas!"

Hana continued to cry so Christy walked faster. As soon as they were inside the house, Christy grabbed her phone off the counter and waved to get Todd's attention. "I'm going upstairs to feed her. Can you have everyone start on brunch? Wait on opening the presents until I come back, okay?"

Todd announced that the food was ready, and he asked Uncle Bob to offer up a prayer for all of them. Christy heard her uncle's voice rise and then fade when she closed the door to the nursery and settled in the glider. She positioned her crying baby in her arms, and Hana did what Hana did best.

Christy breathed calmly. She loved the quiet of this cozy haven. As Hana nursed, Christy noticed that Hana's feet were bare. She had started off wearing tiny red socks that morning. Did David pull them off to tickle her toes? Or had she wiggled her feet out of them during the photo shoot? Glancing more closely, Christy noticed that Hana's little toes were covered with golden sand.

"Look at you, little Sandy Toes. How did you manage to do that? Do you like to get your feet in the sand like your mama?" Christy realized they had just taken Hana to the beach for the first time.

She reached for her phone on the side table and took several shots of Hana's adorable feet.

With a contented smile Christy leaned back. Later that day she would keep an important promise. She would change the screen saver on her phone to a picture of her daughter's sandy toes. She also would send the picture to Shawna and remind her that Christy, Todd, and Hana couldn't wait for her to come stay with them again.

As Christy rocked slowly, she could hear the muffled sounds of laughter coming from her family downstairs. Laughter, mixed with Christmas carols. The sound of love soaked into the walls and swirled around all of them.

How did Shawna describe it? This house breathes love in and out. That's what makes it alive.

That was certainly true today. The carol that wafted up to her next was the one Todd had said was his favorite last summer. Christy thought of the night at the Gathering when he sang it to the group, and Christy had felt Hana flutter inside her for the first time.

Christy hummed along, and Hana opened her eyes. She sleepily looked up. Never did Christy imagine that she would feel such love as she felt at that moment for her firstborn. Never had the Christmas story touched her in such a personal and poignant way.

Christy felt she could grasp a deeper sense now of what happened on that O holy night when God's Son was born. God's gift of life, eternal life, had come to us wrapped in the flesh and blood of a baby. Jesus willingly became a tiny, limited human being so that He could one day become the sacrifice that paid the debt for our sins. Through Him, we can become adopted into God's family.

Such love.

Hana closed her eyes and looked like she was about to fall asleep with a quivering little baby smile on her lips. Christy smiled and stroked Hana's velvety cheek with the back of a finger. Christy's heart felt filled to overflowing with love. She couldn't wait to spend her life pouring that love out on her daughter, the way God had so patiently and faithfully poured out His love on her.

She bent close and kissed Hana's forehead.

Whatever awaited their little family in the days, months, and years ahead, Christy was certain of one thing: God's unfailing love. His presence would always be with them. He was the Everlasting Father and He would never stop thinking about them.

ABOUT THE AUTHOR

Robin Jones Gunn is the much loved author of the popular Christy Miller series for teens and Sisterchicks novels as well as non-fiction favorites such as Victim of Grace and Spoken For. Robin's Father Christmas novellas have been made into a 2016 Hallmark Original Movie titled, "Finding Father Christmas." Her 90 books have sold over 5 million copies worldwide. As a frequent speaker, Robin has traveled extensively in Africa, Brazil, Europe, and Australia. She and her husband Ross live in Hawaii where she continues to write from her heart.